THE HUES OF
ME AND YOU

Praise for Morgan Lee Miller

The Infinite Summer

"*The Infinite Summer* by Morgan Lee Miller brought back a lot of nostalgic memories of my own youth, especially that summer between high school and college...and that really fun summer after high school. I hope it does the same for you."—*Rainbow Reflections*

"There is something about Morgan Lee Miller's writing that gets me every time...but all in all, Miller delivered yet another enjoyable story that made nerd me happy."—*Hsinju's Lit Log*

Before. After. Always.

"Miller tackled the tough subject of grief in *Before. After. Always.* It didn't feel too painful reading, but all the emotions were there."—*Hsinju's Lit Log*

All the Paths to You

"This book made me, a self-proclaimed hater of sports, care about sports. Even sporting events that were purely fictional. That in and of itself is impressive...My God, Kennedy and Quinn are such a cute couple, I love them!! I ship them so much it isn't even funny. Their chemistry is through the roof to be honest."—*Day Dreaming and Book Reading*

"*All the Paths to You* is the kind of romance that makes your heart ache in all the right places."—*Hsinju's Lit Log*

"This book had a lot of feel-good moments and I still have a big smile on my face...this was the feel-good and even a little inspirational book that I needed right now "—*Lez Review Books*

"I can strongly say that this is one of my new favourite books (and series) and is definitely a contender for my favourite book of the year so far... I'm so happy I had the chance to read it and I don't think I could ever recommend it enough!"—*Althea Is Reading*

Hammers, Strings, and Beautiful Things

"There's more going on than first appears, and I was impressed that Ms. Miller won me over with a well written book that deals with some more serious issues."—*C-Spot Reviews*

"*Hammers, Strings, and Beautiful Things* is an emotionally raw read with plenty of drama. The journey Reagan and Blair share is rough in places, but there is a beauty that you won't want to miss out on."—*Lesbian Review*

All the Worlds Between Us

"This book is really sweet and wholesome and also heartbreaking and uplifting...I would recommend this book to anyone looking for a cute contemporary."—*Tomes of Our Lives*

All the Worlds Between Us "deals with friendship, family, sexuality, self-realization, accepting yourself, the harsh reality of high school and the difference between getting to tell your own story and having your own story exposed. Each character plays a vital role...and tells the story of this book perfectly."—*Little Shell's Bookshelf*

"If you're looking for an easy, quick cute f/f read, you should give this a try...This was a solid debut and I can't wait to see what else this author publishes in the future!"—*The Black Lit Queen*

"This book took me straight back to all of my gigantic teenage emotions and got right down to the heart of me. I'm not a swimmer and I wasn't out in high school, but I swear I was right there with Quinn as she navigated her life as a competitive athlete and a queer kid in high school. Experiencing love and betrayal and triumph through her story was bananas. Morgan Lee Miller, you ripped my heart right out with this brilliant book."—*Melisa McCarthy, Librarian, Brooklyn Public Library*

"I'm always up for fun books about cute girlfriends, and *All the Worlds Between Us* was certainly that: a super cute ex-friends to lovers book about a swimming champion and her ex-best-friend turned girlfriend...*All the Worlds Between Us* is a great rom-com and definitely recommended for anyone who's a fan of romance."—*Crowing About Books*

All the Worlds Between Us "has all the typical drama and typical characters you'd find in high school. It's a tough, yet wonderful journey and transformation. The writing is divine...It's a complicated tale involving so much pain, fear, betrayal and humiliation. *All The Worlds Between Us* is a terrific tale of taking what you want."—*Amy's MM Romance Reviews*

"Morgan's novel reiterates the important fact which should be repeated over and over again that coming out should always be done on one's own terms, and how this isn't a thing that any other people, straight or queer, should decide."—*Beyond the Words*

"Finally a sporty, tropey YA lesbian romance—I've honestly been dreaming about reading something like this for a very long time!"—*Day Dreaming and Book Reading*

By the Author

All the Worlds Between Us

Hammers, Strings, and Beautiful Things

All the Paths to You

Before. After. Always.

The Infinite Summer

The Hues of Me and You

Visit us at www.boldstrokesbooks.com

THE HUES OF ME AND YOU

by
Morgan Lee Miller

2023

THE HUES OF ME AND YOU

ISBN 13: 978-1-63679-229-3

THIS TRADE PAPERBACK ORIGINAL IS PUBLISHED BY
BOLD STROKES BOOKS, INC.
P.O. BOX 249
VALLEY FALLS, NY 12185

FIRST EDITION: JANUARY 2023

CREDITS
EDITOR: BARBARA ANN WRIGHT
PRODUCTION DESIGN: STACIA SEAMAN
COVER DESIGN BY JEANINE HENNING

Acknowledgments

I'm a sucker for second chance romances, and I'm warning you now, this isn't going to be my last. I love to write them. I love to read them. It's hands down my favorite trope. Not only are they entertaining to read, but they're very real. We can all relate to second chances in some way because they appear in all facets of life.

While the second chance romance gets all the attention, what I find very underrated are the second chances we give ourselves. As you will soon read, this story centers around the quarter-life crisis, forks in the road, and faded dreams, and the importance of giving yourself that second chance when you run into bumps. I'm so glad I gave myself the chance to pick up writing again when I lost it during my "early 20s self-discovery" (it's a more positive spin on the quarter-life crisis), and because of that second chance, I get to write stories for you.

Always a big thank you and endless gratitude to everyone at BSB, and to Rad and Sandy for seeing something in me and for helping me keep my writing dream alive. To my wonderful editor, Barbara Ann Wright, for continuing to make me a better writer with every story...and for her entertaining commentary when editing my manuscripts.

Thank you to my wonderful support system: Julie, Alex, Ana, Kris, Krystina, Kate, Erica, and Sabrina, and so many others, for all of your unwavering support and encouragement. You make the bad days easier and the good days core memories. I'm very grateful to have you all in my life.

Thank you to my beta readers for all their time providing wonderful feedback and insight.

And as always, a big thank you to you, the reader. You have shaped my love for writing into a dream career. Whether you have read only one story, read them all, or you are just picking up your first, your support means the world to me.

For anyone who feels stuck in life

CHAPTER ONE

"Fucking kill it," Brooke yelled from on top of the couch.

"Why do I always have to be the murderer?" Abby shouted just as loudly while standing next to her.

"Abby, just kill it, and we'll discuss later."

"I don't want to."

An intense shudder snaked through Brooke. Any critter with more than four legs creeped her out. "Please!"

Abby whined, stomped her feet on the couch cushion, and yelled, "Fine." She hopped off the couch and scampered into the kitchen as if fire walking the whole way. She came back out with dish soap and a glass. "Where is it?"

"Soap and a glass?" Brooke said. "You need more than that. Try a shovel or a flamethrower."

Abby walked around the coffee table with the weapons like the brave best friend that she was, ready to look a demon in the eye. She searched low but kept her arms extended as if ready to act at a moment's notice.

"I fucking hate living in the city," Brooke said.

Abby rolled her eyes and crouched. "No, you don't. Last weekend, you were yelling down 18th Street all tipsy on White Claw saying how much you loved this place. Don't lie."

Abby searched under the coffee table, then shrieked, causing Brooke to shriek again. The noise must have scared the demon because it scurried across the old parquet floor. Abby squirted Dawn soap everywhere until it covered the cockroach. As it slowed, she set the glass over it and sat with her back against the wall, exhaling a sigh of relief.

Once it was trapped, Brooke calmed down and sat on the couch. She observed the six-legged brown monster fading away. She tilted her head. "Are we cruel for not scooping it up and letting it back outside? They're pests, right? Serve no purpose in the circle of life?"

"Actually, they clean up decaying shit," Abby said. "Like plants and animals and they nourish growing plants. They're, like, professional recyclers."

"How do you know?"

"Because when we moved into this shithole, I looked it up after the first cockroach you and Stephen made me kill."

"So what you're saying is that we're awful people and should have released it on a plant outside?" Brooke said, shaking her head. "Great. We're murderers."

"*I'm* a murderer since all you and Stephen do is scream. I'm the one with blood on my hands…well, dish soap. I'll tell the landlord he needs to spray this place down. If the cockroach isn't paying DC rent, it's gotta go. This place is too small for us and its family. And don't tell Stephen about this. It will bring back his insomnia."

Brooke zipped her lips.

This was the third time an unwanted visitor had crawled through their apartment. The first time, Brooke had been by herself and had seen one skitter across the kitchen while cooking. She'd shrieked, and when it had disappeared, she'd packed her book bag and headed straight to her art studio. She'd stayed there until Abby had come home from work, and they could face the cockroach together.

A couple of weeks later, the same cockroach—or another one—had visited again. Abby, Stephen, and Brooke were having a Friday night in, a rare Friday where none of them had to work, when a cockroach had scampered across the floor, resulting in all of them huddled in one bed for the night. They'd called the cockroach Roberta and had tried to capture her, but she was too dang fast.

Now, Roberta was dead and covered in tiny soap bubbles.

"While you're at it, you should tell the landlord about the clogged kitchen sink." Brooke checked on Roberta, dead underneath the glass. She was still amazed that dish soap did the trick. She shivered and snatched her purse off the coatrack. "I can't even look at it."

"I like how you and Stephen are going off to the land of the rich tonight and leaving me here in the land of Robertas."

Brooke shrugged. "I picked up this guy's shift last minute. Somewhere in St. Michaels, so we'll be back super late. Stephen should be outside with the truck any minute now."

"Oh, St. Michaels? Schmoozing with the elite?"

"More like making their drinks while they schmooze with each other."

She checked herself in the mirror, making sure the terror Roberta had caused a few minutes ago hadn't ruined too much of her hair, makeup, and uniform: black slacks, white dress shirt under a black vest, and a black bowtie. She didn't necessarily love being a bartender, but it paid her bills, helped pay for her art studio, and was what kept her afloat when combined with her day job as a freelance artist. Enough for her to breathe, at least. But she sensed that her quarter-life crisis was just around the corner. Did she stick to bartending and all the shifts that came with it in order to make enough money to afford rent, or did she move back to the corporate world to get that steady income?

Until creating art paid all the bills, she would spend her nights making drinks for the rich and hopefully making lots of tips.

"I hope you find a beautiful rich woman tonight," Abby said. "Preferably one with a boat. Summer just started, and how amazing would it be if we could go on a boat?"

"I wouldn't have to work two jobs, so that would be spectacular."

"Well, your uniform really highlights all your gayness, so maybe it will all work out for you."

"I hope," Brooke said teasingly and crossed her fingers. She glanced at her phone and noticed the text from Stephen saying he was outside. "Okay, Stephen's here. Be back late. Good luck dealing with Roberta."

Brooke was grateful she had an hour and a half drive with her favorite coworker and roommate. Stephen insisted they blast Taylor Swift and nurse Starbucks venti drinks while enduring the Beltway and Bay Bridge traffic to the other side of the Chesapeake Bay.

"We've got a long night ahead of us," he said, shaking his iced coffee and taking a large gulp through the straw. "And this party is going to be *ridiculous*. We just got the details, and oh my God."

"Ridiculous? How so?"

He raised an eyebrow. "Did Cory tell you what this event is?"

"No. All he said was he desperately needed someone to cover the shift and then offered to take my next Friday event. I didn't care what it was. I was sold. I really need next Friday to prepare for the art exhibit. More than a fair trade."

Stephen's smile widened to a mischievous grin. "We are going to Marc Adair's presidential candidate party…at the Adair Estate. We're going to be in the presence of one of the most powerful and wealthiest families in the area, hell, probably even the country."

Brooke's jaw dropped. Despite the air-conditioning flowing through the car, sweat beaded along her hairline.

"Oh God, you look sick," Stephen said. "Nope, you can't barf in this car. You know I can't handle barf—"

"I'm not gonna barf, Stephen. I just…"

"Then why are you so pale?"

She couldn't tell him the truth. At least, not before the event. She was sure the awkwardness would unfold in front of him, and there would be plenty of time to delve into the whole saga on the way back home.

But for now, she had to mentally prepare herself. She had to remain professional, especially knowing who she would be making drinks for. It was the Adair Estate, which meant she would see all the famous politicians that made up the family: Henry Adair Sr., a four-star Navy admiral and the former Secretary of State during the nineties; Congressman Henry Adair Jr.; and Governor Marc Adair, who had just announced his presidential campaign three weeks prior.

Oh yeah, and Marc Adair's daughter, who Brooke had practically been in love with all through college.

No, Brooke couldn't unleash the truth now. She needed the rest of the time to calibrate her thoughts. This was just an ordinary event with superrich people. She didn't have time to let the past saturate her mind again. She could wait to do that once they were heading back home.

"No reason," Brooke said and cleared her throat. "I just never thought we would be serving the Maryland Kennedys."

The smile landed back on Stephen's face. "I know, right? If Marc Adair wins the presidency, I can scratch that off my bartending bucket list. God, I can serve drinks for the former Secretary of State, a congressman, and the current governor, who could very much be the future president of the United States."

He cranked up Taylor Swift as Brooke slouched in her seat. She checked Google Maps on Stephen's phone and kept her eye on the ETA, noting how much longer she had to mentally prepare.

It was the fastest two hours she'd ever experienced. Before she knew it, Stephen drove under a canopy of trees down the long driveway until it pooled into a motor court. She spotted other workers from their catering company walking back and forth from the vans to elsewhere on the property. In front of her stood an L-shaped, French-country house. It was enormous, everything she'd always imagined the estate to look like.

Stephen and Brooke hurried to the backyard where their colleagues had placed standing tables throughout the lawn. As she and Stephen set up the bar, she took in the view. The Miles River glistened in the early evening sun, and a boat dock stretched a couple of feet out on the other side of the yard; no boats waited there, and two white Adirondack chairs had taken up residence instead. The left and right terrace staircases led down to an elevated lawn where the live band had started to set up.

Right at seven p.m., the guests filtered into the backyard in droves. The men wore button-down shirts and ties, the women an array of colorful cocktail dresses. About a half hour in, Brooke recognized several Adairs. Congressman Henry Adair walked in holding his wife's hand. Marc Adair's oldest daughter, Jacquelyn, walked in with the smallest baby bump forming underneath her sky-blue dress, and her grandfather, Secretary Henry Adair Sr., slowly walked beside her.

The uncle, Congressman Henry Adair, came over to the bar and without making eye contact, said, "A French 75."

No please or thank-you. Just the drink order.

Whenever guests forgot to use manners, Brooke always went easy on the alcohol. She made sure to do that for the congressman.

She was thankful that while she'd collected numerous stories about the Adairs throughout college, none of them knew who she was. It was better that she had never met any Adairs except the one she'd been crushing on. To them, she was just the bartender. All they expected her to do was make a satisfying drink, and that was what she did for all the guests.

They had no idea that she knew stories about all of them.

Luckily, she kept busy for the first forty minutes, making sure every guest had their first round by the time the man of the night, Governor Marc Adair—and his wife Kathryn—joined the party. But it wasn't the presidential candidate who captured her gaze. It was his youngest daughter. She trailed him, a tall blond woman walking next to her, and just like all those years ago, Arlette Adair stole Brooke's attention. It felt as if the evening sun had absorbed all the heat it had given throughout the day and now dumped it all on Brooke.

Her stomach plummeted. Five years later, Arlette had somehow found a way to become even more beautiful than the memory imprinted in Brooke's mind. Her silky, chocolate brown hair blew back in the breeze wafting from the river. She wore a white blazer over a black shirt as well as white jeans that cut off at the ankle.

Brooke tried to focus on the line of people wanting their first round, but half of her kept an eye on Arlette Adair floating through the crowd. Brooke's black vest and long white shirt absorbed enough heat to make sweat trickle down her spine. It wasn't even an hour into the party, and the fabric of her shirt had started collecting liquid nerves.

Her heart thrummed rapidly. She sucked in the breeze to help detangle the knots in her stomach. The anticipation of running into Arlette piled on her in layers of heat. After serving two margaritas, she downed her glass of ginger ale over ice, hoping that would ease the painful stomach knots.

How the hell was she going to get through the night in one piece?

She only had a moment to figure it out because after her ginger ale break, she faced the bar again only to find the most beautiful green eyes locked on hers.

Arlette's dark red lips parted as the breeze combed through her long hair. "Brooklyn?" Arlette said, sounding as if Brooke's sudden appearance had sucked the breath out of her in the same way it had to Brooke.

Brooklyn. The only person to ever call her by her full name.

Although she had practiced what she would say to Arlette so many times since the summer after college graduation, the polished words had fizzled during the lost five years. What was left were the ghosts of them dancing on the tip of her tongue as she tried to figure out what to say back.

With Arlette a foot in front of her, Brooke had never felt so underprepared.

"Hi, Arlette," Brooke said, trying to remain as professional and poised as one could be. She exhaled the feelings balled in her throat while taking Arlette in. She had every part of College Arlette memorized. That was the artist in her. She observed everything and took mental notes on the smallest details.

She had been quick to notice that the boat dock on the other end of the yard was made up of weathered wood, indicating that it was probably unused. She had been quick to notice that the maple tree on the edge of the property had some engraving on it, but she wasn't close enough to make out what had been carved there. Now she was quick to rediscover the beautiful flecks of olive, gold, and amber in Arlette's eyes. It was the first thing she had noticed when she and Arlette had met when they'd moved into their dorm room freshman year, and it was the first thing she noticed now. The details of Arlette's beautiful eyes had never diluted.

When Brooke pulled back her focus and studied this older Arlette, she saw that the five years had beautifully aged some of her features. Her facial structure was more defined, her lips darkened by a rich velvet color. One quick scan of those full lips caused heat to prick at the back of her neck as the air became increasingly warmer.

If it wasn't for those lips, they might have still been best friends.

"What…are you doing here?" Arlette said.

"Well, it looks like your family hired the catering company I work for, so I'm here making drinks. What can I get you?" Brooke put on her professional cap and did what she was paid to do: serve drinks. Arlette was just like the rest of the Adairs. She was a guest, and Brooke was her bartender. Not a former roommate, not an ex-best friend with unresolved history. Just a bartender.

Arlette stood there, seeming as if she was trying to wrap her head around the situation.

Brooke decided to take advantage of the head start. She knew exactly what Arlette needed. "Something stiff?" Brooke suggested.

"Uh…yes, actually. Please."

"Any preference?"

Arlette opened her mouth to say something and then closed it as if thinking twice. "No. Just…anything. I'm not picky."

Brooke went with a Negroni, making sure to add a few extra splashes of gin. She topped it with a sliced orange peel and slid it over. "Here you go, a Negroni. One of my favorites."

It only took her a little under a minute to make the drink, but that still didn't seem like enough time for Arlette to formulate words and power through the extremely awkward moment. She held the drink as if she had no idea what to do with it. "At first, I thought I was seeing things. I thought you just looked like Brooklyn Dawson. I…I had no idea you were living in the area."

"Been here for three years now."

Another woman approached the bar. Brooke pulled her attention off Arlette to make a whiskey ginger. In her peripheral vision, she watched Arlette stand to the side, sipping her drink and still looking as if she had no clue what to do with herself.

"I…I had no idea you would be here…or that we would ever run into each other again," Arlette said after the woman walked away.

Brooke hated how her stare fell to Arlette's full lips, forcing her to study how amazing the matte lipstick highlighted how full and feminine they were.

No, we're not doing this again. Keep her at a distance.

"Well, that makes two of us very surprised."

Arlette faltered. "How have you been?"

That was a loaded question. Brooke was inching toward her quarter-life crisis, debating whether she should sell her soul to the corporate design world instead of doing the freelance work that made her happy. After two internships, she'd decided that being a freelance artist full-time was risky, but it was the most rewarding. Life was too short to follow the money. It didn't equal happiness, anyway. What made Brooke the happiest was creating art that paying customers wanted in their homes.

However, money could create comfortable happiness. Not worrying about missing rent would make her world less stressful. That was why she'd started questioning her decision to freelance. She'd only had to ask Abby to lend her two hundred dollars once. It had been two months ago, and she'd paid Abby back within a month, but it was still mortifying to have to ask her best friend for money. Ever since April, she'd wondered if she should suck it up in order to never put herself—or Abby—in that situation again.

Another pro to switching her bartending job for a normal nine-to-five was that it would give her time to date. Abby and Stephen were amazing friends and roommates and filled half her heart, but the other half was terribly lonely. She wanted to know what falling in love was like. Being lonely and broke really made her consider putting her art on the back burner to have a stable income and schedule. Maybe she'd been too much of a dreamer for the last five years.

But none of that was anything Arlette Adair needed to know.

"I've been great," Brooke answered diplomatically, though she could hear the flatness in her tone.

"That's good," Arlette said and pulled a sip from her drink as the awkwardness saturated the space between them like the humidity in the faint breeze. "Are you…are you doing this full-time, or are you still making art?"

"I'm still making it. This job supports it."

Right as Arlette was about to say something else, the tall blond woman she'd walked in with slid up behind her and brushed an arm up her back to her shoulder. With her presence came the scent of expensive perfume that Brooke was sure could cover next month's rent.

"There you are," the woman said and kissed Arlette's cheek.

Arlette flicked her gaze to her drink. Her smile faded while the young woman remained oblivious. The blonde looked at the bottles behind Brooke and without even a simple acknowledgment said, "A Manhattan, please." Then, without missing a beat, she looked back at Arlette. "I've been looking all over for you, babe."

Brooke snatched a coupe glass, making sure to suppress the urge to roll her eyes. Of course Arlette had a girlfriend. At least one thing hadn't changed in the last five years, and that was women fawning over Arlette Adair. Brooke couldn't blame them, not even the girls in their dorm who'd had crushes on her. She was gorgeous. That was a fact. Rich dark brown hair that made her light green eyes stand out and a structured jawline that had once, and apparently still, captivated Brooke. Arlette's beauty was always the focal point to anyone with eyes.

Once Brooke stirred the rye, sweet vermouth, and bitters together, she poured it in the coupe glass and pierced a cocktail pick through two Luxardo cherries as a garnish. She passed the drink over, and the blonde accepted, still with no eye contact.

"There's someone I want you to meet," the girlfriend said to Arlette.

"Thank you," Arlette said to Brooke.

Brooke gave her a polite grin before she turned back to the blonde. At least she still had manners.

The blonde squeezed Arlette's shoulder. "Come on. Follow me."

Brooke watched the blonde escort Arlette with a hooked arm up the stairs to the left terrace. Once Arlette reached the door that led inside, she turned, cast another glance at Brooke, and went in.

God, it was the hottest evening Brooke had ever endured.

Then there was a warm, heavy hand on her shoulder. "Um…hi. What the hell was that?" Stephen said.

Unfortunately for Brooke, the two of them were finally given a break. No guests approached for drinks, so Brooke poured herself more ginger ale and scooped in a liberal amount of ice to cool down the aftermath of talking to Arlette, sweat still sliding down her back like condensation on a glass.

"What was what?"

She knew exactly what he was talking about, but he was reactive, and she wanted her mind to get off her unresolved past with Arlette Adair and on to something lighter, like making Stephen squirm.

"That." He gestured to the front of the bar. "Whatever it was, made me sweat. So thank you."

"That's because it's humid as fuck right now."

"That's not humidity, Brooke. That was tension. All tension. So spill."

"There's nothing to spill. She was my roommate freshman and sophomore year. We were really good friends."

Stephen's mouth dropped. "Shut the fuck up. Really?"

"Really."

"Have you been here before? Have you met her family?"

"No and no. She met my mom once. Sophomore year during parents' weekend. But I never met hers. They were always busy."

There was a lot more to it, but it wasn't her place to share Arlette's business with the world. The fact that she'd gotten Arlette to open up to her once was rare in itself. She'd never blamed Arlette. When a family was as prominent as hers, people searched high and low for baggage to air to the world. Arlette had kept her world tiny, and the fact that at one point, she'd trusted Brooke enough to let her in meant everything. Even though they hadn't spoken in five years and had left things on poor terms, she would never tell anyone Arlette's personal business.

"How come I feel like there's so much more you're not telling me?"

She was saved by Marc and Jacquelyn Adair. Stephen's eyes widened as they approached. He had a bartending bucket list that he'd literally written in a notebook back at their apartment. This was his moment to serve the possible next president a drink.

He stepped forward, straightened his back, and put on a perfect cordial and professional smile. "Mr. Governor, how are you? What can I get you?"

Marc Adair smiled as if chuckling on the inside. He faced his daughter, and Jacquelyn said, "Two tequila shots and a Shirley Temple, please."

Marc Adair's eyes widened. "Jackie, I don't know about that—"

"Oh, please, Dad. This is your night." She tossed an arm around him. "Where's Arlette? She'll do a shot." Jacquelyn searched the crowd.

"There she is," Marc Adair said and pointed to the terrace. Arlette walked down the steps by herself, and when Brooke turned, Arlette's eyes were on her.

A few moments later, Marc Adair's daughters had lined up at the bar. Stephen fixed two shots and a Shirley Temple. When Brooke met Arlette's gaze again, Arlette's quickly flitted away; she grabbed her shot and faced her family.

Jacquelyn held up her Shirley Temple. "To Dad, for finally pursuing his dream. We're proud of you, and I know I speak for the rest of the family by saying they're all proud of you too."

He smiled. "Thanks, Jackie."

Arlette patted his shoulder. "You're going to do great, Pops."

They toasted, and the shots were quickly downed while Jacquelyn sipped her Shirley Temple. Marc Adair put his arm around Arlette's shoulder. She didn't flinch like Brooke expected. Instead, she smiled at him.

"I hope so. Let's see how this plays out," he said. "Take it easy on the alcohol. And don't tell your mother about the shot." He pointed at Jacquelyn and Arlette. They laughed, and everyone dispersed as some guy in a suit waved for Marc to come over.

However, Arlette stayed. She rested her forearms on the bar and said, "Can I get a scotch on the rocks, please?"

Stephen glanced at Brooke. "I think this is yours," he said. Not quietly enough because it pulled Arlette's attention. The faintest shade of pink streaked across her cheeks, and Brooke felt the embarrassment land on her own face.

When she turned to fix up the drink, she tightened her jaw at Stephen, who suppressed a grin. "Shut the fuck up," she muttered through her teeth.

She felt Arlette's stare as she tossed ice in a lowball glass, poured the Johnnie Walker, and added a few extra splashes. Despite ending things on horrible terms with zero closure, her job was to make sure the guests were liquored up and happy…within reason, of course. Knowing what she did about Arlette and her once strained relationship with her father, Brooke knew she needed the liberal pour.

Brooke slid the drink over, and Arlette was quick to take a long sip. "We've been in the same city for this long and are just now running into each other?"

"Well, we don't really run in the same circles," Brooke said.

"I mean…I can think of one."

There was the smallest hint of a smile tugging a corner of her mouth. Brooke wasn't sure if she thought it was an appropriate time to bring that up or if the alcohol had finally kick-started her buzz. Either way, there was absolutely no chance that Brooke was about to go there. The comment—whether Arlette intended it or not—stung. It was an acknowledgment of their last month of college, the one that had clearly meant significantly more to Brooke than it had to her.

It wasn't like Brooke could do anything about the sting, either. She was behind the bar, in uniform, working for the Adair family, and on the other side stood Arlette in her white blazer and jeans, accepting the drinks Brooke was paid to create. They were not about to take a trip down memory lane when Brooke couldn't do anything but be professional.

"Don't," Brooke said through her clenched jaw, as professionally yet sternly as possible. "We're not doing that."

The tension was palpable. As if sensing the prickly discomfort, Arlette reached into her purse, pulled out a crisp twenty, and placed it in the tip jar to the side of the bar. Brooke cringed at the twenty taking up so much space in a jar filled with ones and fives. She couldn't believe they'd gone from staying up late, talking about everything and nothing while sipping Gatorade and bottom-shelf vodka, to Arlette tipping her for making a drink.

After all that time together, that was where they'd ended up. Their close friendship in college shaken like dice and scattered across opposite sides of the table. Arlette on the side with the money...

...and Brooke on the other side with the tips.

She didn't want the twenty. She'd give it to Stephen, even if that meant taking home less for equal work. She wasn't going to accept pity money no matter how much she needed it.

"Okay...well...thank you for the drink. Hope you have a good night." Arlette gave a forced, cordial smile and headed back to the party.

She didn't approach the bar for the rest of the night. The desperate part of Brooke willed her to come back. As the night progressed, she kept searching for her in the crowd like a game of *Where's Waldo*. Arlette hopped from one circle of wealthy people to another, and when her girlfriend was by her side, their arms locked.

Though as Brooke studied them, she found it interesting how it was always the girlfriend who initiated contact. It was a small detail that she whisked away. Nothing about Arlette Adair was any of her business anymore.

"Okay, spill," Stephen said once they drove off the property around midnight. "Or I'm waking up Abby when we get home because I know that she knows, and you better believe she'll tell me everything."

Brooke rested her head against the seat and closed her eyes for a moment, trying to sort and process everything that had happened. "It's a long story."

"And we have a two-hour drive, and I have a feeling we're not even going to get to talking about how that blond woman with Arlette Adair is Sabrina McKay, as in, the billionaire McKays. She already has more money than I will probably accumulate in this life and the next two lives." Stephen shook his head. "Anyways, one thing at a time. Arlette Adair. Spill."

Brooke pinched the bridge of her nose. She had no idea that the girl kissing Arlette's cheek was from one of the richest families in the country, but of course she was. That was one of three things Arlette's parents wanted for their daughter: go to the Naval Academy just like everyone in their family had done for five generations, go into politics, and marry well. To either someone in the Navy or armed forces, someone in politics or law, or apparently, someone from a billionaire family. Arlette had scoffed at the Naval Academy legacy by going to a Division III college instead and had told Brooke that the last thing she wanted to go into was politics. Brooke couldn't help but wonder if dating a billionaire was to make up for breaking the rest of the rules.

One thing to process at a time, and right now, Brooke was still processing running into someone she'd never expected to see again.

"Arlette and I were best friends in college, and I had a massive crush on her."

"I mean, she's not my type in any way, but I see it. Those eyes." Stephen fanned himself.

"Oh, I know. Trust me. I pined over her for four years. She knows everything about my life, and I know everything about hers."

Stephen peeked over. "Oh yeah? Can you write an Adair tell-all book?"

"Basically, yes."

Stephen's jaw dropped. "I'm sure that would solve your money worries. That could go for six figures, easily. But anyway, we'll work on that later. What happened? Something happened."

As their final month of college resurfaced in Brooke's mind again, she let out a heavy sigh. "Long story short, I pined over her for years. She never knew…because we were best friends, and I knew that I shouldn't have a crush on my roommate and best friend. Arlette dated this girl for six months during senior year, and the girlfriend, Jade, really fractured our relationship. She was easily jealous and was intimidated by our friendship, so Arlette and I sort of drifted apart. Arlette broke up with her a month before graduation, and she told me it was because Jade had never listened to her. Or ever truly saw her…not like I had seen her."

Stephen gasped. "Oh shit."

"I don't know what happened, but that made me kiss her. She kissed me back, and then we had this 'friends with benefits' thing going on for the last month of college."

"Shut the fuck up. Are you serious?"

"Dead serious." Telling Stephen the story was like brushing dust off a novel she'd read countless times, one she once had memorized, and the words fell naturally off her tongue like they had years ago. Remembering the most exciting and the most heartbreaking month of her life sent a dull ache to her chest. She had no idea what the exact word was to describe her feelings about Arlette Adair back then. Love felt too strong a word for a month-long rendezvous that never went past making out in their underwear.

But if it wasn't love, then Brooke had been a step below being in love with Arlette Adair, and God, had those feelings consumed her back then. Five years later, no one had made her heart race, melt, and shatter the way Arlette had so effortlessly.

"But that's all it was," Brooke said, adding a slight firm period at the end of the sentence, trying to convince herself too. She couldn't afford to spiral into old feelings again. "It was casual. She made that very clear."

"But you didn't want casual, did you? You felt something more?"

She blew out the heaviest exhale. She closed her eyes and allowed herself to wander back into the memories of how it had felt being held by Arlette, kissed by Arlette, finally desired by the woman she had wanted for four years.

If it was only supposed to be casual, why had kissing her taken Brooke to places she'd never been with any other woman?

"Honestly?" she said and faced him, her cheek pressed against the headrest.

"Honestly."

"I felt everything. The night before graduation, Abby and I threw this party. I wanted to talk about what was happening between me and Arlette and what it would look like after we moved back home. Arlette agreed, told me to give her a moment. Ten minutes later, her ex-girlfriend, Jade, got sick in our bathroom. Jade's roommate asked Arlette for help, and Arlette took it upon herself to walk Jade home. She said she'd be back, and I waited…and waited…but she never came. Two hours later, I got a text from her that said, 'I'm sorry,' and that was it. She ran away from a conversation we really needed to have. I was devastated. Arlette had promised that she wouldn't let Jade ruin our friendship, but it was strained because of her insecurities. That last night was the final straw. I felt like I was on the back burner yet again for a girl who'd never treated Arlette the way she deserved to be treated."

"Why the hell didn't she come back?"

She shrugged. "I've been asking myself the same question for five years, Stephen. A few days after graduation, we talked on the phone because Arlette was finally desperate to fix things, but by then, I was done. I was so exhausted from the last year of dealing with her girlfriend, who didn't even want us to be friends. I was tired of Arlette using me for something casual, and I was tired of allowing myself to let her when nothing was casual about it for me. I really cared about her. Deeply." She shook her head as all the suppressed feelings from that night came back to life.

"It ended? Just like that?"

"I ended the call by asking her if the last month had meant anything to her and if she'd regretted it. She'd told me that we probably shouldn't have hooked up because things were weird now, which they were. Once she said that, I hung up, and we haven't spoken since. For the longest time after, I thought it was my fault for kissing my best friend and making things weird. I don't know. What I do know is that I felt like she abandoned me on so many levels. It was silly to even think that Arlette wanted more. Look at her dating a billionaire now."

Brooke had a long list of unanswered questions. If she could go back in time, she would have put her heartbroken and abandoned feelings aside to get answers and closure. But she'd let them get in the way of potentially mending her heart and her friendship with Arlette. She struggled to accept what transpired between them for a while but eventually made peace with it. She had to for her own sanity. As time went on, and Arlette Adair had been out of her life longer than she'd been in it, Brooke had forced herself to move on. Sometimes, people never got closure, and this was just one of those times.

Life was filled with the intersecting paths of people who were meant to shape a person. Arlette Adair's path had crossed Brooke's at what felt like the right time. She'd grown up wondering why her father had decided to abandon her and her mother when she was eight. She hated how his absence had shaped her insecurities and molded her relationships with everyone who came into her life. However, when her path had crossed with Arlette's, Brooke had felt something rare. Arlette had made her feel wanted, appreciated, and loved.

While Arlette had helped her discover who she was, for whatever reason, Arlette was also meant to be the person to give her a first taste of heartbreak. There would always be part of her heart that flourished with memories of Arlette; at the same time, the other half would always ache for what could have been.

CHAPTER TWO

A rlette didn't know how to fall back asleep.

Sabrina was asleep next to her. Sharing a queen-size bed with someone when there was no comfortable spot to lie in made her feel like she was being pushed off the bed. She'd tried sleeping on her side, her back, her stomach, but each position was like finding comfort on a bed of nails. So she sat up and waited for the ibuprofen to kill the piercing headache, a result of the strong drinks she had consumed.

Once light broke through the window, she knew sleep was a lost cause.

She tiptoed downstairs and made sure to be as quiet as a mouse so she didn't wake up the rest of the family, all of whom had crashed at Grandpa Harry's house. It had been a long night of celebrating, socializing, and drinking; Arlette probably should have stopped about three drinks earlier, knowing that she and Sabrina were going to look at a house the next morning.

Maybe that was part of the reason she'd snatched a bottle of Dom Pérignon for herself and had hidden in the darkness with Jacquelyn on the boat dock. She was certain that she would have finished the bottle if it hadn't been for the two other drinks right before that, all to help forget about Brooklyn Dawson randomly appearing from her past.

The rising sun scattered streaks of light pinks and yellows through the sky and highlighted the Miles River in the backyard. As she stepped outside, she took in the quiet space freed from all the guests from the night before. Dew clung to the grass, and early morning fog danced on the surface of the water. That was when she made out Grandpa Harry's silhouette sitting in an Adirondack chair on the dock. She smiled. It was his favorite spot on the whole property because of his love for the pocket of peace and silence it offered; it was her favorite spot too.

She brewed some coffee, carefully brought two steaming mugs down to the dock, and took a seat beside her grandpa.

"What are you doing up so early?" he asked through a chuckle, though he didn't question the mug placed in his hand. Most of his life had been spent waking up early while serving in the military. He'd been a lieutenant commander in Vietnam, a four-star admiral in the Gulf War, and had gone on to become Secretary of State for two terms in the nineties. His internal clock had been set to watch the sunrise since his mid-twenties.

"Couldn't sleep," she said and took her delicious first sip. The first cup of coffee was always the best part of the morning, even on the stressful days.

"Didn't you have five or so bottles of champagne? That should have done you in."

She smiled at his teasing. "I had one bottle, and it's your fault for getting the good stuff. You know it's like adult candy. I had to take advantage of the moment."

He grinned behind the rim of his mug. "And did you take advantage of the moment?"

She lifted a shoulder. "Kind of. Jackie and I hid from everyone and sat out here, chatted, tossed around some baby names, vetoed some others."

"Do you have any good contenders?"

"I'd like to think so. I've been patting myself on the back that I suggested a name that made her rethink her number-one choice. So there's that."

"Is it too soon to pitch Henrietta?"

She rolled her eyes teasingly. "She sounds like she'll come out of the womb as an eighty-six-year-old."

He let out a cackle that wonderfully pierced the dawn silence. "Is this really coming from the woman who was named after my mother?"

"Hey, you take that up with my parents. I had no choice in my name, thank you. I took matters into my own hands in middle school and tried making Arlie a thing, but everyone made fun of me for it."

"Hon, you know I love you more than anything, but when you went through your Arlie phase, I might have loved you this much less." He held up an inch of space between his pointer finger and thumb.

She playfully squeezed his arm. She loved how they always teased each other, and it was always within reason. It was their love language, something that made their bond so special to both of them. Grandpa Harry might have been eighty-six, but he knew how to embrace the youth that never left his heart, regardless of all the important titles he'd collected in his lifetime.

As the teasing faded, the silence fell back on them. The small waves lapped the stilts of the dock, and the birds chirped a calming melody. The fun banter gave Arlette a momentary escape from the stacks of worries in her mind. Now, she had to face them again as if the clouds had dispersed, and the view of her anxieties was as clear as ever. She kept defaulting to Brooklyn Dawson on the other side of the bar, someone she'd thought she would never see again. She got the sense that Brooke wished they hadn't reunited because, God, was she aloof. Rightfully so. It was a blatant reminder of how badly Arlette had messed things up with her all those years ago.

"What's going on inside that expansive brain of yours?" Grandpa Harry said.

That was a loaded question. There was a lot happening inside her brain, and she had no idea where to start sorting out her thoughts. Should she start on how stressful her job was right now or the fact that she desperately wanted to escape working on the Hill? Should she talk about how she'd been toying with the idea of breaking up with Sabrina because she could feel it in her gut that they weren't right for each other? She knew it would shatter her parents' dreams of morphing into a superpowered family. Marc Adair's youngest daughter marrying Angela McKay's oldest daughter, who was set to take over the family's real-estate development empire, making them one of the richest families in the United States. Of course, both the Adairs and the McKays drooled over the idea.

Or should Arlette talk about how she was thinking about the girl who got away? The girl who had been randomly spawned from her memories to serve drinks at her father's party.

She exhaled and kept her focus on the water as it absorbed the sunrise coloring the dawn sky. "Do you ever think that if you did one thing differently, your life would be totally different?"

Grandpa Harry chuckled. "The sun is barely above the horizon, and you're already thinking those thoughts?" He shook his head and nursed his coffee. "You really do have a lot going on inside that head, don't you?"

She shrugged. She thought it was a fair question, one he would have many responses to. He was eighty-six and had seen a lot. Besides Vietnam, the Gulf War, and working for two different presidents, he'd been married for sixty-four years, had two sons following in his footsteps, had watched as their family legacy had shaped the lives of his four grandchildren, and was about to become a great-grandfather.

If anyone could give Arlette the perspective she was searching for, it was him.

"Well, not running for president was probably the biggest decision." He'd considered running for president in the late eighties while being an admiral in the Navy. Numerous politicians on both party lines had encouraged him to do it, thinking his moderate stance was exactly what the country was looking for. But ultimately, he'd decided against it.

"Do you regret not running?"

"Absolutely not. Being in politics was never part of the plan. It just sort of happened."

"How?"

"Well...I went to the Naval Academy because my father and grandfather went there. I never really thought of going anywhere else. I was also young and thought it would help make my father, a World War II vet, and my grandfather, a World War I vet, proud. I also thought it would help me see the world." He shook his head. "I saw the world and then some things I wish I could forget. Then, just like that, I served two tours, went up the ranks, and became a lieutenant commander during my second tour. When that ended, I had plenty of military experience, and the jobs the government offered me paid much better. It helped me have enough money for the family I wanted. So my career just fell into place. Secretary of State was an incredibly hard job. I was grateful for it and how my career played out, but that was enough for me. Plus, the game of politics got tiring after all those years. I was excited to retire."

"Contrary to my current job, I also have zero interest in politics," Arlette said and pulled a soothing, warm sip of coffee. She always saw herself doing something else, but like Grandpa Harry, life happened, and accepting very good opportunities was so alluring until she realized how far she'd strayed from her original plan. And now she was stuck and desperately searching for a crossroads to veer off on.

"It's not too late, Arlette. I know you think it is, but you're only twenty-seven."

"I can't abandon Teresa right before she's about to propose the emissions bill to the House. We've worked so hard on that bill. Plus, my dad would freak out if I got off the Hill."

"Your father will get over it. Remember your Christmas announcement when you were eighteen? Didn't he eventually get over that?"

Arlette gave him a half-smile. All the Adairs had gone to the Naval Academy since her great-great-grandpa, Ernest. Her great-grandpa Charles was appointed by the president to be the Chief of Naval Operations—the head of the Navy—during Vietnam, cementing the Adairs' legacy and essentially carving a path for them to follow. But Arlette had zero interest in being in the military. While she inherited her family's love for the water, ocean, and nature, she didn't inherit her family's love for politics, and she didn't bleed navy blue and gold. She knew she didn't have to join the Navy in order to do something that indulged her passion for helping the environment. At eighteen, she was tired of blending in with the rest of the family and being expected to follow everyone else for no other reason than it being a "family legacy."

Instead, she decided to go to Willard University, a small private college right outside of Richmond, Virginia. They had a great environmental science program. There was enough distance between Richmond and St. Michaels for her to form the kind of independence that she'd spent all of her childhood and adolescence craving. And it was small, which meant that hopefully, she would find the close group of friends she'd always wanted but had never had. She'd announced her college decision at Christmas. Back then, she'd wanted so much to have her own life that she'd sometimes made dramatic decisions, like informing the family while opening presents that she would be the first Adair to not join the military. She thought it would be a perfect way to say "fuck you" to them by announcing it then. As to be expected, her father and Uncle Henry had freaked out, while Grandpa Harry had applauded her decision. He'd even worn his burgundy "Proud Willard University Grandpa" T-shirt while he'd hugged her good-bye before her drive to Richmond eight months later.

"Took about four years to get over it, but, yeah, he did," Arlette said. "Uncle Henry, on the other hand…"

Grandpa Harry waved her off. "He has his own two children to worry about, and luckily for him, Christian and Charlotte joined the Navy. So his opinions about your decision are his to deal with, not yours."

Arlette smiled. She loved how Grandpa Harry understood her, always had, and while some of her family looked at her as the black sheep, Grandpa Harry saw her as being the boldest and bravest. That was something she would always cling to.

"I know your father, uncle, and Christian are really into family traditions, but I'm proud of you, your mom and Jackie are proud of you, and I know for a fact that your grandma was proud of you too. You're a smart girl, Arlette. I have no doubt that you'll figure it out. I think it's natural to be a little lost at your age. I sure was. And better to be lost at home than in a foreign country like Vietnam, let me tell you."

She reflected on his words for the rest of the day. They weighed on her like a fifty-pound dumbbell as she and Sabrina ventured over to Annapolis to look at a house. Sabrina was ready for an upgrade. She wanted to move out of her downtown Annapolis condo for more space and a waterfront view. She'd always wanted and hoped that Arlette would move in with her despite her telling Sabrina that she didn't want to commute from Annapolis to Capitol Hill every day. With typical traffic, it would be an hour drive each way, and Arlette already worked long hours as she and Teresa Rosario's team worked on and prepared to propose a new bill to the House. But it seemed like Sabrina took her words lightly, as if she could be convinced eventually, which bothered her so much. But could she blame Sabrina? She had seen firsthand how Arlette's determination had dulled since first meeting when they were sixteen. Arlette seemed to flow wherever the wind took her. Looking back on how her determination faded over the years, she saw it clear as day, and she was so disappointed in herself.

Arlette was willing to look at the house to provide her opinions, but if Sabrina brought it up again, Arlette told herself she would put her foot down on the idea of her moving in.

"Isn't the place amazing?" Sabrina said as she spun around the space. "Look at this kitchen. We can host dinner parties, cook amazing food, host Thanksgiving with both our families. Arlette, how sexy is this kitchen?" Sabrina glided her hand along the white marble counter.

"It's pretty sexy," Arlette said, not able to deny it even if she wanted to.

The house was gorgeous. It had Brazilian wooden floors throughout the first level, and the two-story great room that overlooked the shaded backyard offered beautiful views of the Severn River on the edge of the property. It had six bedrooms, five baths, a theater room, and so much space for two people, let alone one. The only con was that it was all the way in Annapolis.

The longer she took in the house with Sabrina, imagining their life playing out in every single room, the heavier Grandpa Harry's words weighed on her. He usually had all the answers. He had an arsenal of knowledge that had never led her astray in all of her twenty-seven years on earth.

However, that morning was the first time she saw an error in his perspective.

She'd much rather be lost in a foreign country than lost at home where she was supposed to belong.

❖

"We need to revamp this office."

Arlette looked at her boss, Teresa Rosario, who stared at the white walls like they were the most offensive things she'd ever seen, and that was saying something. As a young freshman congresswoman from New York's 13th Congressional District, a huge portion of her job was spent arguing with Republican men who had definitely said more offensive things. She'd even started writing them down. Arlette had thought she was joking at first, until Teresa had actually showed her the collection of insults.

But apparently, the Cannon Building's bland walls were still a close second.

The office had three black-and-white photos of Washington Heights hanging on the walls, part of Teresa's congressional district and the neighborhood she was from in Manhattan. The more Arlette studied the space, the more she realized how badly it needed a dose of color.

"We need something fresh in here," Teresa said, tapping her chin. "There's nothing that screams, 'We love Earth. Let's protect her,' but, you know, artistic enough that it empowers us."

Arlette sensed some teasing in her tone. "Should have had some beautiful art up to help inspire this bill." She pointed at the stack of papers on the desk, their beloved cosponsored emissions bill, one that Teresa was set to introduce to the House the following week. It could drastically cut back on the allowed emissions from public transportation in cities with a population over one hundred thousand. While it might not have been the sexiest bill to the general public, it was an important one, and had been Arlette's baby for the last two months. Boring or not, it would help clean up the air tremendously.

"You're into art, right?" Teresa said. "Your dad told me the story of how you kept skipping classes in high school so you could sneak into DC to visit museums. You seemed to have forgotten to mention that in your interview." Teresa tilted her head back and laughed.

Arlette's face burned. She'd been working for Teresa for two years, and this was brand-new information. Why the hell would her father tell her boss that?

"I skipped classes because I was bored. I learned much more fascinating things at the museums than I ever did in class. I learned all about how doomed we really are from climate change at the Natural History Museum and Newseum. So if anything, you should be thankful that's how you got me. I could have been doing worse things."

Teresa grinned. "This is true. Thank you, Natural History Museum." She shook her hands toward the ceiling as if thanking the museum gods.

"I also learned more about art at the Renwick, the Hirshhorn, and the National Gallery of Art than I ever did in my art classes. I thought it was time well spent."

To this day, on her days off, Arlette loved going to museums on any topics. They relaxed her, and DC had plenty of them. She would refocus off her stress and get lost in an exhibit, channeling her nervous energy into absorbing new knowledge. It was fun and relaxing. She especially loved the art museums that made up her city.

"I'm no connoisseur, but I'd say I'm an art admirer, yes," Arlette said.

"Okay, so with that in mind and based on all the knowledge you gathered from playing hooky, what do you think would liven up this space?"

Arlette did another scan of the room. "Definitely something big and colorful on the opposite wall. Something bold that makes a statement. Something that's a reflection of you and your platform. Our team needs something to remind us of what we're fighting for and why we wake up every morning and come to this office every day."

"Yes. Exactly that," Teresa said with a point. "It has to be a local artist, though. Either from Washington Heights or DC."

"I can do some research when I get home."

"If you really don't mind. Finding something great for this office will be a breeze compared to the Emission Bill, don't you think?"

"Definitely. I need something to cleanse my palate. I'm more than happy to take this on."

Little did Teresa know that Arlette didn't need to spend too much time researching. She had been following a local artist for the last five years.

Once she got back to her English basement, she poured herself a glass of red wine, plopped on her couch, and pulled out her phone. She'd already known that Brooke had been living in DC for the last three years. But despite knowing Brooke's whereabouts, she'd never expected her to be serving drinks in her grandpa's backyard. That surprise did knock the air out of her.

Despite their horrible falling-out, Arlette had always been so proud and impressed that Brooke was doing exactly what she had talked about since the start of college: freelance art.

She thanked social media for that knowledge, although she hardly used it. It was just another window into her life for strangers to peek in and ridicule. She only ever used Instagram, kept her profile private, and only allowed the closest people in her life to follow her. She'd used it the most during college when four years away from home and out of the spotlight had made her open up more. She never posted anything, but she still used it to keep tabs on the friends she'd once had at Willard.

Brooke had unfollowed her after their fallout. At the time, it had really hurt. It was another blow to her stomach that was still trying to let go of the hurt caused by losing her best friend. Even though Brooke had cut ties via social media, Arlette couldn't bring herself to do the same.

A year after graduation, Brooke had promoted her new artist profile on her personal Instagram. Arlette checked it whenever she had the urge to lurk. She had always loved Brooke's art. She created pieces that made Arlette stare in contemplation for the longest time. The kind of art that made her get lost in the world Brooke created on a canvas.

Brooke had wandered to the forefront of her mind since Friday, and once Teresa had mentioned needing some art, Arlette had defaulted to the one artist she'd been admiring from afar for the last five years.

She signed into her Instagram account for the first time in a while and combed through the photos on Brooke's profile. She saw a post from the day before that talked about an art exhibit this coming Friday.

Arlette lowered her phone and let her mind wander. All the what-ifs and what-could-have-beens resurfaced and swelled. What if she hadn't run away from Brooke at the party? What if she and Brooke had actually had that conversation that would have led to Brooke asking for more? What if they had actually explored being more than friends with benefits?

What would her life have been like? Would it have been different at all? Would it have been better? Would she have still felt stuck at twenty-seven?

She knew then what her weekend plans were, and if she played her cards right, maybe she would finally get some clarity on all the what-ifs and what-could-have beens.

CHAPTER THREE

"Oh my God, you really are the next Georgia O'Keeffe," Stephen said as he gawked at Brooke's work on the wall.

"She keeps it a secret," Abby said. "She didn't show me her art once in college until her senior art show. If it weren't for her Instagram or Etsy page, I would still assume she was drawing stick figures."

"I'm loving this Northern Lights painting," Stephen said. "I want it. How much?"

"About two catering events," Brooke said, holding back her laughter.

Stephen's mouth thinned. "Okay...well...maybe I'll get the print of it on your Etsy page. You let me know when it goes up."

"Are all of these...textured?" Abby said as she reached out to one of the pieces.

Brooke snatched her wrist and lowered it. It was Abby's first time at an art exhibit. She didn't know the rules, like how no one could touch the art. This was why Brooke never invited Abby to go to museums. She would probably get them kicked out because she wanted to touch the elephant at the Natural History Museum, and Brooke could literally not afford to be banned from the free DC museums. She really valued that about the Smithsonian Museums.

"The number one rule at an art exhibit: don't touch," Brooke said.

Abby made an I'm-in-trouble-face. "Sorry. It's textured. I thought it was inviting me to touch."

"It doesn't work that way."

"Well, still. These pieces are beautiful, Brooke." Abby turned to

Stephen. "We should go look at some of the other artists. Fully embrace this fancy lifestyle. We can pretend that we're art curators."

"And that we're sipping the fanciest wine from Italy."

"Exactly." She squeezed Brooke's arm. "We're really proud of you, Brooke. You should be too. Seriously. Now, go find them good homes."

She winked, and Stephen blew a kiss before they walked over to the next artist, who had five abstract sculptures. Brooke bit back a laugh as they tilted their heads. They studied one of the pieces while pulling a sip of wine, and then both looked back at Brooke with confused expressions. She couldn't quite grasp what the artist was trying to say in his pieces, either, but that was a huge reason why she loved art. There were a million ways to convey a message, and the puzzling ones were the most fun.

While her friends meandered through the gallery, Brooke chatted with the people who came to her post. Some gave her compliments, some simply admired and moved on, and some inquired about purchasing a specific piece. She passed out business cards to the people asking about buying the pieces, and a handful asked if she did commissions. The excitement of commissions made her heart thrum. It was how she made the most money. Depending on the piece, she could make anything from a few hundred dollars up to a grand or more.

There was always a seed of doubt that she wasn't good enough. Putting her work out there for people to judge was scary, especially when she was still trying to build her name. For the first two years of her career, she'd shied away from shows and exhibits. Growing up in the world of social media had helped. She could hide behind her phone, upload her art, and still have some layer of anonymity to shield her from ridicule. After her account had gained some traction and people had kept commenting and messaging her, asking how to purchase, she'd decided to open her Esty shop. It was where most of her money came in, and it provided a light, yet steady, cash flow. It had also helped build up her confidence to push herself into shows and contact local businesses to feature her art. Now, she had people wanting commissions, offering her some relief from the worry that she wouldn't make rent.

When she turned and admired her paintings, she smiled at how far she had come. In life, in general. She'd been through a lot. Her father had left when she was eight. She'd watched her mom blindly navigate raising a child on an elementary teacher's salary, and still, with the adversity and the hole her father had left in their family, Brooke had turned out pretty decent. At least, she thought so. She'd persisted through the adversity, working hard to get the scholarships that had helped her go to Willard University, a school with a prolific art department. Even though she hadn't grown up in the wealthiest of households, she'd still found a way to live in a big city, doing freelance like she'd always wanted to do, with her art on the wall.

Abby and Stephen were right. She had every right to be proud. It was probably the proudest she had ever been of herself.

"Wow, this painting is really beautiful."

Brooke glanced over her shoulder to find Arlette Adair's striking green eyes staring at the wall.

What the hell was she doing here?

Last week, Brooke at least had two hours to prepare to see her, but tonight? She felt as frozen as Arlette had seemed on the other side of the bar. A prickly heat rapidly snaked around her spine and ballooned in her chest. There stood Arlette, wearing a white blouse tucked into dark skinny jeans and black booties that added about an inch to her normal five-eight height. She stared at the wall for a few extra moments before shifting her gaze to Brooke, and as their eyes connected, a ripple shot through her gut.

"Hi, Brooklyn."

Unlike the weekend before, Brooke didn't have to soak her words in professionalism. She could be as candid as she wanted. "What are you doing here?"

"I came here to look at some art." She gestured to the wall before taking a few steps forward to get a better look.

Brooke dug up all the rehearsed speeches she'd once memorized for if and when she ever spoke to Arlette again. Those lost five years had apparently erased those polished words because she couldn't remember any of them. Even though she'd outgrown those speeches, the residual hurt remained like a scar on her heart.

"You know, once I walked in, before I even saw you standing here, I knew these paintings belonged to you," Arlette said. "They're just so… stunning. The colors, these textures, my God." She took a step closer, getting a front-row view of Brooke's favorite new painting technique:

the palette knife. Arlette studied the paintings for a few more moments before shaking her head, pulling a sip from her beer, and turning back to Brooke with a friendly smile. "They're still a bit abstract, so they snatch your eye instantly but not so abstract that you don't know what the hell you're looking at. It's the kind of art that invites you to try harder to find the meaning, you know? Not…well…" She raised her eyebrows and shot a look at the sculpture that had confused Abby and Stephen. "It's not so much that it scares you away and makes you feel like you're not good enough for not understanding."

And those were the words Brooke had been searching for over the last minute. That was exactly how Arlette had made Brooke feel the last time they'd seen each other. When Arlette had run away, she'd made Brooke feel like she wasn't good enough to be with her. Arlette was an Adair, one of the most powerful and influential families in the country. And Brooke was just…her best friend. Nothing more.

"I can't believe you're here at an art show in a big city," Arlette said as her smile grew. "I mean, this is what you were talking about freshman year, and now you're actually doing it."

All those unspoken words began to materialize in her brain. Brooke truly thought she'd gotten over what had happened between them, but she realized then and there how easy it was to think she had moved on from something, until that something was looking right at her with a beautiful smile. She opened her mouth, but no words came out.

Arlette took another drink and faced the wall of paintings. "I love this one. It's stunning. If I wanted to buy it, how much would it be?" She pointed to *Autumn in New York*.

It was Brooke's favorite piece, but that was a secret. Each original painting was one of her babies, and she couldn't make it apparent that she had a favorite out of any collection. In the background of the canvas, an outline of skyscrapers stood in black oil paint. Off to both sides were trails of trees in fall foliage. She'd slathered bold crimson, amber, and gold with a palette knife and had textured the leaves. In between the leaves stood the silhouette of a female couple walking down a textured white path.

"Um…it's five hundred," Brooke said, the words tumbling out. "I mean…sorry, it's six-fifty." She ran the numbers through her head to make sure her math was right. "Yeah, six-fifty."

"And it's for sale?"

"All of them are technically for sale."

Arlette faced Brooke with determination in her eyes, and the gallery got significantly warmer. "Well, then, I'm interested. I'm sure there are other potential buyers, but I'm willing to go higher than the asking price."

Brooke thought about it and remembered the other people who had stopped and inquired about her pieces. She always cared about who bought her work. She wanted to make sure they got the proper homes they deserved.

Did she really want to sell this one, her favorite of the bunch? Did she really want a painting that meant so much to her to go to someone who had broken her heart?

"There are other people interested in it, yes," she said.

"I'll do seven-fifty."

Brooke hated how she involuntarily coughed at Arlette's offer. She really wanted to say no. Hell, she'd been getting pretty good at saying "no" since the last time Arlette had seen her. It came with both of her jobs. But Arlette came back with an enticing rebuttal, one that made Brooke rethink the "no" dancing on the tip of her tongue.

"I feel like I caught you off guard," Arlette said.

"Uh…yeah, I think it's safe to say that."

"How about I go take a lap or two, and maybe I'll catch you at a better time?"

Why did Brooke want her to leave just as much as she wanted her to stay?

Arlette moved on to the sculptures, stopped, and studied the one that had been stealing everyone's attention. When she seemed lost in observation, Brooke scurried in the opposite direction and searched for Abby and Stephen, catching them on the other side of the gallery chatting up two separate guys. She rolled her eyes because, of course, her two single friends came to the exhibit not only to support her but to also take advantage of the open bar and the men who appreciated art… and who probably had enough money to buy original pieces. But so many weighted memories spiraled in Brooke's head like a cement truck that she didn't care if she was ruining their chances. She grabbed them both and hauled them into a unisex, single-stall bathroom.

THE HUES OF ME AND YOU

"Jesus, Brooke," Abby said, steadying the wine sloshing in her glass. "Be careful with this. It's an open bar. Every drink counts."

"Arlette Adair is here."

A smile curved around Stephen's open mouth. "Seriously?"

"Seriously."

"Don't worry. I can handle this," Abby said and headed for the door.

Brooke caught her arm just in time. "Hold it. You are *not* handling it."

Abby frowned, looking completely offended. "What? Why not?"

"Because you are *not* a fan."

"Of course I'm not a fan. She used you as a rebound and didn't have the decency to have a mature conversation with you. Four years of friendship down the drain just like that, and who had to pick you up off the bathroom floor when you were crying? Me."

Brooke rolled her eyes. "Please, do not do anything. I can handle this."

Abby crossed an arm under the one holding her wineglass. "Oh, yeah? How?"

"I don't fucking know, but I need to figure it out ASAP because she wants to buy one of my paintings. She offered me a hundred dollars over the asking price."

Abby coughed on another sip of wine. "What?"

"I know."

"Well, we know those Adairs have plenty of money."

"Yeah, you should see their house," Stephen added. "It smells like crisp hundred-dollar bills." He faced Brooke. "Are you going to sell it to her?"

The residual hurt expanding inside warned her not to. Arlette had been her best friend at one point, and Brooke had trusted Arlette with her life, and Arlette had completely broken that trust. Did she really want to give her painting of vibrant warm colors to the woman who, at one point in time, had dulled hers?

"I have no idea if I should sell it to her," Brooke said. "The heartbroken twenty-two-year-old who stopped painting for three months because of her says *hell no*. But the struggling twenty-seven-year-old who needs to pay rent says that I'd be dumb not to accept."

"What does your gut say?" Abby said. "Your gut is always right, and even if we're both bitter and need money, you have to trust what it says."

Brooke's gut reminded her that she had once trusted Arlette with everything, and if she found a way to trust Arlette for so long, maybe she could trust her with a favorite painting.

"I really have no idea. I want to sell it to her, but I also don't," Brooke said.

"You can't have both," Abby said. "You want one more than the other. What is it?"

Brooke inhaled deeply until it reached the bottom of her lungs. She'd spent her childhood watching her mom worry about money, collecting every nickel and dime to make sure they'd lived as comfortably as possible, even if that meant giving up time with Brooke to work a second job teaching art to adults. Brooke had spent the majority of her life worrying about money too. As she'd immersed herself in her art and had strived to become financially dependent on it alone, she'd noticed how much her mood affected her work and productivity. It had started after college graduation, when her heartbreak had clogged all inspiration from flowing out of her onto a canvas. The more stress on her plate, the harder it had been to make art. She'd wanted to eliminate all that so she could paint more, make money, earn more to her name. That meant selling more pieces and not getting tangled up in people who had no interest in being with her, like Arlette Adair.

Two other people had inquired about the same piece. Did she protect her heart by selling it to them, or protect her stress and bank account by selling it to Arlette?

She couldn't afford to worry. Not when she'd spent half her life watching her mother take on too much stress.

"I think I need to sell it to her," Brooke finally said and exhaled all the pros and cons she'd compiled in her brain.

"Then go do that," Stephen said.

"And we'll be ready to act if you need to escort her out," Abby said. She gave Brooke's arm an assuring squeeze before Brooke headed out of the bathroom.

When Brooke returned to her spot, Arlette was lost in the crowd. Brooke let out a relieved sigh, knowing that the crowd had bought her more time to process. Half her mind had been focused on the exhibit, talking to potential buyers and making sure her canvas babies found a deserving home. The other half was hyperfocused on Arlette, who she finally spotted weaving around the crowd and soaking up each work of art from the other nine artists. She stood in front of each piece for what seemed like five minutes, as if combing over every detail in order to truly appreciate it.

Arlette had done the same thing at Brooke's senior art show. She had given every piece equal attention and had stayed to the very end. At the time, Brooke thought that must have meant something, that all of their secret hookup sessions meant that maybe Arlette had feelings. But knowing what she did now, Brooke knew that Arlette sticking around now and taking her time with each piece meant nothing. It was just who Arlette was. She moved from piece to piece like she had with girls in college.

Twenty minutes later, Arlette came back around and flashed Brooke a cautious smile as she approached. "Hi," Arlette said and gave a small wave. "How's that painting doing?"

"Pretty well. Quite a few people are interested." That was the truth. While Arlette had been observing, two more people had asked about *Autumn in New York.*

"I'll go up to eight-fifty. I really love this painting, Brooklyn. It's stunning. I'm willing to fight for it."

God, the way she said Brooke's full name still caused her breath to stutter like it had in college. She hated it. She hated how good Arlette still looked too. She was wrapped in a simple, yet sexy, white shirt that dipped to the start of her cleavage. Her bold beautiful eyes, confidence, and swagger hadn't been diluted over time.

Brooke wasn't supposed to still be affected like this. It was inexcusable. Every atom of her being had turned traitorous. Sure, Arlette was fucking gorgeous, the type of gorgeous that made her feel special whenever their eyes met. But she had to remember all the pain and hurt that beauty had once caused. She wasn't going to let herself cave so easily. She swatted those thoughts and locked them out.

"While you think about it, do you do commissions?" Arlette said.

"I do."

"And how would one go about getting a Brooklyn Dawson commissioned piece?"

What was even happening right now?

Brooke reached for her stack of business cards sitting on an end table between her and the sculptures. "All the information is on here. You can email or call, and we can go from there if that's something you really want to do."

The amount of professionalism Brooke drenched her answer in strained her throat. She didn't want to have to be formal with Arlette, but with a gaping hole in their timeline, she had no choice. All the time that had passed had demoted them from best friends to strangers with unresolved issues.

Arlette stared at the card for a moment, and when she met Brooke's gaze, a silent moment passed between them. It was as if the full weight of their situation had finally resurfaced in Arlette by the way she stared at Brooke with regret pooling in her eyes. "Can I just say how great it is to see you again?"

There it was, the hurt swelling in Brooke's gut. College had been several lifetimes ago, several girlfriends ago, but she was still shocked by how much seeing the first girl she'd fallen for, the first girl who'd broken her heart, affected her.

The scariest thing was, there would always be a part of Brooke who was happy to see her too.

"Yeah, it's been...um, it's been a really long time." Brooke tried swallowing the nervous growth in her throat to no avail.

"Are you doing anything after this? I would love to buy you a drink and catch up."

The way she waited for the answer with raised and hopeful eyebrows caused something heavy to sink in Brooke's stomach. Arlette seemed so scared of the huge possibility of rejection, and it was a question with great risk, the kind she had run away from before. Brooke wondered if part of her showing up to her exhibit was to get answers. This might have been the only opportunity for them to get the closure they'd been waiting for after all this time.

"Just one drink. My treat," Arlette added, doing an amazing job of persuading. She still had her charming charisma. That hadn't changed, either.

If Brooke was to get a drink with Arlette—one drink only—she had to remain firm. She couldn't soften as easily as she used to. She needed to use the residual hurt swirling in her stomach to build a very sturdy guard.

"I can only do one drink," Brooke said, and she was proud of herself for setting the boundaries between them...and that dip in Arlette's blouse. She was thankful for learning to draw her own lines and stay inside them. "There's a bar around the corner. I can meet you there at ten o'clock?"

One side of Arlette's smile grew. "Sounds good to me. I'll see you then, and in case someone tries bargaining for that painting, just know that I'll take good care of it, I promise. You know how much I've always wanted a Brooklyn Dawson original."

Brooke remembered a little too well.

❖

Okay, so that could have gone much better, Arlette thought while waiting for Brooke to fill the empty booth across from her.

She sipped her stout and bounced her knee in a steady, anxious rhythm underneath the table. It was clear that everything that had transpired between them still pained Brooke. It pained Arlette too because Brooke had been her best friend, the one person she'd trusted with everything, outside of Grandpa Harry and Jacquelyn. Much like her prolific family, Arlette kept her circle small. She had to when her family had been in the public eye for forty years and had enemies who would do anything to sell dirt on them. Her small circle prevented many friendships from becoming deeper. That was the price of being in the public eye. She'd been taught that the only people she could trust were her family.

Then she had trusted Brooke with everything. Both of them had been so desperate for each other's affection during that last month of college that Arlette had been terrified that not wanting to be in a relationship with Brooke would ruin their friendship. And it very much had. She'd led Brooke on and had broken her heart, and she felt terrible about it.

One mishap had ruined the closest, deepest, and best friendship she'd ever found outside her family.

Arlette downed the rest of her beer and ordered another.

By the time Brooke made it to the bar, Arlette had just taken a sip of her second beer. Brooke's sandy blond hair was a few shades darker than in college and longer, cascading in loose waves to the top of her breasts. While part of her still looked the same, there was so much that was different. She looked a bit older but in a good way. The quiet and insecure woman Arlette had once known had grown in confidence. It wasn't blinding confidence that bordered on arrogance. It was subtle, the sexiest kind of confidence.

Arlette eased her nerves with another drink before sliding a glass of water toward Brooke as she slid into the booth. "I would have ordered you a drink, but I have no idea what you like."

Brooke gave a friendly smile to the approaching server and said, "Hi. I'll have a gin martini. Extra dirty, please."

Arlette raised an eyebrow as the server walked away. "An extra-dirty martini? Okay, that's very different from the Gatorade and Burnett's days."

Brooke gave her the smallest smile, and Arlette took that inch and stretched it out a mile. She'd gotten Brooke to smile, and knowing that eased the clenching in her throat.

"God, I don't know how we did that," Brooke said through the trace of a laugh.

"Right? I don't think I can ever bring myself to drink Gatorade again. All I taste is bottom-shelf vodka."

Instant silence squeezed its way into the booth. As jarring as it was, Arlette never took her eyes off Brooke, and she did the same. It felt as if all the questions settled on the table like long-awaited plates of food. It wasn't until the server handed Brooke her martini and she took an encouraging sip that Arlette found the words to shatter the silence.

"So…how is everything? You seem to be doing well. I mean, your art's hanging on an exhibit wall."

"I'm well."

"And your mom? How's she doing?"

"She's good. Still teaching elementary school art in the day and adult classes at night."

Arlette had met Brooke's mom, Lori, once during parents' week. She'd loved the relationship they'd had. They were so close, told each other almost everything, and Arlette had wished she'd had that with her own parents, especially her dad. "I'm glad to hear it," she said.

"I see your family's doing well too?"

"That they are," Arlette said and took a long sip. "Dad's following his dream. Jackie's four months pregnant with a little girl who I'm so excited to meet. I'm going to spoil that child."

"Aunt Arlette?"

"Her most favorite aunt. Grandpa Harry is older, slowing down a bit, but he's still quick-witted and the same old Grandpa. But anyway, you're making gorgeous art and casually doing exhibits on the weekends."

"You caught me on a good weekend."

"A really good weekend. People were admiring your work. It made them smile, and according to you, a few were interested enough to put offers in. It's really amazing, Brooklyn. You know that, right?"

Brooke gave a half-smile and glanced at her martini. Arlette thought she saw the faintest blush through the dim bar lighting, but she told herself she was just imagining what she wanted to see. "What about you? Are you working for your nonprofit?"

Arlette let out a hollow laugh and took a long gulp. "Honestly?"

"Honestly."

"I'm a bit stuck at the moment, but it could be worse. I like who I work with, who I work for, but it's not at all what I thought I'd be doing."

"But does it make you happy?"

Arlette thought about it. She didn't necessarily feel one hundred percent unhappy. If the House passed the bill she'd been working on day and night with Teresa, then yes, she would absolutely feel fulfilled and happy. But those were temporary feelings, like riding a big wave that lasted for only so long. Politics came with big waves and then none. However, she had always thought happiness shouldn't revolve around tangible things, and that was the problem with her job. It only came with tangible successes.

"At times, yes," Arlette said.

It seemed like Brooke had never wavered on her dream. Arlette wished she could have said the same about herself, but sometimes, it was much easier to dream when reality wasn't outside the window pounding on the glass. Freshman year of college, anything had been possible. But she'd soon realized that not all the opportunities that had come pounding on her door had been good for the soul. Sometimes, even good prospects were a curse in disguise.

"Anyway," she said again and pulled another drink. "How was the rest of the exhibit?" There was so much more she wanted to ask. Did Brooke ever think about her? Did she hate her? Was she dating anyone? She wanted to ask if they could see each other again now that they both knew that they lived in the same city. If Arlette was lucky enough to see Brooke again, she would have to earn those answers.

"It was great, actually. I'm surprised how many cards I handed out. All my canvas babies got offers."

"I'm not surprised at all. You've always been so talented, Brooklyn. I always told you that."

"Yeah, but you were my best friend. Of course you would say that."

Their gazes met, locked and sizzled, but not in a steamy way. Like their cautiously civil conversation had been extinguished by the heaviness of the past tense that had slipped from Brooke's lips, like water dousing a spark.

The use of the past tense shouldn't have felt like a blow to the stomach, but it was the first time Arlette heard it out loud. They *were* best friends.

Everything that she wanted to say in the last five years bubbled up in her throat. Explanations of why she did what she did, apologies for doing what she did. She was about to finally release them until Brooke cleared her throat and pulled a large sip of her martini. Arlette took that as a sign that Brooke hadn't meant to acknowledge the awkward tension, and if Brooke wanted to move on, Arlette was happy to oblige. She needed to tread lightly and not say something that would prompt Brooke to leave.

So she drank her beer, swallowed her apology, and continued. "All I'm trying to say is that I always thought you were amazing, even when you were doodling on your digital drawing tablet back in college."

Brooke looked back up, and the smallest trace of a knowing smile formed on her lips. "I forgot how much you loved that thing."

"How couldn't I? Once you got that tablet, I'd come back from class to find you doodling and all the Swanson girls begging you to draw them, and you did it perfectly, as if you'd been using one your whole life. Even then, you had people lining up for your art. That was my first glimpse of your talent, and look at you now. Selling all your pieces at an art exhibit. Wow, just…wow. I'm really proud of you, Brooklyn. That definitely never changed."

It was a truth meant to counteract the awkwardness from the moment before. The tension reminded her of what they used to be. She wanted to make it clear that, despite what had happened, it didn't change what she thought of Brooke. She still thought the world.

Brooke thinned her lips, and the heaviness between them eased. "Thank you, Arlette," she said softly.

"I mean it. So tell me, how's the foliage painting doing?"

Brooke hesitated as if getting lost in her thoughts. "I had five people wanting to buy it. Yourself included."

"And?"

"And you gave the best offer."

"Eight-fifty for the Brooklyn Dawson original I've always wanted." She remembered Brooke's senior art show. While Brooke had been so anxious and nervous about it, she'd felt the opposite. Finally, she could see what Brooke had been doing while spending late nights their last semester at the art studio. She'd often sneaked into Dietsch Hall and pulled Brooke away from her studio to help inspire her. This had involved a lot of making out in random abandoned dark spots throughout the building. God, they'd had great chemistry. Remembering it warmed her face. Throughout the whole art show, she had struggled to keep her eyes on the art instead of Brooke. They'd tossed stolen glances that she'd guessed had warmed Brooke as much as herself, based on the blush streaking Brooke's cheeks. She was hands down the most beautiful girl in the room with the most beautiful art.

In college, Arlette had walked her back to her on-campus apartment and had told her that she'd hoped one day to afford a Brooklyn Dawson original.

"I promise, I'll give it the best home," Arlette said in one last attempt of persuasion. "I already know where it's going, and it will be the best thing in my living room."

Brooke smiled. "Fine, it's yours. Sold."

"Wait, really?"

"Really. I'll be picking up the canvases tomorrow, so after that, I'm free if you want to pick it up."

"Wow, oh my God, okay. Well, next week is a bit crazy with work, but I can swing by to pick it up on Thursday if that works for you?"

"That works."

"Can you take care of it until then?"

"Of course."

Arlette sighed, rested back against the booth, and crossed her legs. Maybe not all was lost between them. "Mind if I see your phone?"

At first, Arlette thought she would need to do more convincing, but after thinking about it for a second, Brooke slid it out of her purse. "Why?"

"So I can give you my number?" She assumed she wasn't in Brooke's phone anymore. Brooke had unfollowed her on all social media, and an organized person like her wouldn't have someone's number in her phone if she never expected to see or talk to them again.

When Brooke gave her the phone, the new contact form was already pulled up. As she plugged in her name and number, she exhaled in defeat. She'd been right in assuming Brooke had deleted her number, a blatant reminder of how she was going to have to work hard to erase the image and memory Brooke still had of her.

It was a task she was happy to take on. "There." She handed the phone back.

Brooke typed something on her own phone. "There, just texted you," she said, wiggling her phone.

Little did she know, Arlette still had her number.

Once they said their good-byes outside the bar before heading in opposite directions, Arlette pulled her phone out of her jacket pocket and saw "Brooklyn" spread across her screen.

She grinned widely as familiarity settled inside her. It was a sight she'd thought she would never see on her screen again, and just like all those years before, seeing the name still found a way to speed up her heart.

CHAPTER FOUR

Abby plopped on the opposite end of the couch the next morning with a steaming mug of coffee. "So Arlette Adair is relevant again, eh? The woman who sparked, like, half of Swanson Hall's sexual awakening?"

Stephen joined her. "She's sparking *my* sexual awakening, and I've been in love with Jake Gyllenhaal since I was nine."

Abby raised an eyebrow. "Those are two very big statements. I think you lost your Swiftie card."

"Listen, the guy might have been a douche to her, but he is still fucking fine. Those are not mutually exclusive. Anyway, back to the president's daughter."

They faced Brooke.

"It wasn't half of Swanson," she said. "It was literally three of us: me, Jade, and Holly."

"That we know of. I mean, look at you. You were hooking up with her secretly. I didn't even know until you told me after she'd stood you up at the party. There could have been plenty of other girls crushing on her too."

"What does all this mean?" Stephen asked. "You have her number. She has yours. What happens after you give her the painting?"

Brooke shrugged. "I have no idea."

"Whatever you decide to do, can you *please* promise me that you'll be careful?" Abby said. "Remember what happened last time? You couldn't paint for months. You can't afford that right now. Not with the October exhibit."

"I know that, Abby, but she's just picking up a painting. If you're worried about me falling for her again, I can assure you, that's not going to happen, especially now."

After their phone conversation a few days after graduation, Brooke had struggled to pull herself out of bed. She'd wanted to text her best friend because Arlette's quick wit and love for spontaneity had always made her smile on the toughest days. Except her best friend wasn't her best friend anymore, and because of that, Brooke hadn't mustered enough energy to paint. The brush that had once molded perfectly into her hand and had felt like home and peace had turned into a prickle bush and weighed heavy in her fingers. Painting was her outlet, always had been since she was a kid. But in the days after graduation, her mind had been clogged with so many emotions that she couldn't get any colors on the canvas.

It wasn't until she'd started her first internship the following September that inspiration had slowly poured back into her brush, coating her canvases in shades of blue, gray, and black. She'd switched gears momentarily and had even tried charcoal sketching, desperate to capture any feeling that swarmed inside her. After a few months of her painting drought, the colors had slowly started spilling from her brush, and a new wave of inspiration had overtaken her.

While her drought had only lasted about six months total, she never wanted to go back to a time when she didn't have her art. She couldn't afford that. Mentally, emotionally, or financially.

"I'm going to be fine, Abby," she said and shook Abby's knee. "I'm just giving her a painting."

"Which will turn into five more drink dates, and one of those times, you two will get drunk, you'll resume the steamy make-outs y'all used to have, and then you two will finally end up in bed, and boom. It's all downhill from there."

Abby had held on to her grudge like a handbag in a sketchy neighborhood. Despite being friends in college, Arlette had entered enemy territory now, stamped as a "bad guy" for all eternity. That was just the kind of protective friend Abby was. It was a blessing and a curse.

"I think you're getting ahead of yourself. She bought a painting; I'm giving it to her. That's all this is. Plus, I know to keep her at a distance. She's not sparking another drought. On that note, I need to go paint some models." She slapped her knees before getting off the couch to start her Monday.

Usually, her days started by metro-ing up the Green Line to her studio. To shake the Monday blues, she treated herself to an everything bagel loaded with cream cheese and a chai latte from her favorite shop. Something about a delicious bagel and spiced warmth really got her creative juices flowing. She walked the final two blocks from the shop to her studio, a large brick building that dated back to the 1920s and consisted of rented lofts for the artists nearby.

When she stepped inside, the smell of paint permeated the air. She thanked her bartending job for being able to afford the space. She had the taste and sights of inspiration at her fingertips. She was so ready to open up her fresh tubes of paint and start messing up a perfectly white canvas.

First, she needed to get through her daily housekeeping while she ate breakfast and allowed the latte to wake her up. She combed through emails and messages on her Etsy account. Most of her customers came from her online store, where she sold original paintings and prints for a significantly cheaper price. She checked her art Instagram because some people inquired about commissions there as well. When she was all caught up, she prepped her backdrop for the models. It was just a white backdrop that would collect the shadows created by the southern light through the window. She got her pencil ready, set the canvas on her easel, and picked out the colors she planned on coating over the sketch.

She was excited to start the pieces for a new exhibit. Brooke couldn't believe it when the gallery had accepted her submission for an exhibit that explored female sexuality. She was going to have so much fun with it, not only because of the theme, but because she was in a lineup with other local artists whom she admired. She couldn't believe her art was about to share the same walls with talented artists who were going to draw in their own decent crowds. The exhibit was going to highlight Brooke's work to the best people in the area. Plenty of admirers, curators, and collectors were going to be there. When she'd gotten the acceptance email, she, Abby, and Stephen had danced around the apartment and celebrated with maybe one too many mojitos, but the headache the next morning was so worth it.

The models stopped by at one p.m. After Brooke showed them to the bathroom, they came back in their robes. She directed them to the white backdrop and made sure they were comfortable with the poses. That was her main focus when working with models, especially nude models. She'd explained ahead of time about the poses she hoped to capture and then quadruple-checked that they were okay with it.

The two models today were open to all her ideas. In a matter of a few hours, she had captured them on the canvas and covered the sketch in different shades of blues and splatters of pinks. By the end of the day, her first piece was almost done. But she would go back and polish it until she deemed it perfect.

When she propped the piece against the brick wall and stared at it from the opposite end of the studio, she imagined it hanging on a museum wall, a title card next to it with her name. She absolutely loved it. After spending a whole day lost in the canvas and all the colors that coated it, she finally saw her hard work and smiled. She loved that she'd reached the point in her career where she actually liked what she created. She firmly believed that you couldn't be an artist of any kind—visual, dancer, actor, author, director—and not like your work. If you weren't proud of it, how could you expect others to be?

For a while, that had been her problem. What she created hadn't always produced a smile, and it had held her back from letting others see it, even her mom, her biggest supporter.

But those days were long gone. While she still had a long trek to establish a reputation, at least now, she made things she was proud of. That was a foundation for the rest of a career that would lead her to more customers, sales, galleries, and exhibits.

She might not have been rich with money, but she was rich with pride, and that alone put her in a successful spot in her career.

"Okay, I have good news and bad news," Arlette said to Teresa as they walked through the Cannon Tunnel that connected the Capitol Building to the Cannon House Office Building.

Teresa grabbed her arm. "Is this about the Emissions Bill?"

Arlette thought about it. Maybe it hadn't been the best idea to start off with that sentence right after Teresa had spent the morning introducing the bill to the House. "It has nothing to do with the bill."

Teresa retrieved her hand and pressed it to her chest. "God, Arlette. You can't do that to me," she said. "But if it has nothing to do with the bill, lay it on me. I'm ready. Let's get our mind off it."

"It's about the art for your office."

"Oh yes?" Teresa smiled the first smile of the day. "You found something?"

"Close. I found something for myself, which I'm proud of. But that's the bad news. The good news is that the artist does commissions, and she's fantastic. Like, really fantastic."

Teresa raised a dark brown eyebrow. "Oh, really?"

Arlette nodded and pulled out the business card that included Brooke's contact details. She handed it to Teresa. "When you get the chance, you should look at her Instagram. I think it showcases most of her art. You can see if her work is the vibe you're aiming for. I'm picking up my piece on Thursday. You don't even know how excited I am."

"You'll have to show me. I'll go check her out and get back to you. I appreciate you doing the research for me."

"Anything for you, boss."

Right as Arlette reached to open the door into the Cannon Building, she spotted her Uncle Henry running to catch them. She deflated. He was the epitome of how it was a shame that one couldn't choose their family. Anytime he was near, it wasn't a positive experience. He was a judgmental, disgruntled, peevish curmudgeon. That was why Arlette and Jacquelyn always called him Uncle Frank from *Home Alone*. Behind his back, of course. She thought it was fair since Uncle Henry had told her—more than once—that she was the black sheep of the Adair family.

"Ms. Rosario," Uncle Henry said to Teresa and attempted a smile. He looked at Arlette. "Arlette," he said flatly.

She opened the door and begrudgingly held it open for them to head inside.

"That's an interesting bill you've got there," he said to Teresa. Arlette trailed them silently.

"Oh, really?" Teresa said with curiosity. "I'm happy to discuss any part and why it was included."

His skepticism was not surprising in the least. He was one of those longtime politicians who was persuaded more by money from special interest groups than facts, science, his constituents, or what was morally right. He was a moderate Democrat and knew that anything too far to the left regarding the climate would scare off some of his moderate supporters, despite the science, research, and expertise that supported those facts. *SNL* had once mocked him in a skit. Arlette and Jacquelyn had thought it was the greatest thing the show had done since Kate McKinnon had played Hillary Clinton. It even got Henry's son, Christian, to chuckle, and he was deeply obsessed with the family's dynasty and legacy. Uncle Henry, however, didn't let out a single laugh.

"We've got less than seven years to achieve zero emissions, or we cannot reverse the effects," Teresa said.

He chuckled. "You don't actually believe that, do you? It's practically fearmongering."

Teresa stopped walking and gave her famous frown to Henry, the look that warned any challenger she was about to own them. Arlette bit back a grin and watched the entertainment unfold.

"Of course I do," she said confidently and sternly. "Mr. Adair, are you questioning the work of environmental experts who've dedicated their lives to this research? Would you also question an epidemiologist? An oncologist? A dentist? I will happily send you the reports that show the current trajectory we're on. We're heading to very scary times, times that you might not live through, but your kids and your grandkids will certainly live—and suffer—through. I will gladly pull those up if it's what's needed. Your niece has done thorough research, and I trust her and my legislative team. I can have those references in your inbox by the end of the day."

Uncle Henry glanced at Arlette, his expression blank, and she purposely allowed her smile to grow because she knew it would irritate him. She couldn't help but wonder if his skepticism about the bill was fueled by his grudge against her.

"I've seen the report," he mumbled.

"Seeing and reading are two different things. I strongly advise you to take another look. Your younger constituents are relying on you to vote in favor of this. Now, I need to go, but thank you for voicing your concerns. I hope the science will eventually convince you."

This was the part of politics that disgusted Arlette. Getting an idea on paper and thinking about that idea changing the scope of the environment? That was exciting. She loved the research, and she loved being inspired to use that research to solve problems. It was what pulled her into politics in the first place. What she didn't like about her job was that once the bill was verbally introduced in the House Chamber, the other four hundred and thirty-four representatives with their own political agendas would share their two cents, fueled by their parties and special interests. Hardly ever were the two cents based on clear facts.

By Thursday, she was drained. She would stare at nothing, only to realize her jaw had been clenched the whole time. She tacked on fake smiles and shook the hands of other representatives, gauging their interest in the bill to see who would be voting on it and who she needed to persuade. She even had to talk to representatives who'd publicly bashed her family—most specifically, her father—and there was nothing she could do about it except kill them with kindness.

But despite all the draining throughout the week, there was one positive. Not only did she get to pick up her painting, but she got to see Brooke again. The fact that Brooke had accepted her phone number was the smallest hint that maybe their friendship wasn't as dead as she'd thought.

As she metroed to the address Brooke had texted her, she found a message from Sabrina: *So sorry, baby. I have a big project due on Monday. Not going to be able to make it down there tomorrow.* Sad face emoji.

Arlette rolled her eyes and tossed her phone in her pantsuit pocket. She wasn't at all surprised. Sabrina prioritized work over relationships, and, honestly, Arlette didn't quite blame her. Sabrina would one day inherit her mother's billion-dollar real estate development company. Even at twenty-eight, Sabrina had taken loads of work onto her plate. On top of that, the McKay Group was based out of Annapolis, an hour away with the usual DC traffic. Driving almost that far for someone Sabrina barely held on to was too much work. Arlette wouldn't have made the drive either if their roles were reversed.

Arlette wasn't mad at Sabrina. She was upset with herself for being so indifferent about their relationship.

They didn't feel like girlfriends. Arlette and Sabrina could make all their appearances at fundraising events and galas. Sabrina had no problem staying close to her side, hand glued to the small of her back, pecking her cheek with kisses throughout the night when there was an audience. Sabrina had no problem charming her family and making them excited about an Adair-McKay power couple. But when it came to being with just Arlette, Sabrina pulled the work or distance card without hesitation. It had happened so frequently over the last month or so that Arlette never expected Sabrina to come down to DC. The only time they saw each other was when Arlette visited her family in St. Michaels.

They were more like partners on the path to fulfill their parents' dream of merging the two families. That had remained their parents' dream ever since Arlette had come out in high school and her parents had thought to play matchmaker with Sabrina McKay, who had also come out the year before. Their parents had tried. Very hard. At first, Arlette had been grateful that her family didn't care at all that she was a lesbian. She'd felt swaddled in their love and support, and she'd thought they were just trying to make her happy by encouraging her to talk to Sabrina. But the older Arlette got, the more she understood that her parents' support had a murky depth. They wanted more out of her relationship than just her happiness.

For much of high school into college, Arlette hadn't even considered dating Sabrina. They were strictly friends. They were always at fundraisers and holiday parties together and always had a good time. They would sneak bottles of expensive alcohol and find a secret spot to share the drinks while they talked and laughed about the most ridiculous things. Arlette had a friend she could talk to about dating and gorgeous women. They'd swapped stories, and Sabrina had given Arlette plenty of advice while she'd dated Jade MacCleary in college.

After college, Arlette had lost her best friend. Although the depth of Sabrina's friendship had come nowhere near as close as Brooke's, Arlette had needed someone. Sabrina was there for her throughout that summer. She'd listened when Arlette had needed to vent. She'd invited Arlette out with her queer friends to help distract her from her heartbreak. Being around her had made Arlette feel light. Their friendship came easy with fun and laughter, but most importantly, Arlette knew Sabrina understood her and her lack of trust for people outside her family. And she understood the issues Arlette eventually ran into when she'd started dating again. They had talked about all their struggles with dating over the years. Dating women who'd either recognized their last name or who'd eventually put the pieces together and had used them for clout, getting ahead in their career, or money.

Brooke was depth and comfort in a world where Arlette's life had lacked both. Sabrina was fun and understanding.

It wasn't until a year and a half ago that Sabrina had kissed Arlette. She should have known that the spark she'd felt kissing Sabrina for the first time had probably come from all the champagne flowing through their veins. All the events they'd attended together after their kiss involved alcohol, which made it easier for their nights of usual laughter and fun to escalate to sleeping together. How well they'd gotten along over the years had made it easy for Arlette to agree with Sabrina when she'd asked if they should "give this thing a try."

Looking back now, Arlette could see that a decade of pressure had finally forced an illusion of a spark, and Arlette had run with it. She'd hoped that by dating Sabrina, her family would stop seeing her as the black sheep Uncle Henry always referred to her as just because she hadn't gone to the Naval Academy or because she was originally averse to being in politics. She had a job on the Hill, she was dating Sabrina McKay, and as a result, her relationship with her father was the strongest it had ever been.

It was why she was so hesitant about finding a way off the Hill and out of her relationship. She desperately wanted to keep her relationship with her father.

The impact of Sabrina's text swelled in Arlette's chest as she walked a couple blocks to Brooke's studio. It meshed with the lingering anxieties gathered from the work week. Once she approached the brick building, she inhaled a deep breath. She didn't want to worry about all of that right now. She'd been looking forward to picking up her painting and seeing Brooke all week. She didn't want her worries to dim the excitement. Despite their fallout and a five-year gap in their timeline, Arlette still felt a trace of Brooke's depth and comfort.

When she was buzzed in, she walked up to the second floor and knocked on the door to Brooke's studio. Her breath caught when Brooke answered wearing a baggy flannel button-up speckled with a variety of paint, her sleeves cuffed around her elbows, and sexy, clear-framed glasses that made her whole artsy aesthetic pop.

God, Brooke Dawson made paint-stained shirts look as sexy as lingerie.

"Hi," Arlette said with a slight wave. Hearing the wavering in her voice, she cleared her throat to untangle it.

"Hi," Brooke said and gestured her into the studio. "How was your day?"

"It was okay. The week was insanely long and hectic," she said and stepped inside. "But my boss is awesome and practically forced me to take the day off tomorrow, so I'm pretty excited for that."

"That's great. Any plans?"

"Besides sleeping in? I might take myself out on a date. Go have lunch by myself, maybe go to a museum. Then pick up some dinner and binge some Netflix or something."

"You always loved your museums," Brooke said with the smallest grin.

"I really do. There's this epidemiology exhibit at the Natural History Museum that sounds fascinating. Anyway, this studio is beautiful." It smelled like paint and instantly dug up a memory from childhood about how her elementary school art room had smelled.

The space was small, with one wall of exposed brick, and an easel off to the right side where canvases—some completed, some in the works—were propped up against the wall. There had to have been at least twenty to thirty canvases. It was no surprise that all of them were beautiful. Different strokes of bold colors, abstract enough that it made her mind wander through a list of possible meanings hidden in the canvas. She found herself getting lost in each piece. The colors and brushstrokes Brooke used were always unique. She couldn't help but stare. She didn't know anything about art. She knew what her eyes liked and didn't like. She loved staring at pieces and trying to solve the meaning. It was a much more fascinating puzzle than an actual puzzle.

She was so captivated by all the other paintings that she almost missed the one she'd purchased sitting in the corner. She walked over and picked it up, studying it again and feeling her chest swell. She knew how lucky she was that, given their history, there was still a kernel of trust deep inside Brooke that trusted Arlette with the painting. She knew that had to mean something, even if it was to the smallest degree.

She turned to Brooke. "I've been looking forward to picking this up. It's the highlight of my week."

Brooke smiled. "I'm glad it's going to a good home."

"Yeah? I'm going to take care of it and appreciate it every day. It's going to be perfect right above my couch." She set it down and pulled out her phone. "How do you accept the payment? I can do whatever. Check, Venmo—"

"Venmo is fine," Brooke said. She reached for her phone in the back of her jeans pocket, pulled up the app, and showed Arlette her QR code.

Once Arlette sent the money, she slipped her phone back into her blazer. "I remember the first week of school," she said, still staring at the collection of work. "You were always on that digital drawing tablet. Anytime I looked over, you were on it. I'm pretty sure I came home from a party that first weekend to find you with a candle lit—very rebellious, by the way—headphones in, and you were so into what you were drawing."

"I remember that weekend. You smelled like Malibu rum."

They shared a laugh. "Sounds pretty accurate," Arlette said. "You were drawing Abby Hoffman and claimed you had just picked up the tablet a 'few days before.'" She used air quotes.

Brooke let out a small laugh. "It was a few days before. I got it on move-in day."

"I still think you're lying," she said jokingly.

She knew Brooke was telling the truth, but she couldn't believe that the first piece of art she'd seen of Brooke's was on a tool she'd just started using. It looked like she'd been using a tablet for years. She had said that a few girls had asked for drawings, and she'd done them for extra practice.

When Arlette saw how talented Brooke was, she'd requested a drawing and had even offered to pay her twenty bucks. Since Brooke had refused to take any money, they'd finally settled for the payment of one Kit Kat, one Snickers, and a bag of gummy bears from the campus store. That was when she'd learned that Brooklyn Dawson had one massive and permanent sweet tooth.

Arlette faced the brick wall of canvases that served as proof of how much Brooke's talent had evolved. She couldn't believe how talented she was. Brooke had been too good for her senior art show, and five years had perfectly aged and ripened her skills. All Arlette could do was gawk and admire. One in particular stopped her roaming eyes. It was a painting of two women. The one in the front wore a black robe, and the second woman stood behind her, peeling it off her shoulders. The lapels hung halfway down the first woman's arms, revealing her breasts and the rest of her torso. As she took in all the detail, the outside temperatures rushed into the studio and heated her face. In true Brooklyn Dawson fashion, the details were immaculate, the colors were bold, the textured strokes were unique and captivating. Arlette wasn't quite sure the purpose of the piece, but if it was to make her blush, Brooke had succeeded.

"Well, this is a nice one," Arlette said with a point. She didn't face Brooke until the heat dulled on her cheeks. When she did, she noticed the pink dusting Brooke's own face. She suppressed a grin. At least she wasn't the only one who was attacked by a blush. She told herself it was another flickering ember of what they had once been.

"Yeah...I...um, I'm starting this new collection. I was accepted into this exhibit in the fall. It's pretty big, actually. Some of the best local artists will be there. I have no idea how I got in. I just applied to see what would happen, and...well—"

"It happened."

"Yeah," Brooke said, exhaling. "It happened. I'm pretty excited for this one. It's about women's sexuality, so that's going to be...fun."

"Oh! You have my full attention. Go on."

"Right? I couldn't pass that chance up." Brooke let out a laugh, and Arlette smiled at the warm playfulness in her voice. "It's my only piece so far. I'm still sorting out all my ideas for the rest of them."

Arlette looked back at her *Autumn in New York* painting. "Do you remember your senior art show?"

Arlette stared at the palette knife textures while waiting for Brooke to respond. She wondered if Brooke's hesitancy was from the memories of what had happened after that show. She had walked Brooke back to her apartment, and Brooke had snuck her up to her room. She had pushed Brooke onto her extra-long twin bed, crawled on top, and showed her with her lips how proud she was.

As she replayed the memory, she remembered the faintest murmur that had come from Brooke that night. She'd almost heard it like a whisper in the wind, and she'd so badly wanted to grasp it before it floated away.

"I do," Brooke said. Just like with that almost-heard murmur, Arlette could have sworn she heard a quick rasp in Brooke's voice, as if she'd cleared a feeling from her throat.

"Remember when I walked you home and told you that once I had big-girl money, I would buy a Brooklyn Dawson original?" She glanced over.

Brooke's stare carried some weight. It felt more important than the other times they had made eye contact. Arlette knew then that Brooke's mind had to have wandered back to the memories they'd made on her bed just a few minutes after that. Thinking about Brooke reminiscing made her mind sputter. "You did say that, didn't you?" Brooke said.

"I did, and I'm so happy I finally got one." She picked it up and smiled as she admired it up close. All the paintings she'd kept track of on Brooke's Instagram, and finally, one was in her hands. One of them was all hers. "I'm really proud of you, Brooklyn."

She really meant it. Whenever Brooke had interrupted her thoughts over the time apart, she was glad to know that Brooke had at least gained the confidence to sell her work. She had always been shy with her art, and Arlette could only imagine the amount of vulnerability it took to share her creation with the world, opening up to criticism.

"Thank you," Brooke said softly. "It's always nice to hear."

"Why do you seem doubtful?"

Brooke shrugged. "I don't know. The job is hard. Sometimes, I wonder if I should sell my soul to the nine-to-five job just to have a more secure paycheck."

"But you never wanted to do that. You only wanted to do freelance, and you're doing exactly that."

Brooke laughed, but it didn't quite reach her eyes. "Because who hasn't glorified that kind of life? Back then, I didn't have to worry about paying rent. I didn't have to pay my student loans yet. It's easier to dream when you have nothing to lose."

Her statement hit hard. Arlette knew that to be true as well. "Does it make you happy?" she asked, remembering the question Brooke had asked her the night of the exhibit.

"Absolutely," Brooke said without hesitation. "I never went into art thinking I was going to make the big bucks. I'd rather do what my heart wants than work at a miserable place that pays well."

"Feeling stuck is one of the worst feelings," Arlette said. "I'm so glad you didn't do the latter."

Once upon a time, Arlette and Brooke had agreed on the same thing: follow the heart, not the wallet. Those were easier times. Life hadn't quite hit them yet. They had each other to rely on, and the weight of expectations was off in the distance. Dreaming about living had been easy.

Living in those dreams was the hard part. Reality rooted dreams in place. Expectations. Money. Experience. Even though Arlette had been tangled up in the weight of her family's expectations, she was still happy to see that Brooke's dreams had taken off.

"The fact that you're doing exactly what you've been wanting to do since freshman year means that you're doing much better than half the population," Arlette said. "A lot of people cave or think that a job isn't going to be that bad, and it's not until they're smack-dab in the middle of it that they realize they should have always followed their gut."

Brooke frowned. "Did you cave?"

Arlette let out a hollow laugh, a little taken aback that Brooke had read her so easily. Clearly, she had forgotten how quickly Brooke read people. If Brooke could easily find the meaning of an art piece, of course she could see through any disguise Arlette tried on. Apparently, with five years wedged between them, there was still a part of Brooke that had Arlette memorized, as if the forgotten lyrics of her once favorite song somehow found a way to flow perfectly from her lips.

"I'm not sure what I did," Arlette said. "It wasn't intentional. One opportunity led to another, which led to another, which led me to where I am."

"I thought you said your job makes you happy."

"I like who I work for. I like that my work has the possibility to make an impact, but I don't like the world of my job. It's draining." She glanced at her canvas. "I think what you're doing is amazing and admirable, so please don't backtrack to the normal nine-to-five if that's not what your gut is telling you." She felt Brooke studying her. She looked up and offered Brooke a quick smile to mask her own failure that had started to seep into the conversation.

Brooke's stare lingered as she seemed to wrestle with what to say next. "This might be a shot in the dark, but are you doing anything tomorrow night?" Brooke said. "I know you mentioned dinner and Netflix, but Abby and I were going out for drinks if you wanted to join."

That wasn't a question she'd expected at all. She could hope that running into Brooke Dawson after all these years meant more than ships passing in the night, but she'd never expected Brooke to prop open her door. Arlette wasn't complaining. Instead, she enjoyed how the possibility of seeing Brooke again sparked anticipation inside her.

"Drinks sound much better than Netflix. You're still in touch with Abby Hoffman?"

"Yes. She's one of my roommates. I can't seem to get rid of her. We were thinking about maybe going out to U Street. If you were up for it, we could have a mini Willard reunion. Cheers to that madhouse known as Swanson Hall."

"We really had some fun times there, didn't we?"

"We definitely did."

"Sometimes, I really miss those days. Not the classes or studying but having that group of friends. It'd be great to have some semblance of that back. Count me in."

Brooke started unbuttoning her paint-stained shirt. Arlette paused and watched. Underneath, Brooke wore a black V-neck shirt, but it was the action of unbuttoning that had Arlette's mind filling in the blanks as to what was underneath.

"I'll talk to Abby and text you the details tomorrow." Brooke tossed her shirt on the chair in front of her easel, seemingly unaware of the prickling heat that trickled down Arlette's back.

Arlette shook herself out of her tumbling mind. No. She had to stop imagining Brooke unbuttoning her shirt with nothing underneath. She had to stop imagining that Brooke's naked torso would look like the painting of the naked woman in a robe. She had to stop remembering the kissing patterns that made Brooke limp in her arms.

She had to stop entirely.

"Great. Sounds like a plan," Arlette said, though it sounded more like a croak.

CHAPTER FIVE

"Remember, be nice," Brooke said with a direct point as she and Abby weaved through the crowds walking down U Street.

"I'll try my very best," Abby said. "Have you two even addressed what happened?"

"I'm still getting my bearings around her. I'm not going to be like, 'Hey, Actual Stranger now, what the hell was up five years ago?'"

"Um, why not? Get straight to the point and bypass all this dancing around bullshit."

"Coming at Arlette with guns blazing is the last thing I want. I don't need to focus on that when I need to focus on my art and this exhibit."

She wasn't going to admit this to Abby, but she was also scared to hear the truth as to why Arlette hadn't fought for them. It might have happened years ago, but Brooke wasn't sure if she could bear hearing that her ex-best friend and the person who'd made her feel the most had never liked her in return. Hearing the truth would rip open the wound that had taken a long time to heal. So she decided to do what she knew was the safest option: she would avoid it as long as possible.

"So you're just ignoring everything that happened?"

"I'm not ignoring," Brooke said. "I'm keeping Arlette at a friendly distance."

Abby tossed back her head and laughed.

Brooke shot her a glare. "What? What's so funny?"

"You're keeping Arlette at a friendly distance? Is that why you wore this sexy shirt that shows the perfect amount of cleavage?" She pointed to the dip in Brooke's shirt before she reached for the door of the bar.

It was Brooke's favorite going-out top, one she didn't question until she looked at her reflection in the glass door and examined the black tank top to see if it revealed too much. It dropped right between her breasts, the tops of them teasing just a little. She thought about it for a second before deciding that she didn't care if she accidentally showed off the perfect amount of cleavage. It wouldn't be the worst thing in the world if Arlette noticed.

"I like this top," she said as Abby held the door open. "I wear it all the time."

"Yeah, I'm sure Arlette's going to like it too."

Brooke and Abby maneuvered around patrons at the bar and were lucky to snag an empty high-top table. After grabbing a martini a moment later, Brooke heard an, "Oh, hey," coming from behind her.

She turned and found Arlette between her and Abby, and she looked...fucking amazing. Brooke's breath caught as she took her in. In college, they'd worn sweatpants and sweatshirts, the occasional going-out clothes when they went to a party; those clothes had always stolen Brooke's attention more than she cared to admit. But now, she got a full view of what the twenty-seven-year-old Arlette Adair was like in public on a Friday night, and it got her heart racing like their Willard days all over again.

Arlette wore a plain white V-neck that really teased her cleavage underneath a black button-up shirt with white cacti, cuffed around the elbows, dark skinny jeans, and black-laced boots. Her hair was down, and it looked like she'd used a curling iron.

She had been beautiful in her work pantsuits. But in her cuffed shirt and boots, she was fucking hot, and somehow, Brooke had to find a way to swallow her traitorous attraction as quickly as a bottom-shelf vodka shot. If they'd gone to a lesbian bar, Arlette would have had every woman turning her head, especially with those eyes that glued Brooke to her spot when they were on her.

Like now, when Arlette smiled.

She'd aged well, that was for damn sure.

"Hey, old friends," Arlette said and slung an arm around Brooke's shoulders to give her a half hug.

The breeze of her perfume that smelled like one spray could pay next month's rent came with her presence. It was light but woodsy. Memories spawned of when Brooke had been wrapped up in Arlette's sandalwood and vanilla scent after making out for as long as they had.

Her smell wasn't quite the same, more like it aged too. Whatever it was, it was an Arlette smell, and Brooke liked it. A lot.

"Abby Hoffman. Hey, it's been a while," Arlette said and offered Abby a half hug too. "How have you been?"

Like they'd practiced the last twenty-four hours, Abby tacked on a smile and accepted the hug. "Arlette! I've been well. How about you?" She broke the hug. "Probably getting ready for your dad's big presidential run, right?"

The thin smile Arlette had was probably masking the anxiety weighing on her chest from her family living under a microscope. Brooke remembered all the deep conversations they'd had about everything. Arlette's family being a household name made her extremely uncomfortable. She and Abby had been casual friends, so she had no idea about Arlette's disdain of being in the public eye.

"Yeah, something like that," Arlette said. "Anyway, it's good to see you again. It's been a minute. Hi, Brooklyn." She faced Brooke, her beautiful eyes tracing the dip in Brooke's shirt. She'd done it so quickly that Brooke couldn't fully enjoy the moment except by watching it on repeat in her head.

"I'm ready for a drink," Arlette said. "Are we too old for shots or should we do one as an ode to our college days?"

Abby and Brooke exchanged glances. "I could do a shot," Abby said.

Brooke hated shots. She was more of a casually-sip-and-enjoy-the-myriad-tastes girl instead of a toss-something-back-and-taste-intense-regret girl. However, if Arlette was going to look that good at the same time that Brooke was trying to swat her attraction away like a swarm of gnats, she was one hundred percent up for a shot.

"I'll do one too," she said.

"Great. I'll be back." Arlette walked over to the bar.

Abby slid into the lingering cloud of perfume. "Doing a shot, eh?" she said with waggling eyebrows. "I haven't been able to make you do a shot in, like, four years."

"It's for a trip down memory lane. I'm doing it for the nostalgia."

"Yeah, you're fully enjoying all the nostalgia at the table right now. Your face got bright pink the moment she said hello. Ah, it really is a trip down memory lane."

Brooke rolled her eyes and sipped her martini. "You know, for someone who doesn't want me to even reconnect with her, you're doing a lot to try to point out the chemistry."

"Ugh, it's inevitable that Stephen or I will have to make a Safeway run for ice cream in the near future, isn't it?"

"She has a girlfriend, so really, nothing is going to happen."

"That doesn't mean anything. Half the couples in this area are non-monogamous anyway."

"And in addition to her billionaire girlfriend, I've been down that road before. I can find her insanely attractive *and* know not to go down that road. Just trust me, Abby."

"Fine. I'll be cautiously optimistic."

Brooke patted Abby's arm. "Thank you. I'll take it."

Arlette came back a minute later with three shots of tequila and three limes, and then ran back to the bar for the salt shaker. Abby and Brooke tossed another stare at each other. They were really taking it back to the old days with tequila shots. The possibility of the night ending in one piece was rapidly declining.

"Don't worry," Arlette said as she passed out the shots. "This isn't the bottom shelf Montezuma from our Willard days. This is Patrón, the good stuff."

Abby made a sour face. "Oh my God, Montezuma. I can taste it right now."

"It tastes like severe regret," Brooke said. "You know, I've sworn off tequila since senior year."

Arlette lowered her shot. "You haven't had tequila since your twenty-second birthday?"

"You were a witness. There's no way I'm ever recovering from that night. The fact that I even agreed to this is a very brave decision on my part, and I would like us all to recognize it."

Arlette patted Brooke's back, and her breath hitched at the unexpected contact. "I admire you for your bravery, Brooklyn."

Arlette saying her full name like that was the equivalent of a tequila shot.

Brooke offered a shrug, and she hated how part of her deflated the tiniest bit when Arlette took her hand back. "I guess I'm really committing to tasting nostalgia."

"You sure are," Abby said, and that comment slammed a blush on Brooke's face.

Brooke tightened her jaw. Abby laughed and held up her shot glass. Arlette exchanged a glance with both of them before giving up and following Abby's lead.

"To upgrading our alcohol choices and to reconnecting with old friends," Arlette said. "Cheers."

They clinked their glasses. Brooke looked at Arlette, and when their eyes met, Brooke quickly turned to Abby and said, "Cheers."

Brooke downed the shot the fastest. Arlette sucked on the lime, and Brooke continued her journey down memory lane. Arlette's go-to drink in college had been horrible tequila with a lime wedge. She would squeeze the lime juice over her tequila, suck on the remnants still on the wedge, and then toss it all back. It used to make Brooke's mind spin, and Arlette had always been unaware. The end of their senior year, Brooke had finally gotten to enjoy the taste of lime and tequila on Arlette's tongue.

Arlette had kept her same tequila-shot process. Brooke knew how she tasted at the moment, and it made her mouth water and sent instant pressure underneath her underwear.

No, this couldn't be happening again. She'd sworn she wasn't going to allow it; she wasn't going down this road again. If Arlette Adair was going to come back into her life, she needed to stop her feelings from taking over. If they were meant to be together, it would have happened years ago. Arlette had a girlfriend, and no matter how attractive she thought Arlette was, Brooke was not going to be that person.

Unless, if they're open...no! Nope. No Arlette Adair under any circumstances.

Brooke pulled a sip of her martini to tame her thoughts.

The tequila shot was a segue into safe, mutual territory. Brooke, Arlette, and Abby reminisced about the good ol' days, about all the horrible drink concoctions they'd tried, especially during junior year, when their friend group had started turning twenty-one, and they were able to buy alcohol for the rest. That turned into reminiscing about freshman and sophomore year, when they'd lived in Swanson Hall, and all the things they'd done to entertain themselves on the weekends. Sled races down the hallways, capture the flag in the field behind the dorm, and huddling in the common room to tell ghost stories.

"Somehow, Arlette always told the scariest ghost stories," Abby said.

"Yeah, because they were real," Brooke said. "Remember she scared the shit out of all of us when she spent a week collecting Willard ghost stories?"

Arlette tossed her head back in laughter.

Abby shot her a playful glare. "I do remember that because my roommate was gone that weekend, and I had to sleep by myself."

"Abby called out Emma Elliot for telling a lame story, so I made sure I didn't disappoint," Arlette said. "I take my historical stories very seriously."

"You freaked us all out with the Carroll Hall ghost," Abby said and shuddered. "It still freaks me out."

The story about the ghost caused goose bumps to travel down Brooke's arms. "I didn't sleep that night. I didn't even want to get out of bed because in order to go to the bathroom, I had to walk by our mirror, and I was worried about seeing the ghost."

Arlette sipped her beer, clearly unaffected by all of it. "But the Carroll Hall ghost wasn't in Swanson. We didn't have any ghosts that appeared in the mirror on the anniversary of their death. We had a different ghost, but she stayed down in the basement and messed with you while doing laundry."

Brooke tossed her hands over her ears as Abby shivered again and eased it with another drink. Arlette laughed and gently lowered Brooke's hands. Arlette's hands were warm, soft, and gentle, like how she remembered them whenever they'd grazed her skin or rested against her cheek when Arlette would kiss her.

"And what did I do? I protected you from the ghosts," Arlette said. "I turned on the lamp, we squeezed onto my bed and watched *Friends*, and I walked you to the bathroom and made sure the mirror didn't attack you. Didn't I?"

Brooke had forgotten about the ghost stories. For good reason. She loathed scary things and had refused to partake in the friend group's scary movie marathon they'd had every October throughout college. It was more time to spend in the art studio, working on her projects or enjoying the less terrifying parts of the month by doodling cute pumpkins, witches' hats, and black cats on her drawing tablet. But now she remembered that the scary movies and ghost stories came with Arlette making sure she'd felt safe after scarring her mind with such horror.

"You did. And then we got into a debate about if Ross and Rachel were really on a break," Brooke said. "You said they were, and I was about to find a different roommate."

"I only said that because I knew you would debate me, and it would take your mind off the ghosts," Arlette said. "And it worked. But, yeah, they were totally not on a break."

Their eyes met again, and all of their shared memories fell between them. The stare looking back at Brooke with a warm, friendly smile was the same one she'd memorized years ago. Seeing her best friend again for the first time in a long time was like seeing the sun after a long, dark winter. Brooke wondered if Arlette felt the same because she bit her lip as if trying to hide her smile, but she failed. The smile took hold.

There it was. A bit of their complicated history had made itself known at the table, and Brooke wondered how transparent she was based on Arlette's growing mischievous grin. Abby directed a stare at Brooke, making it pretty evident that even she could feel the chemistry.

"And with that, I'm getting another," Abby said, downing the rest of her beer and heading to the bar.

Arlette laughed and leaned into Brooke. A wave of sandalwood washed over her, causing a stutter in her chest. "I think you scared Abby off."

Brooke felt washed in perfume. Her mind stumbled back to the memories of when her body had collected Arlette's smell after all the long make-out sessions. She drank her martini to cleanse the thoughts.

"She's easily scare-able," Brooke said and waved off Arlette's comment.

"I mean, don't hate me but…I'd argue that you're pretty scare-able too."

Brooke feigned shock. "What? The Carroll Hall Ghost in Room 206 is a terrifying story. A girl who was obsessed with the occult dies in her room and then appears in the mirror on the anniversary of her suicide? Fucking terrifying."

"Didn't you get scared when we watched the *Scary Movie* series?" "I know they were comedies, but they still had moments of suspense."

When Brooke looked up, she got a glimpse of the teasing in Arlette's beautiful eyes. How close they stood made Brooke's heart gallop like a racehorse, but it felt good. She was amazed at how quickly they'd fallen back into the same rhythm of innocent teasing.

Arlette bit back her smile again as she stared at her beer. "So, um, I wanted to talk to you about something."

Brooke's heart thudded at all the possibilities. They still had a million things to talk about that they'd been awkwardly waltzing around. She figured that if now was the moment to talk about the past, at least they did a tequila shot and had their first round of drinks to soften the blow. "Oh, yeah? Go for it." Brooke sipped her martini to brace herself.

"My boss has been wanting some art to liven up her office. I told her about you and gave her your card. I hope you don't mind."

Brooke let out a sigh of relief. "Not at all." She paused and then laughed. "You know, I don't even know what you do. That should have been one of the first questions I asked but...I don't know. I was—"

"Scared?"

Brooke winced. "A bit."

"You weren't alone, if that makes you feel better."

"It does, but it doesn't."

"How do you feel right now?"

Hot. Brooke felt really hot, like the bar had turned the heat on despite the fact it was mid June, and the typical DC humidity was keeping the city a hothox. "A little less scared," Brooke said, but she couldn't look at Arlette. Instead, she watched the condensation drip down her pint glass. She cleared her throat. "So your job. You're not a fan of it, and you feel stuck. Those two clues make me wonder if you're in politics? Am I right?"

Arlette gave a smile that didn't quite reach her eyes. "You are. You were always good at reading people. Always good at reading me."

"You left a large trail of breadcrumbs with your work clothes that screamed Capitol Hill. Am I right again?"

"You are."

Brooke pumped her fist. Arlette grinned at the same time that the information knocked through the alcohol that had fogged Brooke's brain. "Wait, you work on the Hill?"

"I know. Shocking."

Arlette had always said she absolutely didn't want to follow in her family's footsteps. She'd never had any interest working in politics because it was a "giant game of money and power," as she'd described it multiple times. She'd said she wanted to work in the field at some NGO where she could help animals, the environment, or social issues like women's rights.

Brooke had always found it insanely sexy that Arlette had the passion to be in politics but the heart to stay out of them. Her dreams and ambition had filled any room whenever she'd talked about them, and Brooke had never had a doubt that Arlette would have been the first one in her family to carve her own path in decades.

Somewhere along the way, she'd gotten stuck, apparently. She was the strongest and most ambitious, determined person Brooke knew. It made her deflate knowing that something had faded Arlette's dreams.

"Wow, I have to say, I never saw that coming," Brooke said.

Arlette shook her head and thinned her lips, an expression that seemed to hold back a lot. "Neither did I. Like I said, the internship I had with the EPA the summer after junior year turned into interning for the UN in New York, which helped me meet a congresswoman from the city. I met her while she was campaigning, met her again when she was at a DC event, and that led to a job offer. She's the only person I would even consider working on the Hill for."

"Oh, a congressional staffer. That's fancy," Brooke said, nudging her arm. "I feel like you're not a true Washingtonian unless you brag about who you work for."

In DC, one of the first questions people asked was who someone worked for, and usually, that answer was that they worked for the government or a nonprofit, or had some consulting job. The unfortunate part was that many people measured someone's worth based on their security clearance.

Not like Brooke cared. When she'd first moved to the city, she, Abby, and her new favorite coworker, Stephen, had joined a kickball league in an effort to make friends. It was the first question people had asked her, and when she'd said she was a freelance artist, a handful of people had scoffed. That was the moment she and Abby had joked that they would stay away from Hill interns and congressional staffers. Another sign that she needed to steer clear of Arlette.

Though the longer she stood next to Arlette, smelling that perfume and witnessing Arlette's gaze drop down to the dip of her shirt, the harder it was to listen to her own rules.

"This is true," Arlette said with the smallest smile. "But you know I'm not a bragger."

"I know. I'll help you. Tell me who you gave my card to."

Arlette faltered for a moment. "Teresa Rosario."

Brooke choked on a sip of martini. She covered her mouth, coughed, and then said, "Wait, seriously?"

"Seriously."

"You're joking."

"I'm not."

Teresa Rosario was one of the most prolific congresswomen on the Hill. The younger generations loved her, the older generations loathed her, and the pundits on Fox News thought she was the spawn of Satan, which meant that she was probably doing something right. It finally made sense why Arlette was on the Hill. Teresa Rosario would be the only person to get her to work in politics.

And now, Teresa Rosario had Brooke's business card.

"You...you handed Teresa Rosario my business card?" Brooke said.

"I did, and she said she would look you up."

Brooke's jaw dropped. She needed another martini to help process all of this. If Teresa Rosario actually called her, she had no idea what she would do. It would be the biggest and most important commission of her career.

"Okay, but surely, she would want someone...I don't know... someone more legit," Brooke said.

Arlette frowned. "Are you doing it again? Are you selling yourself short?"

"No."

"You are." Arlette reached for her wrist and squeezed it. She swallowed the flutter that tickled her throat. "You're talented. That's a fact. I think you're the only one who doesn't believe that." She withdrew her hand, and Brooke felt the loss. "Anyway, I'm pretty confident that

Teresa will be reaching out, and when she does, you need to accept that you're a hell of an artist. Deal?"

Arlette extended her hand again. Brooke contemplated before shaking it, not sure if she could make a promise that her imposter syndrome would disappear if Teresa Rosario requested a piece. But she decided to shake anyway. Her skin burned at the touch of Arlette's hand. Their eyes locked, and the promise that danced between them added weight to the moment. No matter how much hurt had dulled their edges or how much time had chipped away at them, they still found a way to click back into place.

"Hi, I'm back," Abby said, finally returning with a second beer. Luckily, she seemed too preoccupied to notice Brooke and Arlette drop each other's hands and wash the tension away with their drinks. "I was talking to that guy in the navy suit. Got his number. Go me! What did I miss over here?"

A lot, you missed a lot, Brooke thought.

CHAPTER SIX

I'm getting too old for these crab feasts," Grandpa Harry said. A slight pang rippled through Arlette as she watched her grandpa slowly ease himself into his seat at the head of the table.

Every Fourth of July weekend, the Adairs got together at Grandpa Harry's for a crab feast. They brought two serving tables and situated them in the shade of the maple tree that dangled half over the grass and half over the water. They topped them with brown paper and pounds of fresh blue crab coated in Old Bay seasoning. There was plenty of crab, beer, and family socializing to last an entire month.

"You're a Marylander," Arlette said, tacking on a smile and forcing enthusiasm to get Grandpa Harry excited for the family tradition. "You're not supposed to say that. I'm pretty sure that's illegal."

"Wasn't this all your idea anyway?" Jacquelyn said.

"It was my father's idea," Grandpa Harry said. "What was once a fun summer tradition with our family of four has grown into a feast with…" He started counting the Adairs and their spouses. Arlette's parents, Uncle Henry and his wife, Denise. Arlette's cousins: Christian, who was four years older than her, and Charlotte, who was a year younger. Then there was Jacquelyn, her husband, Ben, and Arlette. "Nine and a half reasons why my hair is as gray as it is. Wait, where's Sabrina?"

"Yes, where's your better half?" Arlette's father asked as he pulled out his chair next to Ben, right across from Arlette.

She hated that phrase. She washed it back with lemonade and shrugged. "She said she was going to be late. You can make your speech, Gramps. She gave you permission."

"Well, all right, if that's the case."

He clapped and slowly rose from his chair. It always caused a dull tug when Arlette saw how much he had aged. Though his spirits and humor were as sharp as they'd always been, his body was slowing down, reminding Arlette that so was their time. No Adair had reached their ninetieth birthday. She hoped that Grandpa Harry would be the first, but she couldn't help worrying as she watched him struggle with basic tasks over the years.

"Another year, another feast," he said over the chatter. The family started shushing each other toward the back. "I'm thankful for another year with my wonderful and beautiful family. I'm so proud of each and every one of you for various reasons."

His warm hazel eyes met Arlette's. She wondered if he did that on purpose, knowing she was knee-deep in her quarter-life crisis or if it was a coincidence. Either way, Arlette soaked up her grandpa's words. He'd always been her biggest fan. He made her believe she could truly do anything she wanted, even if it had nothing to do with politics. She had no idea what she would do without him.

"Kind of crazy that at our next crab feast, Jacquelyn will be a mother, Ben a father, and I'll be a great-grandpa. I guess that means I need to stop celebrating the fifty-sixth anniversary of my thirtieth birthday."

"They say your eighties are the new thirties, Gramps," Arlette said. "It's okay to embrace your age."

"Well, I'm excited to meet the little one. I expect you, Jackie, to eat enough crab for the two of you. And everyone else, eat up. We have a lot, so no one better leave hungry. Let's eat and enjoy this beautiful summer day with each other."

Grandpa Harry grunted when he took his seat, and no one wasted any time ripping open their first of many whole crabs. Cracks and snaps filled the warm air; the smell of Old Bay and butter permeated. Grandpa Harry reached for his first crab and struggled to break off the leg.

Arlette leaned over. "Let me help you, Gramps."

He refused to let go. "Oh, I got it."

But he didn't. His hands started shaking right as the smallest crack tore through the leg, barely audible with the rest of the snaps around them. It was a weak break.

"Gramps, let go. You're being stubborn." He finally loosened his grip so Arlette could pull out the meat and place it on the paper in front of him. "That was a hard one to open."

It was a half lie. He hated asking for help of any kind, and she could see his pride wither away the older he got and the more help he needed for little things like eating crab during this beloved family tradition, unwrapping presents at Christmas, or getting up.

If she masked his struggle as something she encountered difficulty with too, like breaking the leg off a crab, it would delay a crack in his pride.

"Thanks, dear," he said, piercing the meat with his fork and reaching over to the small bowl of melted butter.

Arlette pulled the bowl away. He frowned.

"Hey," Jacquelyn said to him. "Don't be bad, or I'll put you in time-out."

"That was good, hon," Ben said through a laugh. "You're definitely ready to be a mother."

She flashed her husband a smile before turning back to the troublemaker. She pointed her fork at Grandpa Harry. "No butter. We need you around."

"Just one little piece of meat," Grandpa Harry said.

"That's not a little piece of meat. That's a whole leg."

"I mean, one piece isn't going to do anything," Arlette said.

He especially hated being reminded of the fact that his doctor warned him to switch to a heart-healthy diet a year and a half before. He used to drench his crab in butter, and then as evening fell, it had been a tradition since Arlette turned eighteen that they shared an Arturo Fuente Opus cigar while sitting in the Adirondack chairs on the boat dock. Last year's crab feast had been the first year without him smoking his favorite cigar, but he'd still bought one for Arlette and had kept her company while she'd smoked it.

She just wanted to see him smile. He used to have so much pride hosting the crab feast, and she didn't want to see it dulled for a second year in a row.

Jacquelyn gave Arlette a stern look. "One."

"Go for it, Gramps. Hurry. Before she changes her mind and tells your sons."

Grandpa Harry flashed a victorious smile and stuffed the whole chunk of meat in the bowl.

Arlette was two crabs in when she heard chatter at the other end of the table. Right as she was about to break into a crab gorgeously covered in extra seasoning, she spotted Sabrina greeting everyone with a bottle of champagne. She started with Uncle Henry and Aunt Denise, and Arlette rolled her eyes at how her girlfriend was able to turn the family's Uncle Frank from *Home Alone* into the cool, fun, and happy Uncle Phil from *The Fresh Prince of Bel-Air*. She knew for a fact it was because she was Sabrina McKay, and he couldn't afford to have the billionaire McKays think badly of him.

"Baby! Hi," Sabrina said by the time she made it to the other side of the tables. She planted a kiss on Arlette's cheek.

Her perfume added to the mix of smells from the crab, butter, beer, and corn. She took the empty seat between Arlette and Arlette's mom and smiled as if it hadn't been almost three weeks since they'd last seen each other.

Sabrina grabbed Arlette's hand under the table and squeezed. "Hi, I missed you." She held her hand and kissed the back. "How are you?"

"Fine. What's the champagne for?" Arlette leaned forward to examine the bottle. She widened her eyes at the Krug Clos du Mesnil label. The Adairs loved their champagne, specifically Dom Pérignon. There was always a bottle or two at a big family event, like her father's presidential party. Grandpa Harry had ordered five bottles of Dom Pérignon Vintage. But those didn't compare to Sabrina's Krug. "You got Krug Clos du Mesnil?"

That pulled the rest of her family's attention. "Did I just hear Krug Clos du Mesnil?" her cousin Christian said.

Sabrina smiled and faced the family. "I have some exciting news."

"Are you pregnant too?" Arlette muttered to Sabrina.

"Arlette," Sabrina said through a small laugh and squeezed her hand.

"What's the news? Share with us," Arlette's dad said.

"Well, first, I apologize for being late. But the reason is…I got the house."

Arlette's mom squealed. "Oh my God, the one on the Severn River?"

"Yes!"

Everyone's congratulations clambered over each other. Arlette dropped Sabrina's hand and wiped her palm on her jean shorts. Last she'd heard on the house front, Sabrina was torn between houses, and she'd told Arlette in a text that she would let her know which she wanted. However, she hadn't. Arlette's family celebrated with Sabrina, and her dad scurried into the house to grab flutes. Sabrina popped the Krug and filled everyone's glasses. While they said cheers, Arlette looked at the bubbles in her glass. Sabrina asking her to move in again was no doubt looming, tainting the rest of the feast and cigars with her grandpa.

"Aren't you going to drink yours?" Sabrina said softly and grazed a hand along Arlette's bare leg.

"I'm not in the mood," she said and took out her frustrations on a crab leg.

"Baby, come on. This is a special occasion—"

"I thought you were going to tell me before you put an offer on a house," Arlette said a couple of notches lower to sneak in an urgent, private moment without the rest of her family overhearing.

Sabrina pulled back. "You made it very clear that it's my house, Arlette. You don't want to live with me. I don't believe I have to consult you on something that I'm purchasing."

Arlette scoffed. She held in her words for a few moments, debating whether she should say anything. She looked around the table, and her family was too distracted by all the crab and champagne. "I feel like I don't matter anymore, and honestly, it's really draining," Arlette said even quieter through a tight jaw.

"What? What are you talking about?"

"You haven't seen me for three weeks. You bailed on me two weeks ago. Then you told me last week that you would keep me updated, and then you don't?"

"Arlette—"

"We'll talk about it later," she said and pulled the meat out of the leg.

This was another reminder that they had a partnership rather than a relationship. Sabrina lived and worked in Annapolis, and despite being able to work remotely, she had no desire to move to DC. Sabrina always put work first. That was fine. Sometimes, work would get too busy for them to see each other. But why was it always Arlette sacrificing her time to drive to Annapolis but never Sabrina?

If it was a relationship, they should both bend over backward, and Arlette wouldn't be able to count how many times Sabrina had made it to DC. If it was a relationship, three weeks wouldn't have gone by since the last time they'd seen each other at her father's party. If it was a relationship, Sabrina would have wanted to share the news privately with Arlette instead of announcing it to all the Adairs as if it was a press release.

Sabrina really made her feel like an add-on to the McKay empire.

Since her father's party three weeks ago, Arlette had done a lot of thinking about their relationship. What had started as a great friendship had turned into fun sexual encounters, and then years of pressure from their parents had made them believe that friends who enjoyed fucking each other was enough for a relationship.

Wasn't Arlette supposed to feel something around her girlfriend? A spark? A rush of adrenaline? Nervous in the best way? Because she never had. She wondered if she tried so hard with Sabrina because she wanted so badly to have someone love her the way her grandparents had spent sixty-four years loving each other.

"Okay, fine," Sabrina said and turned her back to talk to Arlette's mom.

Arlette pulled the butter bowl—now a little too close to Grandpa Harry—back over. She dunked her meat and zoned out, thinking about all the things she'd bottled up and how to say them. She found and discarded sentences, tried to focus on which feelings were the most important. Sabrina got defensive when someone pointed out her shortcomings. She didn't ever say anything awful in return, but when she went into defense mode, it was like talking to a brick wall. Arlette knew she had to simmer in her anger, keep a steady tone, and properly communicate before Sabrina started to shut down.

She snapped out of her trance and realized that her meat had probably absorbed half the butter. When she pulled it out, she caught Grandpa Harry watching her. Had he heard her conversation with Sabrina? He had a stern look in his eyes. He was good at reading people, and as the person closest to Arlette—outside of Jacquelyn—he was especially good at reading her. It felt like he saw right through her. She shifted her gaze away and focused on the task at hand: eating as many crabs as possible.

When night fell, Arlette grabbed the Arturo Fuente Opus off Grandpa Harry's desk and walked past where the rest of the family mingled in the living room. A few minutes after she lit a cigar, she heard Grandpa Harry's slow footsteps creaking along the boat dock. He grunted as he lowered himself into his Adirondack chair.

"You didn't wait for me. I take that personally," he said with a teasing tone.

"Sorry. I've been longing for this peace since…"

"Sabrina arrived?"

She looked at the cigar between her fingers as the tip flickered orange. "Getting straight to it, huh? You really do love your gossip, don't you?"

"Hon, I've been sworn to secrecy about many things. I can't help it."

"Yeah, I'm sure you know all the dirty secrets about this country and the presidents."

"I do, and I plan on taking them to my grave."

"Well, you're kind of obligated to, or you'll be accused of treason."

"What's going on, Arlette?"

She took another puff, and the sounds of the summer night blanketed them: the frogs chirping, crickets singing, and the water lapping at the dock.

"You can stall all you want, but I know something is wrong," Grandpa Harry said. "You seemed fine until Sabrina came and told everyone about the house."

Arlette let out a hollow laugh. She and Sabrina still hadn't talked. They'd eaten their crab, Sabrina had showed off pictures of the house, they'd gone inside for dessert, and Sabrina had gotten roped into conversations about Jacquelyn's pregnancy and Charlotte's new job in the Navy. Once she finished the cigar, Arlette would have to pull Sabrina into her room, the one she always stayed in whenever she spent the night, and rip off the Band-Aid.

She couldn't keep holding in her feelings. They were starting to accumulate so much that she hated how tight her chest had become. "Nothing is wrong with me except that I ate way too much crab just to appease you."

"Consider me appeased. Is something going on between you and Sabrina?"

Nothing was going on between them. Literally nothing. No sparks. No conversations. Apparently, no respect, either. She took another long, relaxing puff while picking her next words carefully. She exhaled and let the smell of summer and water from the river ease the clenching in her chest. "Remember the crab fest the summer after I graduated college? You gave me that amazing Cuban cigar, and we sat out here for, like, two hours?"

He chuckled. "I do. You were pretty heartbroken, if I recall."

She lowered the cigar. Grandpa Harry had a wonderful memory. She'd brought up the memory not to remember the heartbreak but the story of when he'd met her Grandma Dot. Arlette had been home for a month and still hadn't shaken the pain of what had transpired with Brooke.

"I was pretty heartbroken, good memory," she said.

"You said you ruined your chance with a girl?"

She nodded. "Yup. And then you told me how you met Grandma Dot when you were at the Naval Academy. You met her during a night out, found out she was a nurse, and then faked an injury just so you could see her working at the hospital."

He laughed, which naturally made Arlette smile because his laugh was so full, as if he had so much happiness inside that a bit slipped out and shined with each laugh. "I couldn't help it. She was the prettiest nurse in town, and I chatted with many nurses, I might add."

"Oh, okay, sure," she said, going along with however he wanted to paint himself.

"She had the best dimples, and she smelled good too."

"You told me back then that you always knew with her. You felt it. Always felt it."

"I did. I can't really explain it, but there was something in me that knew she would be my wife."

"How did you know she was the one? You two were married for sixty-four years. How does that even happen?"

"I knew it in my gut. I just sensed it."

"But how?"

"Anytime I was near her, I felt it right here." He tapped a spot on the left of his chest. "Every dang time. It never went away. In fact, it got stronger the longer we were together. I had always heard that starting a family takes the fun out of a relationship. At least a few of my friends in the Navy said that after we got married. Told me to enjoy not having kids as long as I could. But I never believed them and good thing I didn't because watching her become a wonderful mother, well...I fell in love with her all over again." He nodded and looked at the dark mass of water. "We were married for sixty-four years, and you can roll your eyes as much as you want, but I really do feel like I fell in love with her sixty-four times."

She smiled. She loved how Grandpa Harry wore his heart on his sleeve. Always had. The Navy and his high-ranking career in the military and in the White House had never shoved his heart further up his sleeve. It was always there, dangling for people to see, and he was never ashamed of it. He knew there was no reason to be. She never had to question his love for her grandma. He made sure everyone knew how much he'd loved her throughout their marriage. Since her passing two years before, he hadn't ever been shy about how much he missed her.

Her grandparents' love had made her such a believer in it. Their relationship had set the bar for what Arlette wanted in her own life. She'd never gotten tired of watching the way they stared at one another or how they'd stolen sweet pecks when they'd thought no one was looking. During family functions, they had sometimes snuck away to Grandpa Harry's study and danced to their favorite songs from their younger years.

Now, at just the mention of her, that sparkle appeared in his eyes again, one that faded without his wife keeping it alive. Arlette didn't think it was possible for Grandpa Harry to love his wife more, but his love for her had grown even after she was gone.

Theirs was a timeless love story, and that was the kind of love she wanted.

Grandpa Harry never talked about money. The only thing that showed off his wealth was the house that he'd inherited after Great-Grandpa Charles had died when Arlette was seven. The only time he discussed his wealth was when he spoke about his family. "I'm well-off because of my father, but I'm rich because of your grandmother," he had always told them. "Make sure you find someone who makes you feel rich with love."

The feeling of being a McKay add-on was the exact opposite of what he had always told her to feel. The last few months, she'd wondered if she'd been setting unrealistic expectations with Sabrina. Arlette wasn't a needy person. She liked her space and alone time, but it was nice to be wanted and prioritized, like she mattered to someone when no one else was watching.

And never once had she felt it in her chest like Grandpa Harry had described.

"Why are you asking about this, Arlette?" His voice was low and stern, as if he already knew the answer and used his tone as a lasso to get the words out of her.

She was afraid to admit it out loud because that would make it true and official. She hated disappointing people. She hated disappointing her parents. She didn't want to disappoint the McKays, who had been nothing but warm and welcoming to her and her family since she was a teen. And she cared about Sabrina. She really did.

But she wanted a sixty-four-year-long marriage. If she couldn't imagine spending all that time with Sabrina, then why waste more of her time?

The admission stung her eyes; a wave of disappointment would wash over the people she cared about. "I…" She stared at the flickering cigar tip.

"Arlette?"

The stinging intensified. *Damn it.* "I don't think I feel it with Sabrina," she said. "Actually…I know I don't feel it."

"Oh, hon, I'm so sorry."

"I thought we could get there. We were friends. We had a lot in common. She was so much fun, and she made me laugh. After college, I had a pretty dark time, and she made it better. But a friendship doesn't necessarily equal a relationship. I shouldn't feel like she's more like my business partner than my girlfriend. She only felt like that for the first two months, and even then, I didn't feel a spark. I've never felt it in my chest."

"I know," he said softly.

Arlette frowned. "Wait…you do?"

"Of course. I saw it earlier. I've seen it for a while."

Only two people in her life made it impossible for her to mask her feelings. Brooke had every part of her memorized, and Grandpa Harry read her like a psychic reading a deck of tarot cards. She wasn't sure if she should be upset that he'd been reading her for so long and hadn't said anything or if she should have been upset with herself for being so transparent to the two people she wanted to hide her feelings from the most.

THE HUES OF ME AND YOU

She rubbed her head. "God, what a mess."

"You need to tell her, Arlette."

"Mom and Dad are going to be so upset. The McKays are going to be upset."

For the smallest fraction of a second, she almost understood why Uncle Henry sucked up so much to Sabrina and her family. Even thinking about a powerful family like the McKays having one remotely negative opinion about her was daunting.

"My parents wanted me to marry a nice Catholic girl and were very upset that Grandma Dot was a former Protestant who didn't go to church. Imagine breaking the news to your parents that you weren't going to baptize your children in the fifties. Trust me, I know what you're feeling. No one wants to disappoint their parents."

"I already disappointed Dad with my college choice."

He waved that off. "Parents have an idea of what their children's lives are going to be, and sometimes, what their kids decide they want to do is vastly different from what the parents hoped. It doesn't mean that what you want is wrong, and it doesn't mean they love you less. I know your father is big on traditions and was disappointed you didn't go into the Navy, but I know for a fact that he still loves you and only wants you to be happy. But he sometimes mistakes your happiness for his happiness. Yes, he had a dream of you being in the Navy and yes, has a dream of you marrying Sabrina McKay, but it's really not going to make that much of a difference in his life if you don't. The McKays will still be close family friends. Not marrying each other isn't going to change that. But you need to understand something, dear. Your dating life has nothing to do with your mom and dad. You shouldn't ever live your life for someone else. That's exactly what I told you when you first said you didn't want to join the military. It's what I told you when you said you didn't want to work in politics, and I'll stress it again right now."

Arlette exhaled deeply. "I know. It's just that…it was easier to make my college decision because Dad and I weren't close. But we're doing really well now. We're the best we've ever been."

"You and your dad are more similar than you think. You're both dreamers. You live in the clouds. It's very easy for him to lose sight of what's in front of him. If he took a break from the clouds, he'd easily see what's happening down here and that you're not happy. You deserve someone who makes you feel it in your chest." He squeezed her shoulder.

"I know." She took another puff and thought back on the last five years, trying to pinpoint when she'd lost sight of the ambitious dreams that had once colored her world. When did they fade? How did she lose the grip on them? Why did she watch them float away?

"You better believe you deserve that feeling," he said. "I know she's out there, Arlette. Go find her."

She needed to start living for herself. Grandpa Harry was right again, her voice of reason. She wanted to see those colors once more, and it started with listening to the heart that she'd muted years ago.

CHAPTER SEVEN

B rooke propped the second piece of her collection for the fall exhibit against the brick wall and scurried to the opposite side of the studio. After the model had visited in the morning, she'd immersed herself in the playlist that inspired her the most and hadn't looked up from the canvas until it was finished. She hadn't gone to the bathroom, she'd only taken a few sips of water, and she hadn't had anything to eat except for the everything bagel she'd treated herself to in the morning. She couldn't remember the last time she'd been so in the zone that she'd forgotten to hydrate and use the bathroom.

But it was worth it. She folded her arms, observed the painting and found that same feeling of pride in her chest that she'd felt after finishing the first one. She snapped a picture and sent it to her mom. Sure, the painting was a bit on the sensual side. A woman sitting on a chair, head tilted back, her hair draped over one breast while the other was as exposed as the long column of her neck. One foot rested on the chair with a knee tucked into her chest. The penciled outline was hidden under splashes of warm crimson, gentle carnation, and brushes of amethyst. A few minutes later, her mom called.

"Hi, Mom."

"Honey, that painting is stunning. I love the colors. They add to the sensuality. It's absolutely breathtaking."

Brooke smiled. "You think all my stuff is stunning. You're allowed to provide critical feedback. You know what you're doing."

"Hon, I teach little kids how to color between the lines and then tell them not to lick the scented markers."

"You need to give yourself way more credit. You have adult drawing classes—"

"And that time is spent teaching adults to not draw stick figures."

Brooke heard the smile in her tone. She loved self-deprecating humor. Most of their weekly phone conversations started with her mom telling funny stories about her students, kid or adult. She always found a way to make Brooke smile when she needed it the most. "You practically have a whole mini sculpture garden on the back patio. You're talented too."

"I'm decent. But you're a professional. You create art worthy to hang on walls, to be admired. Not for your own personal enjoyment in your tiny backyard."

Her mom had introduced her to art. Whenever she'd gotten sick as a kid, her mom had bought her a coloring book, and she'd spent the whole time in bed filling the pages with color. When her dad left, her mom had to sell the house since she could no longer afford it. They had moved into a condo a few miles outside the Charlottesville city center, and somehow, they'd still found a way to pack all the emptiness her father had left with them. So Brooke's mom had needed a getaway.

It was Brooke's first time in DC. They'd spent a week soaking up unfamiliar sights, and those had included all the art museums in the city. Brooke had carried her coloring books in her book bag and had filled in the black-and-white pages with her favorite colored pencils as her mom had focused on all the beauty that surrounded them instead of all the grimness back at home.

Brooke remembered looking at one painting and telling her mom she wanted to be an artist like her. Her mom had squatted to eye level, had placed both hands on Brooke's tiny shoulders, and had said something Brooke had carried with her for the last two decades: "You can be whatever you want to be, sweetie. I'm sure you'll be like one of these artists if you work hard enough and have patience. You think you can do that?"

Brooke had nodded even though she hadn't known exactly what that meant.

She couldn't help but remember those almost twenty-year-old words while hearing the pride in her mom's voice on the other end of the phone.

"Your work has always been beautiful," her mom said. "I always knew you had something special. That I wasn't just biased when I went to your elementary school's open house and saw how the usual kid draws and paints. You were never ordinary, and being unordinary is the best thing a person can be."

Just as Brooke was about to only half accept the compliment, her phone went off in her ear. A New York number. It could have been anyone, someone who'd stumbled across her Etsy or Instagram and wanted to inquire about a custom painting. It wouldn't have been the first time. A small percentage of customers still called, and she prayed to the freelance gods that it was a commission. It didn't matter what time it was. If someone was willing to pay for a custom piece at three a.m., Brooke would roll out of bed and get started.

"Mom, someone is calling me. I'll have to call you back."

"Okay, sounds good, sweetie. Keep making the masterpieces. You're one step closer to being in the Met."

Brooke smiled. Her mom always said good-bye like that. It had been their thing since Brooke was in high school. And her response was always, "And you're one step closer to retiring. Love you." She hung up and accepted the incoming call, switching to her professional voice, "Hello, this is Brooke."

"Hi, Brooklyn? Brooklyn Dawson?" a younger female voice said.

Brooke stopped fiddling with her book bag zipper and straightened. The formal voice and an unknown number was definitely a commission. Her heart picked up speed like it always did when dealing with a potential customer. It was exciting. She could let her creativity splatter on a canvas and had the promise of money cushioning her bank account. "Yes, this is her."

"Hi, Brooklyn. My name is Teresa Rosario, and I'm calling because one of my colleagues referred me to you for a custom painting. I've looked at your website and Instagram, and I'm in awe. Your work is absolutely beautiful."

Brooke lowered her pencil. Teresa Rosario was on her phone? Saying her name? Talking about her work? Brooke took a seat to stabilize her legs as the starstruck feeling turned her knees to putty. "Wow...th... thank you so much." She held the phone away for a second to clear her throat. No, she was not going to sound like an eighty-year-old chain-smoker when speaking to Teresa Fucking Rosario. "I'm...I'm so glad you enjoy them. That means so much coming from you."

"I really do enjoy them. I don't know much about art, but I know what I like to look at, and it's whatever you're able to capture. I think your work would be perfect to add some life into my really bland office. One of my colleagues just purchased a painting from you and keeps talking about how much she loves it."

Brooke smiled as she pictured Arlette rambling to Teresa Rosario about her work. If her mom was one of her biggest cheerleaders, Arlette had always been her cocaptain. Brooke was amazed that, after all they had been through, Arlette's support had never wavered. She'd always clung to Arlette's compliments, and she could only imagine what she'd said to Teresa Rosario.

"I would love to talk to you about commissioning a piece…if you're accepting clients and if it's not too late."

Brooke put her phone on speaker, rested it on her easel, and fumbled around for her notebook. "It's not too late at all. I'm happy to chat with you." She asked Teresa Rosario every question needed to outline what she was looking for. Before she knew it, Brooke had a page of notes: something abstract, colorful, and most importantly, something that made a statement about social rights or the environment.

After the call, Brooke called her mom on her way back to her apartment. As she burst through the front door to find Abby and Stephen watching *Love Island*, Brooke dropped her bag on the floor to get their attention. "Guess who I just got off the phone with?"

Abby and Stephen exchanged glances.

Brooke couldn't contain her excitement long enough to hear their guesses. "Teresa Fucking Rosario."

Their mouths fell open. "Are you kidding me?" Stephen said.

"Not in the slightest. She wants to commission a painting. I have all the details in my book bag…this is big."

"Hell, yeah, it's big. This is Teresa Fucking Rosario!"

Abby sprang off the couch and tossed her hands in the air. "My best friend is going to be famous!"

Stephen followed. "Everyone, get dressed. This calls for a celebration."

"Fuck, yes, it does. You." Abby pointed at Brooke. "Get changed. Meet us in the kitchen in fifteen."

"Drinking on a Thursday? How rebellious, given our age," Brooke said.

"We are resurrecting Thirsty Thursday for this special occasion," Abby said. "Just like the good ol' days."

Once Brooke swapped her yoga pants and purple racerback tank top for jean shorts and a floral tank top, she grabbed her phone, plopped onto the bed, and decided to use the spare thirteen minutes to text Arlette:

I can't believe I'm painting something for Teresa Rosario. TERESA FUCKING ROSARIO!

As she waited for a response, she quickly checked her bartending schedule for the rest of the month. A black-tie affair on Saturday at the National Building Museum. That most likely meant a fundraiser. Black-tie anything was either a business party, gala, or fundraiser, and since most business parties were during the holidays, the process of elimination was easy. But she didn't mind because black-tie affairs translated to green dollar bills. Two weddings, a corporate party, and a retirement party would be the biggest events she had scheduled for the rest of the month.

She started mentally planning how she would tackle all the art projects under her belt. Between Teresa's painting, working on her exhibit collection, three small custom pieces from her Etsy account, and fulfilling the print orders that were a slow but steady stream, she had a very busy couple of weeks. An amazing problem she would always welcome.

But when her phone dinged with Arlette's response, she shelved the planning for the next morning. Everything would get done. She was allowed to go celebrate her newest customer with her best friends.

Arlette's text said, *And can you believe how excited Teresa Fucking Rosario is? I can. Because she told me about it.*

Brooke bit her lip. *Did she???*

The gray texting bubble appeared, and Brooke's heart picked up; Arlette had her full attention. *She did. She texted me that the painting was all squared away and said she already knows where she's going to put it.*

Brooke didn't realize she'd been smiling until she started typing back. She forced the smile to fade. She couldn't let Arlette make her beam so easily.

"Brooke? You ready?" Abby called from the other side of the door.

Brooke stood, still writing her text. *Thank you for telling her about me. I'm forever indebted to you. Next time we have drinks, it's my turn to treat you.*

You don't owe me anything. Just go make a masterpiece like you so effortlessly do. You got this, Brooklyn.

For one of the first times in her freelance career, Brooke thought she might actually be a bit better than she'd originally thought.

❖

Was there something in the air that had made two of the biggest events of Arlette's summer incredibly awkward?

First, it was the surprise reunion with Brooke Dawson at her dad's party. While that was still unfolding as a blessing in disguise, she struggled to find the same outcome with the fundraiser she had two weeks after breaking up with Sabrina.

God, their breakup still remained a strong presence in her brain. There had been lots of crying on Sabrina's end. A lot of "I love you," and "we can make this work," empty words and promises since Sabrina's actions had failed to support them. Honestly, Arlette hadn't even known how much Sabrina cared about her until they were breaking up, and that spoke volumes about their compatibility.

She hated that the breakup had unfolded in her room at her grandpa's house. As Arlette had finally voiced everything she'd been suppressing, her family had been downstairs to watch the fireworks pop and sizzle in the sky. Sabrina had never looked more offended than when Arlette explained that they had felt more like partners in fulfilling their parents' wishes than girlfriends. By the time the show was over, Sabrina was gone, and Arlette's family had asked where she was. Arlette had known better than to say they'd broken up. While breaking the news about not joining the Navy had been mildly entertaining at eighteen, she had grown since then and wouldn't find the same enjoyment saying that she'd broken it off with Sabrina McKay. She wanted to tell her parents privately, hoping that would minimize a strong reaction from everyone else. She told her parents several days later, and watching her father take it in had reminded her of the utter disappointment in his eyes when she'd told him she wouldn't join the Navy.

Although he'd never said the words, she could hear all the unsaid thoughts by the look of extreme disappointment contorting his face. She had ripped the Adair Navy legacy right down the middle and shattered his dreams of an Adair-McKay family. She didn't regret either decision, but still, seeing the look of disappointment in her father's eyes packed a strong punch.

Now Arlette would have to face Sabrina for the first time in two weeks. If she had to endure the rest of the night drenched in awkward tension, she was at least going to look amazing. She'd curled her hair in waves and wore a black off-shoulder mermaid dress with a slit that ran just past the knee. It wouldn't have been the worst thing in the world if she found a cute girl to chat with during the auction. God, it had been so long since she'd had sex—hell, since she even had a wonderful make-out session—that she would consider the dreaded night a success if she found someone to distract her from her newly crowned ex-girlfriend, someone who at least made her feel like the smallest ember to Sabrina's smoke.

The McKay Foundation hosted the fundraiser every summer to collect money to distribute to local charities within the DC metro area, charities that ranged from food banks to LGBTQ+ centers to homeless shelters and low-income public schools. The event was always in the Great Hall of the National Building Museum, a gorgeous venue with Corinthian columns that extended seventy-five feet up the three-level atrium. It was one of Arlette's favorite buildings in the city. Every year, she snuck away to one of the three floors to study the lights cascading up the gorgeous columns. She'd already started planning her escape to a secluded part of the building to admire the architecture in secret while getting some air.

The fundraiser drew in hundreds of people each year. Arlette's entire family always went, minus Grandpa Harry, who was too old to endure the event. He'd been writing checks to the foundation in place of his presence. Other socialites, politicians, and businesses always showed up. Arlette arrived with Jacquelyn and Ben, and she immediately eyed one of the four bars stationed throughout the Great Hall.

"Well, considering I'm about to be around Sabrina and her family for the entire night, I'm getting an early start at the bar," she said.

"I'm going to join you," Ben said, in his Navy dress whites. Another reason why Arlette needed a drink was because for any formal gathering, Jacquelyn, Ben, Christian, and Charlotte wore their Navy uniforms, a reminder to the rest of the family that Arlette was the only one who hadn't joined. "Need anything, babe?"

"I'll have a club soda with a lime," Jacquelyn said. "I'll pretend it's a gin and tonic."

Ben was a big introvert. Like Arlette, he was more comfortable off to the side as a wallflower. They'd bonded during large gatherings in tandem silence, throwing glances at each other whenever someone said something inappropriate or bizarre. At the very least, she could hang out with Ben tonight, and together, they could disappear into the crowd.

Several people said hi to Arlette or waved, and while she always waved back, she was determined to get a drink to help ease her mild social anxiety. But once she approached the bar, she spotted a familiar face straining a drink into a lowball glass. Seeing Brooke unexpectedly behind one of the bars eased the clenching in her chest. If anything, it was a little breath of fresh air, a vastly different reaction from five weeks ago. It also helped that Brooke looked ridiculously cute in her uniform. Arlette had a special appreciation for the bowtie.

After handing a woman a fruity-looking cocktail, Brooke's eyes landed on Arlette. She did a double take, then smiled. "I should have known you would be here."

"Well, well, well, we meet again, Ms. Dawson."

And just like that, she had something to look forward to that evening.

Brooke's gaze scanned her dress, her brown eyes seeming to linger on Arlette's bare shoulders before snapping back up. But no matter how she tried to play it off, Brooke had always failed at being subtle, which was one hundred percent all right. It straightened her back and filled her with confidence.

"What can I get you?" Brooke said.

"I'll have a Jack and Coke and a club soda with lime," Ben said.

"Two limes, please," Arlette added. "Ben, take care of my pregnant sister. The number of limes matters."

Brooke fixed up the drinks, handed them to Ben, and then looked at Arlette, who loved the way Brooke's mouth quirked into a little smile. "And for you, Ms. Adair?"

"Something very stiff. Dealer's choice."

Brooke snatched a lowball glass. "Okay. I know you like tequila shots and beer. But beer is too light. And tequila doesn't really fit this whole charity aesthetic."

"I love whiskey. Does that help?"

Brooke pursed her lips as if running through the menu in her head. "I think I can make something that meets your approval."

As Brooke fixed the drink, Arlette told Ben she would catch up with him in a few, and she proceeded to skim the audience for other familiar faces. She found Uncle Henry and Aunt Denise talking with another couple; a few feet away, Charlotte mingled with a young guy in a Marine uniform, nibbling on her black straw while she listened to him. Her parents were talking to Sabrina's parents, Angela and Ron McKay. With no sign of Sabrina, Arlette turned back around at the same time Brooke presented a dark drink with a lemon peel resting across the rim.

"Oh, this is fancy," Arlette said and sniffed the glass.

"A fancy drink for a fancy lady at a fancy party."

Arlette glanced at the drink, trying to hide the heat crawling across her cheeks. "Thanks for the…"

"Sazerac," Brooke supplied.

Another wave of people migrated to the bar. The other bartender greeted them, but Arlette knew that she needed to step aside and let Brooke work, as much as she wanted to stick around and talk to her.

Arlette smiled and leaned in. "I'll stop by when you're a bit slow to say hi again." She wandered back to Jacquelyn and Ben and stuck around them until she felt the full effects of her Sazerac before committing to socializing. She said hello to the people she knew and allowed short conversations with the people who stopped her along the way. Then she found her dad.

"You look nice, hon," her dad said and slung an arm around her shoulder for a quick hug.

"Thanks, you don't look too bad yourself."

"Have you talked to Sabrina?"

That prompted another drink. "No. I haven't even seen her."

"She's right over there," Uncle Henry said, joining the conversation without an invitation.

Arlette took a large swig of her drink to brace herself. She followed his nod to Sabrina, who stood with her father and a senator from Virginia. Apparently, Sabrina had been keeping a close eye on

Arlette for God knew how long because she was quick to make eye contact, which prompted Arlette to turn away.

"I think you two should talk," her dad said.

"I think we shouldn't."

"Why not?"

"Because we broke up."

Her dad was knowledgeable on many things. That was why he was currently a top Democratic candidate in the polls. He knew American and world history through and through and had a strong knowledge of international relations and foreign affairs. However, in this moment, he was very much like any other clueless dad, not fully understanding how breakups worked.

"I still can't believe you thought our family crab feast, the day she'd just purchased a house, was a good time to break up," Uncle Henry said with a scoff. "Should we scratch 'marry someone good' off the list as well?"

Arlette tightened her grip around her glass. She didn't expect anything less from Uncle Henry. He sure had a lot of opinions about every choice Arlette had made for her life. She just wished that after twenty-seven years of unsolicited Uncle Henry opinions, she had learned to brush them off without feeling bruised.

"Not like my love life is any of your business, but I don't think the last several months of our relationship constitutes a 'good' one. I deserve better."

"You should still go say hi, Arlette," her dad said. "You've known her for longer than you were together. It's a decent thing to do."

"Sabrina hardly spoke to me the last three weeks we were together. Clearly, there's not much to say."

Just then, Angela McKay walked onstage, and everyone hushed. While Angela gave her speech and highlighted everything the foundation did in the last year, Arlette took another sip and found Brooke at the bar. Most people were focused on the speech, and the lines for all four bars were thin. Brooke rested her back against the railing, head moving as if she was searching for something in the crowd of tuxedos and gowns. Soon, her wandering eyes locked with Arlette, who flitted back to her ex-girlfriend's mother. But after thinking about it, she found it silly to act embarrassed because she'd been caught. She was freshly single, and that meant she could finally marvel at how Brooke Dawson made everything look beautiful.

Arlette glanced back, and a prickly heat crawled up her spine when she found that Brooke hadn't flinched at all. She gave Arlette a half-smile, and Arlette returned it with a slight wave, then faced the stage again, biting her lip to contain a grin.

As she tried to distract her analyzing brain, something in her peripheral vision snagged her attention. Sabrina, still in her same spot on the farthest left in front of the stage. At the sudden eye contact, Sabrina's eyes flitted away. Sabrina had lost her vibrant smile, heartbreak written all over her face. No matter how much the last few months with Sabrina had bothered her, the breakup still wasn't something she was proud of. No matter what had come between them, she still cared about Sabrina. Just because they weren't right for each other didn't mean she wanted for her to feel poorly.

She decided it was best to slip out of the crowd. Being between her father, Uncle Henry, and Angela McKay with Sabrina's eye on her, she felt like a specimen under a microscope. Plus, Angela was set to speak for at least ten to fifteen minutes, as she did every year. It always went: cocktail hour, Angela's speech, the auction, and then dancing. This was the ideal moment to head over to the bar and steal a moment with Brooke.

"Hi," Arlette said, resting her arms on the bar.

Brooke grinned and set what looked to be a glass of Coke off to the side. "Hey, there. You need another drink?"

"If you're offering the same one as before, then, yes, please."

Brooke took the empty glass, worked her bartending magic, and brought Arlette's Sazerac back to life. "Does this help?"

"Much better. Tonight's going to be a long night."

"Why do I feel like there's a story behind that?"

Right. Arlette had been a little MIA between late work hours and her breakup. She and Brooke had texted about a few things, mostly about how beautiful Arlette's painting was in her living room or Brooke freaking out over the fact she was making something for Teresa Rosario. Arlette used that as a way to keep texting, and whenever she saw that she had a text from Brooke, her stomach celebrated with backflips.

It hit Arlette right then in front of the bar. That was what she'd never felt with Sabrina. Whenever she'd seen a pending text from Sabrina, a weight of dread had washed over her from knowing Sabrina was probably blowing her off. She shouldn't have to feel dread from her girlfriend's texts.

She'd never felt that way with Brooke, though. Getting a text from her was the best part of her day.

"Because there is," Arlette said. "What are you doing after this?"

"Cleaning up, packing up the van, heading home."

"Want to bring back our late-night walks for old times' sake?"

Brooke smiled, and Arlette hoped that meant all the memories that came with the question had floated to her mind. It had started freshman year when Arlette and Brooke had met up for study dates at the library. They'd usually stayed until the library had closed, which meant walking back to Swanson Hall around midnight. On evenings that they hadn't felt like trekking to the library, their study dates had convened in the common room, and after immersing themselves in books, homework, and essays, sometimes they'd felt the need to walk off all the material they'd absorbed, stretch their legs, and get fresh air, even if it was almost time for bed.

There was something about the night that had encouraged depth. Some of their best talks had happened while lying in bed with the lights out or wandering campus when it was settling in for the night. There was also a different kind of beauty that emerged from the grounds in the moonlight. Willard was beautifully haunting with its two-hundred-year-old buildings and history.

"Wow, it's been years since we did that," Brooke said through a laugh. "We didn't really have much of those later on in college."

"We know the reason why," Arlette said, thinking of her ex-girlfriend, Jade, who wanted all of Arlette's spare time. She scoffed at the memory. *You really know how to pick them.*

"I would love a late-night walk if you can wait for me to pack up."

"I have nowhere to be after this. Now, how much do those bottles of wine go for?"

Brooke frowned and pointed at one. "You mean this?"

"Any."

"I'm not sure. Maybe forty bucks? Why? How come I feel like you're up to no good?"

"Why do you say that?"

Brooke leaned in. Although there was still a bar between them, a whiff of floral perfume made Arlette's heart twitch. "I used to be really good at reading you, remember? Apparently, I still am."

"You were, but I'm not up to anything bad. Just figured I'd buy a bottle for us to drink."

Brooke laughed. "Arlette, this isn't a store."

"What? The McKays already bought it from you, right? You said forty bucks." Arlette reached into her purse, pulled out a fifty, and placed it in Brooke's hand. "That should be enough to cover the whole thing and then some. I'll hang around here until you're done working."

For the rest of the event, Arlette cheered on her parents during the auction. With a few drinks in her, she mustered the courage to say hi to Angela and Ron, though, as expected, they kept it short and cordial, probably upset with Arlette for breaking up with their daughter. Arlette even waved at Sabrina from a distance, trying to maintain the peace, and Sabrina forced a not-so-pleasant smile and turned around. Arlette was thankful she was next to her parents so they could see her attempting to be friendly and getting denied.

She was glad when the event was over. It wasn't until eleven thirty that Brooke was finally done working. They met up in the alley where the catering company van sat. Arlette rested her back against the building as Brooke wrapped up, told the other bartender she was metroing home, and then rounded the corner with two water bottles filled with dark liquid.

"Your wine, Ms. Adair." She presented Arlette with a water bottle.

Arlette opened it and was greeted by the sweet scent "Ah, this is way better than a wine bottle," she said and took a swig.

"And smarter. If I'm ever going to get arrested, it's not going to be for something as stupid as an open container."

"You really understood the assignment, Ms. Dawson. I'm impressed."

"There's a reason I made the dean's list every year of college," Brooke said and did a proud hair flip.

"Follow me," Arlette said. If it wasn't for the drinks that had filled her with a happy buzz, she probably wouldn't have had the courage to lock arms with Brooke.

"Wait, hold on." Brooke used her free hand to gesture to Arlette's gown. "You're going to walk around in a floor-length dress with no sleeves?"

"Do you have a change of clothes?"

"No. I don't usually bring one with me, but you're really making me question that whole philosophy."

"Good. Next time, bring a change of clothes. Now, come with me."

Honestly, she had no plan. She wasn't sure where the adventure would lead them, but she found that part exciting. It was going on midnight, and the stiff drinks Brooke had poured made her limbs feel warm and tingly. She had tipsy energy flowing through her veins. And she had Brooke hooked to her arm.

She didn't want the night to end.

So she kept walking down Sixth Street with her only mission being to keep the night going. The columns of the West Building of the National Gallery of Art came into view, a beacon to the National Mall. A white hand on the crosswalk signal flashed for them to cross. They walked in silence until they reached the steps of the National Gallery of Art. Lights cascaded up the columns. Like many buildings in DC, the museum looked gorgeous against the fallen night. It was just as beautiful as the art inside.

"You know, this is one of my favorite buildings in the city," Arlette said, her arm still locked with Brooke's as she admired the museum's neoclassical architecture.

"Why's that?"

She caught Brooke studying her while drinking more wine. The lights from the building contoured her beauty, shining a spotlight on the smirk forming behind the rim of her water bottle. Arlette loved the fact that their arms hadn't separated despite their coming to a stop. She sure as hell wasn't going to be the one to let go. She'd done that five years ago and had regretted it. Massively. She planned on continuing their stroll and acting like she'd forgotten that their arms were linked.

"For one, it's absolutely gorgeous," she said. "You know the architect of this building also designed the Jefferson Memorial? The rotunda was inspired by the interior of the Pantheon in Rome."

"Was it really?" Brooke looked back at the building as if viewing it from a brand-new perspective. "Wow. I had no idea. What else do you know about it?"

Arlette guided her along the sidewalk in front of the building. The familiarity of their past squeezed between them. Brooke had always encouraged Arlette's random facts in college. Arlette had realized back then that she gave too many unsolicited fun facts and stories, something Jade had pointed out and asked her to stop doing. But when she'd told Brooke, her face had contorted into a frown. She'd grabbed Arlette's hand and said, "Well, fine. You can share everything you know with me, then."

"I think there's something hauntingly beautiful about this building," Arlette said as she took it in for the millionth time. "This museum opened on the eve of World War II as all the national museums in Europe were closing because of the war. While Hitler and the Nazis were burning paintings and Europe was being bombed, this museum rose up. I see it as a symbol of democracy, and back then, that symbol was like a beacon. It went up when everything else was crumbling."

"Wow," Brooke said and stared up at the columns as Arlette stared at her and wondered what she was thinking. She seemed to be scanning the building as if searching for something hidden behind the columns.

"What are you thinking about?" Arlette asked.

Brooke gave her a smile, but it was too faint to reach her eyes. "My dad."

Arlette didn't expect that response at all. She'd known Brooke since she was eighteen, and out of all their shared moments, only two or three involved talking about her dad. Although Brooke rarely mentioned him, it was clear his leaving had affected her deeply, especially in her childhood and adolescence. And his abandonment made her question her own worth, and Arlette couldn't help but wonder if the only trace her dad had left was the seed of doubt inside his daughter. She hated how Brooke always questioned herself. She had always wished Brooke could see herself through her eyes.

"Why are you thinking about him?" Arlette said.

"You know that after he left, we had to move. My mom could no longer afford the house. So we went from this beautiful two-story house to a little two-bedroom condo, and despite it being smaller, I felt like it had so much more emptiness."

"I remember you saying that."

Brooke faced the building again. "I don't know if I ever told you, but when we first moved, I really struggled. I mean, obviously. I was eight, and my father had left us without ever looking back. My mom thought we needed to get away for a few days. Something to clear our minds. So she drove us to DC before we spent a few more days in Ocean City. And I remember that we stopped at this museum. I remember holding her hand and staring up at the pictures, and at some point, I got bored, sat on a bench, and colored while my mom looked at the paintings. I told her that I wanted to be an artist, and I wanted to be on the walls, which was a pretty empty wish as an eight-year-old. I wanted to be a million things growing up, but the only thing that stuck was being an artist. My mom never questioned me. This was where she told me that I could do anything I wanted as long as I never gave up, and I guess I've held on to that since."

Arlette thought she'd heard all the significant stories and moments that had shaped Brooke Dawson's life, but she'd never heard the one that had taken place in one of her favorite buildings in the city. That piece of knowledge was like weaving a frayed piece of string back together. Brooke had always locked her father in a vault, and Arlette knew how painful it was to talk about him. It was why she never asked. But the fact that Brooke brought him up now, her arm still tightly fastened around Arlette's, meant that though she'd caused some deep cracks in Brooke's trust, she hadn't shattered it completely.

"Your dreams started growing at a time when your world was crumbling," Arlette said.

Brooke gave her a soft, knowing smile. "Yeah, I guess it did."

"I'm glad you never gave up on yourself. I know back in college, you were scared to let people in, especially with your art, but now you're putting it out there for people to see, and I admire you so much for it."

"Thank you." Brooke cleared her throat. "Want to keep walking?"

"Of course."

They continued down the sidewalk, arms still locked while drinking their wine, enjoying the silence that had fallen over the city. Arlette was always amazed by how quiet DC could be at night. During the day, people crowded the sidewalks, cars consistently honked and stalled in the roads, sirens and the occasional helicopter or motorcade added to the ruckus. But at night, all of that went away. The roads and sidewalks cleared, and peaceful silence filtered through and added even more beauty to the glowing monuments, memorials, and buildings.

"You know, I've been meaning to come here," Brooke said. "I need some inspiration for Teresa Rosario's painting and for the rest of my pieces for the fall exhibit. Would you maybe want to come back with me? You can tell me more about your favorite building, and I can tell you some art facts? I know a few things from my art degree."

Arlette's chest tugged pleasantly. If Brooke invited her to watch paint dry on the canvas, she would have agreed to it in a heartbeat. Any moment shared with Brooke had always been exciting to her, even the smallest ones. "I would absolutely love that."

"Great. I was thinking about going on Sunday. You free then? You're not working or have plans with your girlfriend?"

Arlette laughed and thought that was the perfect time to drink more wine.

"What?"

"That's the story behind why tonight was an incredibly long night. I broke up with Sabrina two weeks ago, and this was the first time I've seen her since."

Brooke choked on her sip. She pulled her arm away, put a fist to her closed lips, and coughed again. "What? Why? I mean, you don't have to answer. It's none of my business. I'm sorry, I just—"

"Easy there, Brooklyn," Arlette said, laughing, and patted her back. "This is not something to choke over."

"I'm sorry." Brooke washed the cough with more wine. "Are you okay?"

"I'm fine, actually. I mean, part of me is upset, but that's more at myself than anything."

"What do you mean?"

"That I let it go on as long as it did when I knew there wasn't much between us. I wasn't in love with her." Brooke stared back with rounded eyes. "Simple as that. And no matter what she tells me, she wasn't in love with me, either, and I'm mad at myself for sticking around hoping that one day, she'd feel something, or I'd feel something, or she'd at least act like we were something."

Brooke's stare held sympathy. "I'm sorry she made you feel like that."

Arlette shrugged. "I should have done this much sooner, so that's on me. I think it's very apparent when someone's in love with you." She paused to think about her words. "Well…at least, it should be apparent. I wouldn't really know, and I don't think anyone has been in love with me, but I'd like to think that it's blatant when they are."

She sat on a bench that faced away from the National Gallery of Art and toward the darkness that had fallen over the National Mall. Across the lawn, through the trees and the occasional lamp, stood the Air and Space Museum. Arlette chose to focus on how close Brooke sat to her, her black dress pants resting against where Arlette's dress draped over her leg.

"Can I ask you a personal question?" Arlette said.

"You can ask me anything, Arlette. That hasn't changed."

Arlette nodded as she processed the knowledge. She was afraid of the question she was about to ask, and she couldn't exactly pinpoint why Brooke's impending answer made her feel uneasy. "Have you ever been in love?"

Brooke pulled back and let out an empty laugh. "Wow, that's a deep question."

Maybe they were at a point where they could reference the secrets they'd once shared, like Brooke's father, but Arlette should have known better than to assume she could ask Brooke about her personal life, especially before they had yet to muster up the courage to address what had happened years ago.

Arlette shrugged and shook her head. "I'm sorry, you don't have to answer."

"I'm not sure," Brooke said softly. It wasn't quite the response Arlette expected. "I feel like I've been close, like knocking on its door but not being invited in."

Arlette realized she'd been holding her breath, and when Brooke was done, she exhaled, hot and heavy, leaving a pile of nerves in her gut. She wondered who the woman was who hadn't let Brooke in. Part of her couldn't help but wonder if it had been her, but they'd been so young then. They had a five-year hole in their timeline, and Brooke Dawson was so beautiful, intelligent, deep, and warm. She radiated beauty inside and out, and Arlette was positive she'd attracted many other women. She didn't doubt for a second that there had been other women since their short-lived fling who hadn't cowered about making Brooke theirs.

The streetlamp cast the smallest light on Brooke's face, illuminating all the things Arlette had walked away from way back when. The light must have had some magical powers because the longer she studied Brooke's features, the more she felt twenty-two all over again, remembering how those perfect lips used to dance across hers, the column of that neck that held all the magical spots to make Brooke whimper when kissed, and all the sounds that had escaped her. Brooke had been the shortest, yet the most significant, physical relationship she'd ever had because no matter how much time had passed, it still clung to her like a large presence in the corner of the room.

"So you haven't ever been in love?" Brooke asked, snapping Arlette out of the trance of her lips.

"What? Oh…no. I…um…" She nervously ran a hand through her hair. "Do you think falling in love is supposed to be hard?"

"I don't know. I'd like to think that when it's with the right person, it actually happens pretty easily."

Arlette had never viewed love that way, but when she let Brooke's perspective marinate, she saw it clearly. She'd really tried to fall in love with Jade and Sabrina, the two longest relationships she'd had. Arlette and Sabrina got along. Sabrina made her laugh. Arlette's family loved her, and the McKays loved Arlette. Sabrina could have given her everything she'd wanted if it could be purchased. Sabrina had millions and she was twenty-eight, and once she inherited the company, she would be a billionaire. But even with all the material things Sabrina had in the palm of her hand, it wasn't enough to give Arlette the sparks, safety, and love she desperately wanted and deserved. Love was the one thing that couldn't be bought.

Arlette and Brooke decided to walk back to the front of the museum once they finished their wine. After calling their Ubers, they turned back to each other.

"So Sunday?" Arlette said. "You still want to look at some art together?"

Brooke smiled. "If you're still willing to tell me more about your favorite building in the city."

Arlette stuck out a hand. When Brooke's soft fingers wrapped around hers, she felt her stomach tighten. "Deal," she said, pushing through the welcome discomfort.

As she lay down later that night, her head spinning from whiskey, wine, and confusion, she knew Brooke had been right. Those butterflies, nerves, and sparks should have been there all along if Sabrina was the right person. Arlette went home that night positive, for the first time since the breakup, that she had made the right decision.

She deserved sparks. She deserved to feel it in her chest.

THE HUES OF ME AND YOU

CHAPTER EIGHT

Arlette found the art in the West Building of the National Gallery of Art very boring. She loved modern art, and everything else wasn't as exciting or as pleasing to the eye. But if she had to look at thirteenth-through-sixteenth-century art to help Brooke collect inspiration, she would do it without a fight.

Brooke soaked up the paintings through those adorable, clear-framed glasses Arlette loved so much. Being near her was all the entertainment Arlette needed until they reached the modern art in the East Building. She spent more time watching Brooke study each piece than she did looking at the paintings. She loved how Brooke's eyebrows furrowed with each detail and how her head tilted to the side. Witnessing Brooke nerd out to thirteenth-century art was the most adorably sexy thing Arlette had ever seen.

Brooke seemed completely unaware of how unfocused Arlette was on the paintings, which allowed her to keep stealing glances at Brooke being unintentionally attractive as hell. She continued to each painting, repeating her same process of eyebrow raising and head tilting. Occasionally, she asked what Arlette thought about the art, how she felt, as if Brooke truly believed she had something profoundly deep to say about it. Any time she asked, Arlette had to suck in a grin. After all this time, Brooke still valued her opinion. She had limited specks of knowledge about art, and yet, Brooke still wanted to hear her thoughts. Brooke had always validated her feelings. It was as if she hung them up like a frame on a wall and admired them as much as the art surrounding them.

Arlette wished she had never let go of that.

"It looks great," she said to every piece, and every time, she winced at how lame she sounded. Since Brooke had invited her and asked her about her thoughts, she clearly expected more than a rudimentary response.

But for some reason, Brooke never reacted to the dumb things Arlette supplied. She just continued reading, studying, analyzing, and Arlette fought every urge to tame the smile that wanted to claim her whole face. Brooke was in her element, and that made her smarter than ever, more confident than ever, and sexier than ever.

It wasn't until they went to the East Building that the art attracted Arlette's gaze. Abstract, vibrant colors and shapes. This time, Arlette found herself reading each title card like she did in history museums that were more up her alley and in her realm of knowledge.

"This one looks sad, don't you think?" Arlette said and gestured to an oil painting in royal and baby blues, lavender, and black in the forefront.

Brooke studied her for a second and then looked at the canvas. "I can see it. It's the darker shades and the black in the middle. It's what your eyes see first."

"All of these paintings remind me of yours." Arlette gestured to the art that made up the surrealism and abstract expressionism section. "All of these are just so…beautiful."

"These are my greatest influences right here. This is what I'm thinking about capturing for Teresa Rosario. Do you mind if we do another sweep? I want to really take it in again for her piece."

"We can stay here as long as you'd like." She meant it. She could watch Brooke in her element all day. There was no need to rush when it made Arlette fully content just being in Brooke's presence.

They went around the East Building again, getting lost in each piece. It wasn't until they reached a Matta painting that Arlette stole a glance at Brooke. "I knew you had something special the moment you showed me those digital drawings of our Swanson friends," she said, pulling Brooke's gaze off the Matta. Brooke lifted an eyebrow. "And then you drew me, and it took you, like, two weeks to finish it, and I swear, in that small amount of time, you'd gotten significantly better."

"It took two weeks because I took my time," Brooke said. "You were much more patient than everyone else in the dorm, so I might have taken advantage of that. But hey, you got a better picture, so there's that." Brooke laughed and elbowed Arlette's arm.

"I guess patience really is a virtue."

"Exactly. You also have pretty unique features, so I used your patience as time to get all those details right."

Arlette raised her eyebrows. "What do you mean?" This was the first time she'd heard anything about her "pretty unique features," and repeating those three words caused her heart to quicken at the thought that it might have alluded to Brooke's old crush.

Their stare locked and made Arlette feel so much closer, despite the two feet between them. "Your eyes alone are something to talk about."

Another rush of heat cascaded down her neck. "What's going on with my eyes?"

"The real question is, what's not going on with your eyes?"

"I don't know. I don't really stare at them."

"Well, I had to study them in great detail, so I feel like an expert. Or at least, I was once."

Something about Brooke studying her in great detail caused feelings to swirl inside her. It made Brooke so much more intriguing than any of the paintings. "You were once an expert on my eyes?"

"I'd like to think so," she said it so confidently, with unwavering eye contact, that it warmed the back of Arlette's neck despite the constant blast of air-conditioning.

"Can you describe them to me?"

Brooke erased a foot between them. The cold air held a palpable charge. By the way her eyes flitted all over Arlette, Brooke was taking her in all over again, as if it was the first time she'd done so. "You have a very pronounced limbal ring, which is the black ring around your eyes. You basically have an outline. At first glance, they look a soft olive-green in color, but you have bursts of amber around your pupils that meet with a thin layer of gold that dissolves into the green you see from a distance. Once I noticed the ambers and the golds, I couldn't unsee it. It's, like, the first thing I notice now."

"Do...do you see it now?"

"I always see it, Arlette. It was the first thing I noticed again when we saw each other at your dad's party."

A lump appeared in Arlette's throat. "It was?"

Brooke nodded. "I think your eyes are chartreuse. It's a rare color. A very beautiful color. They're…they're really something." She was quick to turn back to a title card, as if she hadn't meant to say the last part and was embarrassed by her lack of filter.

No matter how fast the recovery was, Arlette held on to the last comment for the rest of their time in the museum, her heart never quite easing up from hammering against her rib cage at all the possible meanings those words had held.

As they stepped outside, they silently agreed to walk around the National Mall. But right as they started walking, someone shouted, "Go Beckett!"

Arlette turned and found a man in his mid-thirties wearing a gray shirt with Kendra Beckett's campaign logo. He waved, quickly followed it with the middle finger, and then continued walking in the opposite direction.

Kendra Beckett was one of the other democratic candidates running, her father's biggest competition. They were the top two in the polls. Honestly, Beckett's political views were more aligned with Arlette's. She appealed to the younger generations and had branded herself a proud progressive; the more moderate liberals tended to favor her dad. Teresa Rosario was about to announce her endorsement for Beckett, which was not a huge surprise to Arlette. She really wasn't upset by that.

What upset her was being accosted in public, drawing more attention to her. People glanced over, and a few seemed to recognize her. Someone pointed, and Arlette wanted the summer sun to melt her right there on the sidewalk so she wouldn't be looked at as if she were a street performer. The familiar tingling warmth climbed up her spine and spread on top of her head, the feeling she always got when panic started bubbling inside her. There was something uncomfortable that sewed through her limbs and yanked on her too tightly.

It was a personal attack, and while the encounter was over and done within a few seconds, discomfort poked and prodded at her skin from knowing that she had been targeted in public.

Brooke's soft, gentle hand grabbed her arm. "Hey, are you okay?"

Arlette glanced over at the man but couldn't find him in the crowd. Her mind sputtered while trying to center back in the present. She looked at Brooke's hand and focused on how nurturing the grip was, as if guiding her away from the anxious thoughts.

Growing up in a prominent household had helped mold her anxieties. It wasn't the first time a stranger had shouted at her while walking the DC streets. She'd had plenty of exposure as a kid at school, and her classmates had repeated all the lines their parents had said behind closed doors. Kids had casually told her on the playground how their parents hated her dad, uncle, or grandpa. Sometimes, she wouldn't be invited to birthday parties because the parents didn't want to be associated with her last name. She'd also grown up with her dad, grandpa, and uncle receiving death threats, which became a normal part of her childhood. All of that had shaped her discomfort for large crowds. When she was little, she'd been terrified of one of those threats actually happening. Anytime they went to an event, her mom always pointed out the security personnel. The few times she'd attended events when the president was there, her mom had told her that everything would be all right because of the Secret Service.

Though some of her anxieties had eased as she'd grown up, they'd never fully left her. She thought a lot about how her abnormal upbringing in a political family had shaped the way she saw the world, the way she presented herself, and the way she let the world in. It was why she kept her circle so small, why she'd rather be off to the side with Ben at a party than as the center of attention, and why she absolutely had no interest in politics.

The criticism always made her feel like she was an inch tall, so easy to step on. But she was thankful for the safety Brooke provided in that moment. At least Brooke knew and understood, and while Arlette's mind started drowning in her anxieties, Brooke was the life vest pulling her up.

"How about we get out of here," Brooke said and ran her fingers up and down Arlette's arms.

Arlette paused for a moment to enjoy Brooke's touch, and if it wasn't for the fact that she was so focused on calming her racing heart, she would have been embarrassed by how easily goose bumps broke out on her skin, completely revealing her cards about how much she enjoyed the soothing touch.

Arlette thought of the closest thing she knew that would cloak her from the public. "Can I show you one of my favorite spots in the city?"

"You've already shown me one of your favorite buildings. I would love to see one of your favorite spots."

Arlette smiled. "Follow me. We're scootering over."

The National Mall was littered with electric scooters. It was the best place in the city to ride one. The Mall stretched two miles from the Capitol to the Lincoln Memorial, with the Washington Monument smack-dab in the middle, offering pedestrian paths that made it much easier to go full speed.

They hopped on and scooted from the National Gallery of Art toward the Lincoln Memorial. The wind whipped Arlette's hair, lightness filled her veins again, and occasionally, she glanced back to make sure she hadn't lost Brooke, but there she was, her blond hair also billowing back and a smile on her face.

They zipped down the length of the reflecting pool and stopped at the base of the steps leading up to the memorial. Groups of people always surrounded the memorial at all times of the day. Arlette couldn't really blame them. It was a gorgeous and iconic memorial that supplied beautiful views of the city on all four sides. Luckily, most of the people only stayed on the front side to take in the sights of the pool, the Washington Monument, and the Capitol Building in the distance. They were too focused on that shot to notice there was an equally beautiful view behind the monument if you went at the right time of the day. It was one of Arlette's favorite spots that offered the best sunset views.

"Should I be worried about where you're luring me?" Brooke asked as they marched up the steps, weaving in and out of groups of people snapping pictures of the monument and the reflecting pool.

"No, you should be excited because I'm about to show you something amazing."

"Is it a big statue of Abraham Lincoln? Because I've seen it countless times."

They finally reached the top, and the enormous Lincoln greeted them through the two rows of columns. Arlette reached for Brooke's hand. She ignored the swirling in her stomach when Brooke's fingers latched on to hers, and guided her to the back of the memorial that overlooked the Potomac River, the Arlington Memorial Bridge, and Rosslyn, Virginia. The back was significantly less crowded. Only a few people had traveled there to watch the dying sun.

Arlette took a seat and dangled her feet over the side, and Brooke cautiously joined her. By the time they got situated, the hues of the sky had become bolder. Deep golds and wispy streaks of orange cirrostratus clouds painted the sky.

"Wow, this is...amazing," Brooke said as she stretched her legs, and her right leg naturally fell and rested against Arlette's.

"Isn't it? Shh. Don't tell anyone. This is our secret," Arlette said and nudged Brooke's arm.

"I promise, I won't tell a soul."

"If I make it out of work early enough and the sky looks like it will give us a good show, I will scooter or even walk over here to watch the sunset. This is one of my happy places."

"I feel like you probably have a lot of secret happy places."

Arlette marveled at how the sky cast at least five different yellows on Brooke's face, making her hair look even more golden. "I have a few, but this is my favorite." Her grandpa's boat dock, the back of the Lincoln, and any place next to Brooke.

"I feel like you must also know a fun fact about this if it's your favorite spot."

Arlette smiled at the excitement bubbling in her chest. Brooke had always encouraged her stories. She'd made Arlette feel so safe, so free at Willard. She could wander and let her dreams float to the sky knowing she would have a soft fall back to Earth.

"Of course I do," Arlette said.

Brooke rested her back against the column behind her. "Lay it on me."

Arlette followed and moved to square her body to Brooke's. "You said you've seen Lincoln countless times. So have you noticed the typo on the wall inside?"

Brooke furrowed her eyebrows. "There's a typo?"

"Yes. Instead of an F for 'future,' it's an E. They've tried fixing it, but I still think it's pretty noticeable. People sometimes don't notice it, but once you do, it's hard to unsee."

"Kind of like your eyes?"

The comment stopped Arlette in her tracks and pulled something low in her stomach. "Kind of like my eyes." Arlette swallowed the lump in her throat. "So...yeah...anytime you make a mistake, you should tell yourself that at least your mistake isn't permanently etched into the limestone that makes up Abraham Lincoln's memorial. That's what I tell myself, and I instantly feel better. We will have to check it out before we leave."

"That will definitely help me gain some perspective on my next mistake."

A couple walked behind them and rounded the corner to the front of the memorial. Arlette glanced back and smiled to see there was only one other couple at the opposite end. She and Brooke had a front-row view all to themselves.

"So the first debate is coming up," Brooke said and pulled Arlette's gaze. "How is everything going with that?"

She shrugged. "It's going. I know my dad has been working hard to prepare for it. He seems excited and happy, so that makes me excited and happy for him."

"Why does it sound like there's a but coming?"

Arlette let out an empty laugh. Brooke Dawson was at it again. She had memorized Arlette so well that it was foolish to try to mask her feelings. "He wants me to go to Miami next week for the first debate, and I agreed to go, but now…I really don't want to. If I back out, does that make me a shitty daughter?"

"Absolutely not."

Arlette ran a hand through her hair. "We've made so much progress over the years. I feel like he's actually proud of me now. It's really nice. I haven't felt that way in such a long time, and I don't want to lose it. I know he's upset about me breaking up with Sabrina, but I worry that if I don't go to his first debate, we'll revert back to old times."

"Do you think you've only made progress over the years because you started following the path he wanted you to be on?"

The question packed a punch. It was a fair one and something that had been lurking in Arlette's mind for years. Constantly ruminating on it had made her see how far she had strayed from the path she thought she would be on by now. She wasn't supposed to be in politics, and while it had surprisingly made her content for a few years, it didn't anymore. She was flying through life on autopilot, swiping past her dreams like a plane jetting through clouds.

"I do think that," Arlette said, blowing out a heavy breath and looking back at the sun inching closer to Arlington National Cemetery across the river.

"You can wish for others to be different, but you can't change a person. I know because for years, I wished my father wasn't the kind of person to leave his family and not look back. Constantly worrying about how people will react to you is exhausting and takes so much from you. Once I let all of that go, there was so much weight off me. You can only control your own happiness. You should focus on the things you can control."

"My dad's happiness affects mine too, though."

"My mom wasn't too thrilled when I told her after my internships that I was going to do freelance. She was worried about me because we've always struggled with money. Single mom raising a kid on an art teacher's salary was extremely difficult. So, of course, my mom was concerned about it at first and kept telling me she didn't want me to struggle with money. But as much as it concerned her, I knew what was right for me. What I'm trying to say is that your life is yours, not anyone else's. Your dad has to accept that your life is something he can't control."

Brooke's words settled in her. She knew everything Brooke said was right. Her dad might have dreams of being the leader of the free world. One day, he could possibly control the nuclear codes, but he had no right to control her life. She was twenty-seven, old enough to make her own decisions, old enough to know what she wanted and needed in her life.

"I really admire you, you know that?" Arlette said.

"For what?" Brooke sounded genuinely surprised.

"For being so confident and adamant about what you want to do. You took a huge risk, even went against the comfort of a stable paycheck, and you own it. You're very admirable, Brooklyn."

"I'm not really. I just know how it feels to be uncomfortable in the one place you've sought solace. When my dad left, he took the feeling of home with him. The one escape I had was in my sketchbooks. Art gave me comfort and safety. It became what was comfortable for me."

"But you stayed on the path you've always wanted to be on. I strayed because having my parents proud of me was something I've always wanted, and I chased that instead of my dreams. I know my parents love me, but their expectations cloud it."

"It's okay to want unconditional love. It's absolutely normal. When a person places conditions on their love, you'll never feel safe."

To the Adair family—and much of politics—power equaled success, and success equaled happiness. Arlette had grown up and absorbed her family's beliefs. Now that she was an adult, she saw how distorted it was and needed to untangle it. Happiness was the ultimate success. It was as simple as that.

She exhaled deeply. "I wandered off the path just a little bit and never found a way back. But you always followed your gut, even though it might have been scary. Now look at you. People really want your paintings. Your art is going up in exhibits. You're doing what you always wanted to do. That's impressive, Brooklyn. I really admire that. I think it's amazing. *You're* amazing."

"You can do it too, Arlette. I don't think you're as lost as you think. You broke up with Sabrina because she wasn't making you happy. That's much harder than telling your dad you're not able to make the debate next week. I know saying no is hard, but losing your sanity is much harder."

Arlette loved and admired her dad. Grandpa Harry had helped her see that she and her father weren't all that different. They were both dreamers. However, she'd realized that there were two kinds of dreamers. Ones who continued soaring despite the strong winds that forced them in one direction, and ones who got caught up in the wind. Arlette was the dreamer stuck in the wind, and her father was the one who remained in the clouds and soared. He was admirable too. She wanted his strength and determination as much as she wanted Brooke's.

She stopped daydreaming when she felt Brooke's hand on her thigh. When she met Brooke's gaze, it generated another stare that scorched the humid air around them. A stare that seemed to hold Brooke captive as much as it held her.

This moment felt like when they had opened up to each other for the first time freshman year. Arlette felt raw in the sunset, and while it scared her a bit, there was some comfort in knowing that she was being real in front of Brooke again. Something had shifted during their conversation, and wherever it had taken them, it made Arlette's heart beat faster, the dancing around their past more prominent. It was becoming impossible to ignore, especially as the deep conversation reminded Arlette of all those they'd had in college. Falling back into their old patterns highlighted their past like the sunset streaking across the sky.

"What's going through your mind?" Brooke asked with the smallest grin, taking back her hand. "I feel like you went somewhere just now."

Arlette looked at the ground. "I've really missed you."

"What?"

Arlette couldn't ignore the past anymore. It was as bright and prominent as the orange, wispy cirrostratus clouds, and quite frankly, she was done avoiding it. Each conversation they had brought them closer to their past, like digging up a deeply buried time capsule. It was right in front of them, waiting for one of them to pick it up and hold it up for the other.

Arlette shrugged and glanced at the buildings across the river. "I thought about you. All the time, really." As she removed the last layer of vulnerability, she felt the ground below her getting harder and making her uncomfortable. The sun shifted, reflecting off the buildings across the Potomac River and shining directly in her eyes. The last two months had gifted her with a second chance she'd never expected to have. No matter how uncomfortable it made her feel, she was going to fight for that chance. "Still, to this day, I've never had a friend like you, Brooklyn. The four years at Willard were the best years of my life, and once I lost you, I lost all of that too."

A long silence fell between them. Arlette was too afraid to look over while the pause grew. But once Brooke quietly said, "I thought about you too," Arlette looked.

"Really?" She hadn't expected that response. She was the one who'd messed things up. She was the one who'd run away. Brooke had made it clear that their friendship—or whatever it had morphed into—was over. All of it. Brooke had drawn the line in the sand. Arlette wouldn't have ever guessed that missing her was mutual.

"Of course I did," Brooke said matter-of-factly, looking at Arlette as if she should have known better. "You were my best friend. Of course I thought about you."

The weight that washed over Arlette landed in her stomach like a brick plummeting to the bottom of a pool. It was Brooke handing back that dug-up time capsule. They had been dancing around, and she had been constantly wondering when they would dig through enough safe conversation topics until finally reaching the vault of all the answers and unsaid things.

"Losing you was really hard," Brooke said, the vulnerability loud in her voice.

"I know."

"Do you? Because while I was something casual for you, you were everything to me. I spent those four years falling for you. I was always there when you needed me. Even when Jade was in the driver's seat, and our friendship started fading senior year, I was there."

The nerves strained Arlette's arid throat. They were really about to look through the time capsule in great detail. "I never meant to hurt you, Brooklyn. I truly mean that. You were my best friend. Actually, you were the closest friend I've ever had."

"Friends," Brooke said, nodding in defeat before looking back at the sunset. "Was that all we were? Listen, if you didn't have feelings for me, that's fine, but I'm going to disagree that we were only friends. I could tell by the way you kissed me that you felt something too. I know the difference between kissing for the hell of it and kissing when you're really into it."

Arlette looked away as her face burned with guilt and embarrassment. It was Brooke reading her perfectly, just like she always did, and no matter how much Arlette tried running away from her feelings, somehow, they continued to grow.

"When you two broke up, you told me that Jade never looked at you or listened to you the way I did. I thought that you saw what I'd been seeing since we met. I thought, 'This is it. This is our chance,' but you left me standing there, waiting, alone."

"Brooklyn, I had every intention of talking to you—"

"But it didn't happen, Arlette, so does it really matter when you never followed through?"

Arlette glanced at her lap. "I had an internship lined up at the UN that started in the fall. I never told you, but my dad had called to tell me how proud he was that I'd accepted such an amazing opportunity. That comment roped me in because it was something he'd never said before. It made me focus on the future and finally appeasing him, and I wasn't mentally in a place to be in a relationship, especially one that involved distance. I was afraid that I would lose you to that distance. A connection like what we had was so rare for me."

She was also terrified that her make-out sessions with Brooke had weaved a complicated web they wouldn't have been able to untangle themselves from. So she had walked away, understanding that sometimes leaving things unsaid was easier than a truth no one wanted to hear.

"It was rare for me too," Brooke said. "We talked about everything, even the painful things we hadn't told anyone else because it was too hard. But somehow, with each other, those topics were easier. We could talk about everything and anything, except for when it came to what was happening between us? That's the thing that scared you the most?"

Arlette heard the lingering hurt in her voice, and seeing it reflected in her eyes would be more than painful, so she avoided her gaze. Brooke had every right to be upset. Arlette was upset with herself too. That was what made her so heartbroken after that phone conversation...well, yelling match. Brooke had raised her voice and cried on the other end. Arlette had never heard so much hurt and anger from her before. That was when she'd known how much damage had been done, something beyond repair. All of this would have been easily prevented if Arlette hadn't been so afraid.

"I was young, scared, and so fucking confused." Arlette finally mustered the courage to meet Brooke's gaze. Looking directly at all the pain she'd caused was as blinding as the sun bouncing off the buildings across the Potomac. Brooke's eyes, hidden behind a thin layer of gloss and resignation, softened her once-furrowed brows. The tension washed over her with another wave of guilt. She still felt so much shame for letting go of the one person she'd trusted the most, the one person who she'd opened up completely for, that the shame had never dissipated from her chest. "I'm sorry for everything that happened. I'm so sorry for how it changed us and what we once were to each other."

Brooke thinned her lips, glanced at her lap, and nodded. "Yeah, me too."

"I don't like what I did to you. If I could go back and change it, I would redo it in a heartbeat. You meant the world to me, Brooklyn. I know I didn't always do a good job of showing it, especially that last year, but you really did. You still do, for what it's worth."

Brooke nervously pierced half moons in her thighs with her fingernails. Arlette wanted more than anything to stop that nervous tic and hold her hands. "You know I couldn't paint for months after graduation?"

"What? Really?"

She nodded. "That never happened to me before. The one thing that helped me through my saddest times couldn't help me through that one. It's really scary when you lose your outlet. It's debilitating. When I was able to paint again, all my paintings were in black and blue, and now I have about eight pieces hiding in my studio that I don't know what to do with. I feel like they're too personal to sell."

A pang rippled through Arlette. She had no idea that their fallout had affected her that greatly. "I'm so sorry," she said, shaking her head and glancing at her dangling feet.

The drop below felt exactly like Arlette's emotions: careening over the edge, waiting to hear if Brooke had forgiven her for all the hurt she had caused.

"I think the reason they're so visually dark is that because of that whole last year, I felt abandoned. I trusted you with everything."

The pain from that statement hung in Arlette's chest like her feet over the memorial. The emotion was bare in Brooke's eyes; she was afraid of being abandoned again. She had spoken about her fear multiple times throughout college when their conversations had traveled deep, and the fact that Brooke had labeled Arlette as someone who'd abandoned her like her father...it tore through Arlette.

"I kept telling myself that you wouldn't push me aside for a girlfriend," Brooke continued. "You were just stuck in a really shitty situation, but the more I thought about it, the more I thought that was bullshit because you could have easily stopped it."

"I did stop it—"

Brooke looked up with a detailed frown. "It lasted six months. Being pushed aside by your best friend for six months does a lot. I was already hurt long before we started making out."

Knowing that was how she'd made Brooke feel stung her eyes. She blinked back the moisture and cleared the tension balling in her throat. "I'm really sorry. I promise, that was the last thing I ever wanted to make you feel."

"I forgive you."

Brooke's hand landed on Arlette's wrist, and a flutter zipped through her chest. She looked down at the connection before meeting Brooke's eyes with a frown. How had Brooke found a way to forgive her when she had such a hard time forgiving herself? "You do?"

Brooke nodded. "I know you, Arlette. You're a people pleaser. Always have been. I know you didn't go out of your way to hurt me." "I really didn't."

Brooke retracted her hand, and Arlette felt the loss. "For what it's worth, I'm glad we've run into each other again. It kind of feels like the good ol' days all over again, doesn't it?"

Arlette smiled as the clenching in her chest finally loosened. "I don't plan on fucking it up this time. Turns out, I really need you in my life. You make things seem...I don't know. Easier. Lighter. More exciting."

The words fell from her lips before she could stop them. Her mind flicked back to the morning she'd spent on the dock with Grandpa Harry, when she'd asked him if he ever thought about how different his life would be if he'd done one thing differently. Something clicked inside her as she looked her past straight in her beautiful eyes. Brooke was the one thing she wished she had done differently. She had changed Arlette's life for the better, and Arlette had let her go. Arlette couldn't help but wonder, if she had allowed her heart to fully open for Brooke, how different would her life have been?

"Me? I make things more exciting?" Brooke said with a laugh. "I'm pretty sure all the exciting things we've ever done were all your ideas. Late-night walks? Roaming the city with a bottle of wine split into water bottles?"

"You go along with it. That's what makes you exciting. Moments are only adventures when you have someone to share them with."

"Then let's keep the adventure going," Brooke said and stuck out her hand.

Arlette studied it for the smallest moment, biting her lip to contain a smile. She accepted the handshake and met Brooke's stare. The relieved smile on Brooke's face pushed her heart back into place.

She had her best friend back, and amidst the stress and anxieties that had been piling on her chest for the last several months, Brooke had come in at the right time to give her much-needed air.

CHAPTER NINE

B rooke had always loved her studio. She loved the brick wall, the large south-facing windows that bottled all the sunlight in the room, and how the air smelled like old wood and paint. She loved her studio even more when she woke up feeling eager to get out of her comfy bed and get to work so inspiration could be brought to life.

Recently, she'd had a wealth of inspiration pooling inside her, ready to drip onto the canvas as bold colors and beautiful brushstrokes. She stopped to get her everything bagel and chai latte, and once her stomach was satisfied, she was ready to take on the Teresa Rosario piece. She put her earbuds in, turned on her favorite playlist, and got lost in the canvas.

In two long days, Brooke had finished Teresa's piece. Dots of paint stained her hands and arms like a sleeve tattoo, and her button-up shirt looked like she'd mistaken it for the canvas. Her back and butt ached from sitting for so long, but it was absolutely worth it, like being sore from an amazing workout.

She admired the piece from the other side of the studio. It had turned out better than she'd thought it would. Sure, the mini she'd sent to Teresa to make sure she liked the concept had offered a tiny preview. But when it was on a twenty-by-thirty-inch canvas, Brooke stared for a good ten minutes, uninterrupted, as if she'd never seen the piece before.

God, she'd done really well, and even patted herself on the back for a great job. She couldn't take her eyes off it, which meant something because if she couldn't admire her own work, how did she expect others to?

She snapped a picture of her new paint baby, and she surprised herself because the first person who popped in her head to share it with was Arlette.

That feeling hadn't happened since college. She lowered her phone and sifted through the emotions running wild in her. Part of her was nervous that after finally getting answers to her questions just days before, she was quick to let the excitement that came with Arlette's charm lower her guard. She wanted to let Arlette in despite the fact she had told Abby and Stephen that wouldn't be the case.

Should I even send this...yes...yes, I should. She's the reason I have Teresa Rosario as a client anyways.

She texted Arlette the photo first.

Arlette responded within a minute. *Wait. Is that Teresa's painting?*

Brooke pressed her lips together and smiled. The feeling of having Arlette's full attention caused her to slide in her chair and forget about everything else. She texted back, *Told you the museum would help inspire me.*

Holy shit, this is GORGEOUS, Brooklyn!

Brooke allowed her smile to grow. She sent her mom a text as the heat swept across her cheeks, but her mind didn't allow time to soak up her mother's shining approval when Arlette's still had ahold of her.

Brooke responded, *You think she's going to like it?*

Absolutely!

When Teresa Rosario emailed back saying she could pick up the painting that Thursday, in two days, Brooke questioned everything about herself, her studio, and her art as the panic set in. Teresa Rosario would be inside her studio, collecting art that she had made. Did she need to rearrange all her finished pieces against the wall in a more organized manner? What would she even wear to the studio when a congresswoman was going to come by? Her usual yoga pants and T-shirt, or did she need professional clothes? Did she call her Ms. Rosario? Congresswoman? When was the last time she'd even worn professional clothes outside of her bartending uniform?

What the hell was she supposed to do?

When Thursday finally came around, she texted Arlette a couple of hours before she and Teresa were due to come by to pick up the painting. *I'm so nervous.*

She's said that this painting is getting her through the day. You shouldn't be nervous when Teresa Rosario is excited for something

YOU created. Enjoy the moment. Also, I got you a present, so if you're free later, you should come over to my place to claim it.
    A present? Why do I get a present?
    Arlette quickly responded, *For being amazing.*
    Brooke's day got more exciting from there. Because she had so many nerves about meeting Teresa Rosario and excitement about whatever Arlette had up her sleeve, she hardly did anything productive for the rest of the day. She nervously cleaned her studio, responded to emails, and shipped her print orders to pass the time. Then at exactly seven p.m., when Teresa said she would arrive, there was a knock on the studio door.
    So many feelings fluttered behind her sternum, Brooke didn't know which ones to sort through when she opened the door. Should she process the fact that Teresa Rosario stood a foot away, flashing a wide smile, or should she process how sexy Arlette looked in her navy power suit and matching slacks? Her hair fell in loose curls down to her collarbone, and those striking eyes were firm on hers. She looked important and powerful, and Brooke's imagination ran wild about the hot woman in a suit at the most inappropriate time.
    Brooke cleared her throat and stuck out her hand. "Ms. Rosario, it's so nice to meet you. I'm Brooklyn."
    Teresa shook her hand, a sturdy and professional move that told Brooke she meant business; however, the friendly smile was also personable. "Brooklyn, it's so nice to meet you. And please, call me Teresa."
    Brooke stole a quick glance at Arlette, who held her stare with a suppressed grin. Brooke quickly turned away at the connection and gestured the two of them inside.
    "Is this the masterpiece?" Teresa said, pointing at the painting resting on the easel.
    By the rapt tone, Brooke sensed she was impressed. She straightened her back and walked over. "Yes, it is."
    "Oh my God, I absolutely love this. Arlette, don't you love this?"
    When Brooke made eye contact, it was Arlette's turn to flit her gaze to Teresa and then the painting, as if Brooke wasn't supposed to catch her staring. "It's gorgeous, isn't it?" Arlette said, leaving Brooke to join Teresa in front of the easel. "The blues and greens are entrancing, don't you think?"

"The whole thing is entrancing," Teresa said and tilted her head.

Brooke eagerly watched from the side as Teresa and Arlette took in every detail of the abstract painting covered in turquoise, sky blue, and cerulean that swirled together to resemble a wave of spilled resin. The blue wave mixed with layers of black and dubonnet. Brooke wanted the painting to symbolize the ocean. On the surface, you saw beauty and calm, represented by the blue hues, but underneath lay the dark shades of pollution, a reminder to Teresa, Arlette, and the rest of their team of what they were working to fight against every day.

"Water pollution?" Arlette asked and glanced over.

Brooke held back a smile. She'd sensed that Arlette wasn't a fan of all art, like the art in the West Building of the Natural Gallery of Art. Brooke might have been a little too preoccupied with all the art on the museum's walls, but she'd still regarded her from her peripheral enough to know that Arlette had been focused on her more than the thirteenth-through-sixteenth-century art. She'd sensed Arlette going with the flow until they'd entered the East Building and the modern art took over the walls. That was when Arlette's art enthusiasm had finally taken control of the room. Just like now, when she read the painting as well as Brooke read her.

"That's what I was going for, yes," Brooke said.

Teresa's mouth parted as if it had just hit her. "I see it now. Brooklyn, this...this is amazing."

"I'm really glad you like it. It means so much to me."

Teresa turned and smiled. "This painting means so much to *me*. I can already see it disrupting the monotony of the day-to-day. Don't you think so, Arlette?"

"Absolutely. It's going to add a lot to the office, for sure. I feel like this is exactly what you were looking for."

"It is, and then some."

"I had a lot of fun with this one," Brooke said. "It's one of my favorites that I've done in a while. Getting to paint this for you...well... it's really an honor."

Teresa waved her off. "Thank you, but the honor is all mine. I'm glad my wonderful colleague recommended you." She wrapped an arm around Arlette, squeezed her, and then let go. "And I'm excited to have a local artist be part of our team."

"I'm excited too. And just to let you know, I put a coat of varnish over the painting, so it will protect the colors and prevent the paint from cracking. That means it's prepped to serve multiple terms."

Teresa laughed, and Brooke couldn't believe her attempt at a little joke had made Teresa Rosario laugh. She was just as proud of herself for doing that as she was of the painting.

"I hope it's our good luck charm," Teresa said as she wrote Brooke a check. "Thank you so much, Brooklyn. Once I hang this, I'll make sure I tag you on Instagram. Does that sound good?"

"That…that would be amazing."

"Great. And if I meet anyone else who needs a piece for their office, I know who to recommend. Take care, Brooklyn, and thank you so much again."

As Teresa walked her canvas to the door, Arlette surprised Brooke with a hand on her back as she leaned in. "I'm going to help her pack this in her car. Still want to claim your present tonight?"

The smell of sandalwood and fresh chewing gum washed over Brooke as only a few inches existed between her and Arlette's beautiful eyes. A shudder started at the back of her neck and snaked down her spine. "Of course," she answered, a little hoarsely for her own liking.

"Great. I'll meet you outside in a few."

Once Teresa and the painting were on their way, Arlette and Brooke metroed to Capitol Hill together, passing the travel time by chatting about their days: the highs, the lows, and the weird.

Arlette lived in quaint Capitol Hill, a neighborhood Brooke had admired countless times but knew she would never make enough money to afford. Colorful nineteenth-century row houses lined the quiet streets, and families strolled the sidewalks. The adorable character of the neighborhood and the peace that settled over it juxtaposed with the political games and debates at the Capitol Building just five blocks over.

Brooke followed Arlette down the steps of a powder blue, three-story house to the English basement, the nicest English basement she'd ever seen. With gray laminate floors, bright gray walls, and more windows than most basements, it was also equipped with stainless-steel appliances, a full kitchen, and a decent-sized living area. Her *Autumn in New York* hung above the couch, and seeing it as the focus of the main room made happiness swell in her.

Brooke had lived in an English basement during her first four months in DC, until Abby's lease had ended, and they'd moved in together. However, Brooke's experience was nothing compared to Arlette's. She bet that Arlette's apartment repelled cockroaches, unlike her current apartment *and* her old English basement.

"Your place is amazing," Brooke said, envious of how elegant it was. Then she had to remind herself she shouldn't have expected anything less from an Adair.

"I wish I could take credit, but this was all my sister and brother-in-law. They live above and were nice enough to renovate for me. I do love it, though." Arlette tossed her keys on the kitchen table, right next to a bottle of champagne and two large brownies wrapped in plastic wrap.

"Oh, what's all this?" Brooke asked.

Arlette responded with a smile. "Your present. Brownies are still your favorite dessert, right?"

"Obviously. Name a better one."

"See, I tried doing that once sophomore year, and I lost the debate."

"Which baffled me, by the way, given your history in politics. I figured an Adair would hold a solid debate."

"Hey, I did a decent job. Don't even lie."

Brooke shrugged and supplied her with a grin. "Eh, I made you believe that, but it was me who shined."

"You know what? I'll save round two of the dessert debate for another time because right now, it's about celebrating how much of a badass you are."

Brooke placed a hand over her heart. "Champagne and brownies? That's, like, the key to my heart." She stepped forward to observe the bottle of champagne. When she read the label, her eyes widened, and she backed away. "Arlette?"

Arlette came back with two flute glasses. "Yes?"

"Dom Pérignon?"

She smiled proudly. "Yeah. The good stuff, I know."

"I can't accept this."

It hit Brooke all at once. How different her upbringing was compared to Arlette's. While they shared similarities, there were also stark differences, like Arlette casually opening a bottle of champagne worth a couple hundred dollars when the most expensive drink Brooke had ever consumed was a forty-dollar bottle of wine she'd shared with Abby when she'd sold her first commission piece as a freelance artist.

Arlette frowned. "Why not?"

Brooke laughed at how oblivious she was. She must have been so used to expensive champagne that she couldn't understand why Brooke was hesitant to accept it. "Because it's a third of my rent."

"Don't you think you deserve it?" Arlette said, unwrapping the foil around the bottle. "You sold a commissioned piece to Teresa Rosario. She freakin' loves it. She's been talking about it ever since you signed your contract, and now you're going to have an original piece hanging in a congresswoman's office. Tell me why you don't think you should have this?"

"Yeah, I think I deserve that brownie and a pat on the shoulder, but that's an expensive bottle of champagne…"

Arlette sandwiched the bottle between her legs and twisted the cork until the pop echoed through the basement. She poured it, and as she did so, Brooke couldn't help but imagine how each bubble must be worth at least fifty dollars.

She patted Brooke on the back and presented one of the brownies and a flute. "A pat on the back, a brownie, and some delicious champagne. Please treat yourself. It's very well-deserved."

"But—"

"No buts, Brooklyn." Arlette sighed. "Okay, if it makes you feel better, my grandpa gave me this bottle for my birthday. I've been saving it for a special occasion, and this is it, so let's enjoy and celebrate."

It did make Brooke feel a little better that Arlette hadn't gone out and purchased the bottle herself. But it was such a sweet gesture, she felt almost guilty for accepting it. However, there were two reasons why she accepted. One, because Arlette was so excited, and Brooke wanted to keep a beautiful smile like that around longer. And two, drinking the bottle bought her more time with Arlette.

"Okay, fine. Thank you for bringing out your special champagne for this occasion."

Arlette smiled. "It's so worth it." She held up her flute to toast. Brooke followed. "To selling Teresa Rosario a painting that she's already in love with. You're kicking some ass, Brooklyn, and it's only going to get better from here."

THE HUES OF ME AND YOU

Brooke pressed her lips together, but she couldn't help but smile. She loved that she had her other cheerleader in her corner again. Arlette's unwavering support was contagious. She could feel that Arlette was as proud of her accomplishment—if not more—than her. Arlette was as excited about Brooke's successes as if they were her own, and she felt incredibly lucky to have someone in her life who supported her that much.

"And to reuniting," Brooke added. In that moment, she was so grateful that she'd followed her gut and sold Arlette the painting.

"To reuniting."

They clinked their glasses together, and their stares remained steady as they sipped. Brooke was reminded about the superstition about maintaining eye contact during a toast to avoid seven years of bad sex. She wasn't necessarily a superstitious person, but she wasn't about to risk it when it had been several long months for her…and when Arlette Adair was back in her life, staring at her with those luminous eyes that had the power to undo her. Like it was right now.

She broke eye contact in an attempt to stop the spread of warmth covering her face. She turned and took a seat on the couch. "I can't believe we're celebrating with Dom Pérignon."

Brooke was grateful that Arlette followed and sat as close as possible, despite all the space the couch provided. As she settled, her leg relaxed into Brooke's and made her breath catch and release. For a moment, her mind glitched back to the short-lived days when she'd known what it felt like to have Arlette draped over her, her entire body perfectly molded into Brooke as they'd lost themselves in hours of kissing. The memories alone sparked the electricity Arlette always made her feel and cascaded lower, exactly how it had back then.

"Well, I'm honored to take your Dom Pérignon virginity," Arlette said.

Brooke coughed up her drink. Arlette let out a laugh and rested her hand on Brooke's wrist. The contact threaded warmth throughout Brooke's entire body, as if stitching back those deep feelings that had engulfed her in college.

"You're funny," Brooke said sarcastically.

Arlette looked over and laughed again. "And you're beet red. Practically a fire hydrant. Take a sip of champagne. It will cool you down."

God, Arlette had noticed. How mortifying was that? Brooke had managed to get through almost all of college while taming her feelings to make sure she masked them before they turned into blush, and what? Now that Arlette was back in her life, they came rushing out like from a broken dam? What had happened to keeping her at a distance, protecting her heart, and her art?

Those eyes and that smile, that's what.

"And don't forget about this amazing brownie," Arlette said, wasting no time unwrapping hers. The smell of chocolate prompted Brooke to do the same. She was desperate to divert and forget about the moment, while at the same time, she knew that once her body temperature went back to normal, she would relish the feeling for the rest of the night…maybe days, even. "It will help too. I picked these up at Eastern Market. You know how much I love frozen yogurt and think that's the best dessert, but this brownie is a close second. Makes me wonder if you were right all along."

Brooke lowered the brownie. "Did you just admit dessert debate defeat? Wow. That's really saying something."

"I might have." Arlette bit in and moaned her pleasure. It yanked Brooke's attention, and she replayed the sound as if it was her favorite line in a song. "Okay, so I have an idea, but you have to hear me out."

Brooke looked over, intrigued. The part of her mind that had been activated by Arlette's moan was now running wild with fantasies related to that sound, but the other half begged for a distraction. Arlette had an idea for some kind of adventure, and she never had disappointed. "Oh, you have my attention as always, Ms. Adair. Please continue."

"You can veto it if you'd like since this is your celebratory night, but…want to watch an episode of *Jeopardy!*? For ol' times' sake?"

Brooke smiled at all the memories of them crowded on their twin beds in the dorms, procrastinating while sharing a bag of Flamin' Hot Cheetos and watching *Jeopardy!* Brooke had always thought *Jeopardy!* was for middle-age people trying to squeeze in one last show before they went to bed at eight. But Arlette had strongly disagreed and had said it was a much better way to learn than in class.

Studying can be put on hold for another learning experience, she'd said.

"You know, I'm really liking this summer filled with all the old times' sakey things," Brooke said.

"Oh, yeah? Me too." Once Arlette pulled up a recorded episode, she reached for the blanket that rested on the back of the couch. She fanned it out and covered them.

Brooke's legs were starting to get a little cold from the air-conditioning blasting through the basement and shielding them from the early August humidity outside. But while sharing a blanket, Arlette's knee pressed against her thigh, and the blanket trapped the tension and heat Brooke felt at the connection.

She washed it away with another drink of champagne. "I still can't believe you watch this," she said through a laugh as Arlette pulled up the episode.

"Of course I do. The show is still on, isn't it? Though I know it's not the same without Alex Trebek." Arlette looked at both of the brownies. "And the Cheetos. I forgot them."

"But we have brownies and fancy champagne. We've upgraded from Flamin' Hot Cheetos."

Right as she said that, a contestant chose the first category, a thousand-dollar world history question about the Reign of Terror ending in someone's execution. In typical Arlette fashion, she raised her right hand in the air and yelled, "Who is Robespierre?" And did a little dance when she got it right.

Brooke laughed, shook her head, and picked off another brownie bit. "There are some ways you haven't changed at all."

"What do you mean?"

"Any time you know the answer, you raise your hand and then do something to celebrate. A hop, swaying from side to side, or looking at me with a little grin, like you're all proud of yourself. As if you don't know, like, ninety percent of the *Jeopardy!* questions. I should be the one celebrating. I'll be lucky if I get five."

When Double Jeopardy came around, Arlette scurried to the kitchen to grab the champagne and topped off both flutes.

"I'm not fancy at all," Brooke said, allowing the slight buzz to loosen her up a bit. She wiggled her fingers for the bottle. Arlette raised an eyebrow but handed it over. "We don't need the flutes." She drank a large gulp, and Arlette smirked.

"Yeah, fuck it," Arlette said, chugged what remained in her glass, and then snatched the bottle to take a swig. "This is how we're going to watch *Jeopardy!* from now on."

Brooke held her hand out. "Deal?"

Arlette settled back in her spot and sat closer than she had a moment before. Her leg molded perfectly into Brooke's again, a common occurrence Brooke would never complain about. And then there was the wave of sandalwood that always elicited an undertow of tension in Brooke's stomach.

Arlette shook her hand and held it a little longer than expected. As if she felt the same thing, she glanced at their shake before saying, "Deal. You can come over anytime you want to be my *Jeopardy!* partner."

"I might hold you to that."

"Please do."

Brooke helped her catch up on the four recorded episodes. They took turns shouting the answers, high-fiving each whenever one of them shouted the right answer, and rewarding each with a large swig of champagne. Four episodes of *Jeopardy!* and a fancy yet delicious bottle of champagne was all it took for Brooke to safely land back in the comfortable and steady rhythm she hadn't felt in years.

She left Arlette's apartment perfectly buzzed, and it wasn't all from the champagne. She sensed that she was getting her best friend back, and the smile stayed intact for the entire Uber ride home.

Arlette told herself she could at least go to the first presidential debate. She knew the family being there for her father's first debate meant the world to him. She sat next to her mother, Jacquelyn, and Ben in the first row. The other nine candidates put most of their ridicule on her dad, one of the top candidates in the polls. Arlette was actually proud of her father for handling the criticism with as much grace as one could have with that many targets on his back.

After the debate, her dad took them—and his campaign manager, Todd—out for dinner. Todd filled everyone in on what the press was saying, and apparently, Arlette's dad had come out strong. About half the comments and articles said he was even stronger than his biggest opponent, Kendra Beckett.

While Arlette had survived the night in Miami and was genuinely proud of her dad, she knew that she couldn't attend the other debates.

If he became the Democratic candidate and went up against the Republican candidate, she would, of course, go to that debate. But until then, she knew what was best for her and her mental health. She had to rip off the Band-Aid. Brooke had been right. If Arlette wanted to start living the life she wanted, she needed to be the one in the driver's seat, not her father. And that started with drawing boundaries, as hard as that conversation would be. So after a long night of tossing, turning, and practicing the conversation in her head, she went to her father's hotel room right before her flight back home.

On her walk over, she felt the anxiety stacking in her chest, knowing how upset her dad would be. She feared that this would cause a break in their relationship again, and when the thought swiped through her mind, she faltered as she stepped out of the elevator and questioned if she should even follow through with it.

Did he really deserve the disappointment as his lifelong dream soared through the clouds? Arlette had so many great moments with him as a kid. She loved the memories of taking Grandpa Harry's sailboat out on the Miles River and her dad teaching everyone how to sail, hearing her grandpa and dad reminisce about their best moments on the water or in the Navy. She loved how he'd always volunteered to help her study for history tests if he wasn't working. He'd tell her additional stories that weren't in her books, and she learned more interesting historical facts from him than she ever did from textbooks. He was the reason why she sought knowledge beyond the classroom, understanding that there was so much more fascinating and important history than what was taught in schools.

However, those good memories were often tied to unpleasant ones, like when he'd refused to listen to her feelings, as if she'd made them up to create drama. What Grandpa Harry had said rang so true: if her dad grounded himself occasionally, he would see his family in front of him instead of criticizing them for not joining him up in the clouds. The more attuned he was to his family, rather than his work and ambition, the more empathy he had. He listened, observed, and understood. But since her dad was preoccupied with the campaign trail, Arlette already knew she wouldn't get that empathy from him when she voiced her feelings. His head was too high in the clouds to take note of the obvious things on the ground, like Arlette's anxiety that had never gone away.

"Hey, honey, are you all packed?" her dad asked, putting his watch on as Arlette stepped inside the room.

"Yeah, Jackie, Ben, and I are leaving in a half hour. I…um…I was hoping we could talk about something before I left."

"Sure. What's on your mind?"

He poured two mugs of coffee, handed one to her, and sipped the other. She sat on the edge of the bed, stalling for several moments as she picked up and discarded a decent first line. She had only gotten four hours of sleep because she'd been so worried about how he was going to react, and now it felt like she'd wasted the whole night practicing.

"Arlette?" His stern voice pulled her away from tumbling. "What's wrong?"

The faster she did it, the less painful it would be. "You did really well last night," she said. "I'm really proud of you."

"Oh, thank you. That means a lot," he said with a genuine smile. "You know, all I want to do is make the family proud…at the very least, even if I don't win."

"I can assure you, no matter how far you make it, we're all proud of you."

"Well, that's really good to hear. I'm glad. Is that what you wanted to talk about?"

She nervously scratched the back of her head. "Um…no, not really."

"What's bothering you? Something clearly is."

She could really feel the August Miami heat crawling into the room. Sweat started trickling down her back. "Listen, Dad, I'm really glad I came to this debate. It was great to see you shut down your opponents. You really did an amazing job, and I'm really proud of you." Arlette paused, realizing she had already said that. He raised an eyebrow as he sipped his coffee. She had to do this. This was the first step into getting back on that path she'd imagined she would be on back in college. She was so close. "However, I can't make it to the others. I'm sorry."

He lowered his mug as his eyebrows folded tighter. "What do you mean you can't make it?"

"There are going to be a lot of them, and work is getting busy, so I can't make it to all of them."

He hesitated. "Okay…I thought we all agreed that the family would be together."

That was true. Jacquelyn and Arlette had agreed they would be present at the debates, but Arlette had only agreed because she had to. But now she saw that her presence wasn't necessary at the million-and-one debates the DNC had. It made much more sense to attend after he was the official Democratic candidate.

"Honestly? Because it's giving me major anxiety. You know how much I hate public events—"

"And you know how important this is for me. Arlette, crowds should be something you're used to by now. It's only going to get worse."

She rolled her eyes. Here comes the drought of empathy, she thought. "I can't just turn the anxiety on and off. Trust me, it would be so much easier if I could. Look, I know I'm disappointing you, but I have to do what's right for me. There's no reason to subject myself to additional anxiety when I have a million other problems on my plate right now."

"I don't understand why this is such a problem," he said, the anger rising in his voice.

"My being absent isn't going to ruin your 'family man' image. Jackie is only going to one—"

"Jackie is six months pregnant. It's obvious why she can't make the later ones."

"I've swallowed my anxiety for years because it seemed like that made it easier for everyone. But, Dad, I'm the most anxious I've ever been, and that's not okay."

"I have no idea what's making you so nervous."

"Because you don't ask," she said sternly, refusing to go with the wind this time. Brooke's voice swept through her mind, reminding her it was perfectly all right to do what was right for her. She straightened her back as all the words she had practiced in the middle of the night finally came back. "This anxiety has been with me since I was a kid, when the whole family told me to get over it when kids didn't invite me to their parties, told to ignore the kids who talked shit about all of you, told to get over it when you, Uncle Henry, and Grandpa Harry were getting death threats and the family had to literally evacuate to a safe location. That's not normal. We shouldn't normalize that. That really sticks with you growing up, and I felt like I had to hide my feelings to appease everyone. I think that's why I'm so anxious now. I grew up with this idea drilled into me that happiness and success would only be accomplished if I went down the family path that everyone wanted me to be on. To just blend in with everyone for the sake of clout and legacy. But actually, Dad, it makes me very unhappy, and now I'm stuck."

He set his mug loudly on the dresser. "How are you stuck? You have the opportunity to do whatever you want."

"I do, but it comes with the price of disappointing you. I got a job on Capitol Hill because I thought that would make you proud of me. I dated the girl you'd been trying to set me up with for years. She didn't treat me like I was someone she actually wanted to be with, and when I finally ended things, knowing I deserved more than what Sabrina gave me, I disappointed you. I've been so worried about disappointing you that I've massively disappointed myself."

"Arlette, all I'm asking is for my family's support. Your flights and hotel will be paid for—"

"See, I just told you how I felt, and you're basically telling me that I need to ignore that and appease you. I'm sorry, Dad, but this is nonnegotiable. How I feel matters, and honestly, I'm tired of ignoring my own wants and needs. I know that sounds selfish, but I don't feel like I've been selfish enough."

"Arlette, this is absolutely unacceptable," he said authoritatively, as if she was a little girl fighting with Jacquelyn again.

"It's not. It's actually the opposite, and if you can't see that, I'm not sure what else to say to you. I'm sorry, but I have to go now. I'll see you later."

His anger and disappointment were all she could hear when she replayed the conversation over and over as she Ubered to the airport with Ben and Jacquelyn and then waited at their gate. Her dad sent a text that she refused to read until she was in the Uber heading home because she knew that she would just dwell on it.

The text read, *I don't even know where to begin. All I asked for was my family's support. You know how much that means to me. But what I got was being accused of never listening to your feelings.*

A wave of dread washed over her, collecting in her chest. She quickly responded. *If you had listened, you would understand completely how I feel. Jackie and Grandpa understand. I'm not sure why you can't.*

And she tossed the phone aside for the rest of the Uber back.

Jacquelyn wanted to talk about the conversation, but as grateful as Arlette was for Jacquelyn always making herself available for support, she just wanted to be an introvert. She plopped on her bed at home, sucked in the wonderful smell of clean sheets, and grunted out the frustration into her pillow.

Her need to be alone disappeared with the chirping of her phone about an hour later, signaling a text from Brooke: *Did you survive the debate?*

She smiled and typed back, *Barely. Told my dad I wasn't going to the rest of them.*

Brooke: *You did? That's amazing! Do you feel better?*

Arlette: *Eh...the convo didn't go well, but I feel a bit relieved, yes. I'm still processing. Did you survive back-to-back bartending events?*

Brooke: *Barely.*

Arlette: *I have three Jeopardy episodes I need to catch up on. Wanna detox from our stressful weekends and watch them together?*

Brooke: *Give me one hour.*

Arlette: *Great, I'll leave the front door open.*

Brooke was as punctual as always. An hour later, she walked through the door armed with two seltzer waters and a bag of Flamin' Hot Cheetos. "I come with the goods," she said and jiggled the bag.

Arlette scooted over, and Brooke sat in the empty spot on the couch. "Cheetos? Does that mean we are officially reviving *Jeopardy!* night?"

Brooke handed her a bottle of her favorite black cherry seltzer water and then opened the bag. "The champagne and brownies were amazing. Don't get me wrong. But I thought about it a lot, and I think why I failed so badly last time was because I didn't have the spice to awaken my knowledge."

Arlette grabbed a handful of Cheetos and held one up to Brooke's mouth. "If that's what's needed, we must nourish you."

Brooke snatched the Cheeto with her teeth, and as her tongue scooped it into her mouth, Arlette felt a hit to her core. She blinked back the feelings rising in her and decided that was the perfect time to start watching TV.

They settled under the blanket like last time, sharing the bag, blurting out answers, and laughing if it was wildly incorrect. Ten minutes later, upon reaching Double Jeopardy, Arlette discovered that her whole left side touched Brooke's right. She straightened and thought about scooting over.

Brooke was still fixated on the TV. "Oh, oh," she said after the next question. Arlette was too interested in the smile on her lips. "What is Germany?"

Arlette heard the answer: Estonia. Brooke laughed, shook her head, and reached in for another Cheeto. A lightness floated into Arlette's chest as she held on to that laugh and realized that the beautiful woman cuddled next to her was so content that she either hadn't noticed that they were pressed against each other, or she had noticed and didn't mind at all. Arlette decided to play dumb and looked back at the TV. She sure as hell was going to enjoy the moment and wasn't going to move an inch.

Halfway into the second episode, the front door flew open. Both Arlette and Brooke jumped when Jacquelyn appeared in the doorway with a plate of chocolate chip cookies.

"I brought something to cheer you up—" Jacquelyn glanced between Arlette and Brooke and grinned impishly. "Oh, hello. I didn't know you had company."

Arlette straightened. "This is my friend, Brooklyn. Brooklyn, this is my sister, Jacquelyn. She apparently doesn't know how to knock. It comes with pregnancy brain."

Brooke smiled and waved. "Hi, Jacquelyn. It's nice to meet you."

Jacquelyn eyed Arlette as if asking what the hell was going on. "You too. I just made a batch of cookies to cheer up Arlette, but I see now that it probably pales in comparison to what she actually needed."

Warmth threaded through Arlette's entire body. "Thanks, Jackie," she said through a clenched jaw, seemingly encouraging Jacquelyn's grin to widen.

She set the plate on the kitchen table. "I'll leave this here and let you two get back to your...whatever this is."

"It's *Jeopardy!*"

"Uh-huh. Sure it is. It was nice meeting you, Brooklyn. I'll be texting you later, Arlette."

When Jacquelyn shut the door, Arlette settled back. Brooke looked down, now clearly aware of how close they were. But Arlette wanted Brooke to acknowledge their closeness, to do something. If she was feeling any discomfort, Arlette would immediately move to the other side of the couch, noting not to do it again.

"Sounds like you're going to get questioned later," Brooke said, a gentle teasing in her tone. She sank back into her spot, stretched out her feet, and relaxed into Arlette's side.

Arlette smiled. That meant Brooke wanted her close as much as she wanted and needed to be close. "Sometimes I forget how nosy she can be. I can handle her...I think."

Brooke reached in the bag and held up a Cheeto for her. "Take some Cheetos to help you formulate your response."

For Arlette, it was more than just a snack offering. It was an offering for another moment, one that clicked them back into place before the interruption, one that continued to charge the electricity between them.

Arlette held Brooke's stare as she plucked the Cheeto with her teeth, and the bottom of her lip grazed Brooke's finger. Brooke's eyes fell to Arlette's lips before she blinked rapidly and looked away.

Arlette pressed play on the TV and settled back into Brooke's side, and they resumed watching and never flinched from their spots.

CHAPTER TEN

B rooke looked up at the Adair Estate standing bold against the late-August sky. Unlike at Marc Adair's event two and a half months ago, she was now a guest in the mansion. She stepped out on the motor court and took in her surroundings again, collecting a clearer image rather than a bitter one, knowing that this time, she was welcome in the house.

"What do I call him? Mr. Adair? Former Secretary Adair?" Brooke said.

Arlette laughed and grabbed two grocery bags from the trunk of Jacquelyn's white Audi. "You call him Grandpa Harry. That's what we call him."

"But…you're family. I'm…the general public."

Arlette placed a hand between Brooke's shoulder blades. It was becoming her designated spot on Brooke's body, one she welcomed. "You're going to be fine. Ever since Jackie snitched to Gramps that she found me with a girl on my couch, he's been telling me to bring you for a visit. I'm glad you decided to come. Don't worry. Gramps is fun, I promise."

Right. When Arlette's sister had walked in on them cuddled up on the couch, Brooke had frozen like a deer in headlights. She'd had no idea what to do or how to react. She'd been breathing shallowly the whole time Arlette had fallen into her, afraid that one deep breath would make Arlette aware of the intimacy and push herself onto the other side of the couch when that was the last thing Brooke wanted.

The inside of the house was as beautiful as the outside. She was greeted by a crystal chandelier reflecting rainbows onto the white walls and a circular staircase that led up to the second floor. She followed Arlette, passing a den on the left that had a bookshelf as a wall that was completely filled with books. The kitchen opened up to the living room, with large windows overlooking the gorgeous backyard and river.

Grandpa Harry sat there in a leather chair with a book. When he saw them, he smiled and slowly rose. "There's my favorite granddaughter," he said, walking over.

"Gramps, you're going to make Jackie and Charlotte jealous. You need to be careful."

He waved her off. "I tell them the same thing, just less often because you're the one who visits the most. And you brought a guest."

"Pretty sure she's as much your guest as mine. This is Brooklyn."

He shook her hand with both of his. "It's very nice to meet you, Brooklyn," he said with the warmest grandpa smile, reminding her less of the former Secretary of State and more of her own grandfather. "You're the famous roommate Arlette always spoke so highly of?"

Brooke turned to Arlette, who already wore a silly grimace. "Is this true?"

"It might be," Arlette said.

Grandpa Harry chuckled. It was full and happy, a laugh that filled the large room. It instantly coaxed a grin from Brooke. "It definitely is. She's the artist, right?"

Arlette squeezed his shoulder. "You have a good memory, Gramps."

"I might be old, but my mind is as sharp as a tack."

"Okay, both of you sit," Arlette said and gestured at the kitchen table. "I'm going to get dinner ready."

They had stopped at the fish market to pick up three salmon meals. Arlette had said she wasn't the greatest cook, but this market had Grandpa Harry's favorite quick-and-easy meal. Oven-roasted salmon and creamy feta cucumbers. Brooke didn't care what was on the menu. She was just thankful to spend the evening with Arlette and her beloved grandpa.

"So tell me everything, Brooklyn. How was Arlette as a roommate?" Grandpa Harry said, piercing the salmon with the side of his fork.

"Geez, Gramps. I bought you your favorite meal, and this is how you repay me?" Arlette said playfully. "I was an amazing roommate."

"We'll let Brooklyn be the judge of that," he said.

Arlette turned to Brooke. "He loves gossip, by the way. Full disclosure."

"I'll feed into it," Brooke said. "I was really nervous about my roommate. You hear a bunch of horror stories. At least, I did from my cousins. The first night, after all our freshman orientation things, Arlette whips out this Greek mythology book…on a Friday night, I should add. That's when I had the suspicion that she wasn't going to be a horror story."

"Ah, I remember the Greek mythology phase," Grandpa Harry said with a chuckle.

Arlette leaned in. "I had a lot of phases. I don't know if I ever told you that."

"Well, I know about the guitar phase," Brooke said. "You had it in our room freshman year, and then it never made an appearance again."

"Which led into the record phase," Grandpa Harry said. "I bought her all these used records one Christmas. Led Zeppelin, Bob Dylan, Bennett and Sons, and then randomly, a Marlie Rose greatest hits album."

"Which sparked my Broadway phase," Arlette added. "I don't think anyone was complaining when we went to see *Hamilton* with the original cast, just saying."

Brooke smiled as Arlette went on about her different phases. She'd mentioned a few of them in college and had told Brooke that her phases were a bit tiring for her family to keep up with. She liked to know a little bit of everything, and Brooke loved that about her. She was a collector of knowledge. Five years could do a lot to a person, but that part of her would always remain the same no matter how many years had passed.

"I think the Greek mythology phase was my favorite, personally," Grandpa Harry said.

"Honestly, Brooke, I swear, at least a third of the *Jeopardy!* questions are tied to Greek mythology," Arlette said. "I have that book in my apartment if you want to borrow it."

Brooke playfully nudged her arm. "Are you saying I need to get better?"

Arlette held up her pointer finger and thumb, spaced out by a centimeter. "Just a bit."

After dinner, Arlette insisted that she clean up and ordered Grandpa Harry and Brooke to save her a seat on the porch. If Brooke had come to St. Michaels knowing she would be escorting the former Secretary of State onto his own back porch to spend a few minutes alone with him, she would have panicked. But in the last two hours, all his accolades had disappeared, and all she saw now was Arlette's grandpa with the full laugh and comforting presence.

He let out a grunt as he sank into his rocking chair that faced the river, the boat dock, and the maple tree with the carvings. She sat in the chair next to him. "I'm glad I forced Arlette to bring you here, Brooklyn. It's so nice to finally meet you," he said.

"It's nice to finally meet you too. Arlette always talks about you and Jacquelyn. Never any bad things, I promise."

"So all my secrets are still safe?" When Brooke nodded, he threw a hand over his heart and let out a playful sigh. "Oh, thank God. I was worried for a second."

There was a silent moment, and even though Grandpa Harry was still practically a stranger, the silence wasn't uncomfortable at all. It was like a moment enjoyed with a friend she'd known for years, and in a way, she had known him since she was eighteen.

"I was on the phone with Arlette's sister, and she told me that Arlette had a friend over," Grandpa Harry said. "She said it was the really good friend from college who Arlette used to tell us all about. I had to invite you over. I'm glad you accepted." He looked over and smiled, the kind of smile that felt like a giant hug.

"Of course. I'm so honored to be here. I mean, you're the famous Grandpa Harry. You were Arlette's first best friend. I had my competition cut out for me, that's for sure."

"I hope this isn't me overstepping, but Arlette hasn't brought anyone else to meet me. Except for her ex-girlfriend, who was a family friend, so it doesn't really count. Honestly, I expected her to decline my invitation, but she didn't. The point of me saying this is that you must mean a lot to her, Brooklyn. I already knew that based on how she used to speak so fondly of you. I don't know every detail, but I know you two had some kind of falling-out. I also know how important you are to her, and I'm just glad she has a good friend like you. Don't get me wrong, I love the relationship I have with her. She's one of my best friends too, and I love her relationship with her sister, Jackie. But it also makes me very happy that she's found someone to trust outside of her own family."

His honesty threatened Brooke's eyes. She turned away to hide it and stared at the clouds as they started absorbing the colors, getting ready to create a spectacular sunset. "You're not overstepping at all," she said softly. "Thank you for telling me. She's really important to me too. She's still one of the closest friends I've ever had."

"What are we talking about?" Arlette asked as she stepped onto the porch and handed Grandpa Harry an iced tea while carrying a glass of ice water in her other hand. She took the empty seat next to Brooke and pulled it out so she had a better view of the conversation circle.

"You. I'm telling her all your secrets," Grandpa Harry said.

"You wouldn't dare. If you can take the country's secrets to the grave, I know for a fact that you can keep mine."

He chuckled and stared out on the water. Arlette settled in and did the same. Even though there was a generation between the two, they shared so many mannerisms and qualities. They both sank into rocking chairs the same way. Both rested the back of their heads against the chair, and they even rocked in the same slow pace. They stared at the yard and the beautiful summer scene. A few speedboats jetted across the water, and one sailboat traipsed along in the distance. Doves cooed from the trees, and the night bugs had already started chirping in the distance, adding a perfect soundtrack to the evening.

Arlette seemed in her element. She had the smallest curve forming on her lips, as if she was at peace. Brooke had the chance to truly understand the peace settling on Arlette's features.

Arlette turned, and Brooke quickly flitted her gaze back to the river, but Arlette's smile caught her eye. "What are you looking at?" Arlette said in a teasing tone.

"I'm just observing. Taking it all in, one small detail at a time."

"Ah, the artist observing. I've never heard that one before," she said with a wink before turning back to the river.

Grandpa Harry asked Brooke all about her art, and Arlette bragged about the Teresa Rosario painting, showing it off on her phone. Anytime Arlette talked about Brooke's art, the pride that filled her chest was reflected in Arlette's eyes. It was moments like this that made it so hard for her to ignore her past feelings. Arlette went on about how talented she was, glancing over and giving proud little smiles as she did so. Every compliment dug up the remaining feelings from the past. Something unrecognizable rose within her. Something heavier than attraction and lust. Something deeper than desire. It was a feeling that someone saw all of her, knew all of her, and understood her entirely. It felt like possibility was opening the doors and introducing itself after all these years. Falling for Arlette had been the easiest—and hardest— thing Brooke had ever experienced, and Arlette had no idea of the power she wielded.

They swapped funny stories, shared plenty of laughs, and Brooke found an unlikely partner in Grandpa Harry when they started to lovingly poke fun at Arlette. Like the trouper she was, she handled it with grace and a smile.

"You know what? I need to separate you. You two are quite the team," Arlette said.

"I like her," Grandpa Harry said and hooked a thumb at Brooke. "Bring her back, will you?"

"He just replaced you as my new best friend," Brooke said and patted him on the shoulder. He smiled at Brooke and then directed a victorious look at Arlette.

She shook her head, but a smile still remained. She hopped out of her seat and held out a hand. "Okay, that's it. I need to steal one of you, and I'm going with you, Brooklyn. Sorry, Gramps, but she's cuter."

The compliment was like a lasso around Brooke. She placed a hand in Arlette's and allowed her to pull her up. She'd follow Arlette anywhere if that meant she heard more compliments like that.

Grandpa Harry tossed his hands up. "Hey, I can't argue with that."

"I need to show Brooke the best spot on the property."

"I apologize if my granddaughter is a bad tour guide, Brooklyn," Grandpa Harry said. "I hope you find it in yourself to forgive her."

"I don't know, Grandpa Harry," she said. "I'm not sure if that's forgivable."

"Trust me, it's so amazing that I think you'll forgive me," Arlette said, placing a hand on the small of Brooke's back. Brooke let out a relieved sigh at the nurturing touch. Those soft touches were her peace, just the same way that the backyard was Arlette's. "Think you'll be okay for a bit, Gramps?"

"I'm perfectly content right here in this chair, just enjoying the evening. You two go. I'll be here."

"Let's go," Arlette said, guiding Brooke down the steps.

As much as Brooke loved Grandpa Harry, the farther they walked from him meant more possibilities of sizzling moments. After having a few already that evening, Brooke craved more. The late August air was heavy with humidity, heat, the weight of compliments, stolen glances, and soft, secretive touches. She knew that a moment alone would add another charge in the air.

"This is my favorite spot on the whole property," Arlette said as they approached the boat dock. There was that soft touch to Brooke's back again, gesturing for her to walk first. "This is where Grandpa Harry and I like to smoke cigars. Well…used to. Gramps has to be easy on his heart now, much to his dismay."

"Is he okay?"

"He's just getting old. But he's been eating heart-healthy food for the last year and a half. I feel bad because he insists I still smoke the cigars, and he gets secondhand enjoyment from the smell."

Brooke sat in one of the Adirondack chairs. "I had no idea you smoked. A girl who likes cigars and whiskey?" She fanned herself.

Arlette laughed and sat. "Does that do something for you?"

"Apparently."

"Well, damn, if I would have known that, I would have gotten a cigar and some whiskey for us."

"Maybe next time?"

Arlette looked over, smiling. "Next time, I promise."

Small waves lapped against the wooden beams. Off in the distance toward the right, other large homes dotted through the leafy trees. Two herons swooped toward the water and landed gently on the surface. It was easy to understand why Arlette loved it here. It was absolutely peaceful. And Arlette's mind seemed anything but quiet. Brooke could see her thoughts tangling in her eyes on bad days. Arlette hadn't had to say anything back in college, and she didn't have to say anything now. Watching her on the boat dock was like watching all her walls crumble.

Arlette's world seemed to ease while immersed in her favorite spot. Her eyes softened. Her mouth curved. Her presence was lighter. This wasn't the same Arlette who had broken Brooke's heart all those years ago. This wasn't the same Arlette who was once her best friend. This wasn't even the same Arlette who was becoming her friend again. This was Arlette in her purest form. Brooke watched as the scene softened Arlette's sharp edges, and because it gifted her with this version of Arlette, it was quickly becoming one of her favorite spots too.

The horizon yanked the sun down, leaving a melted path of marigold and maize in the Chesapeake sky. As beautiful as it was smeared on the surface of the water like an oil painting, Brooke couldn't pull her gaze off Arlette. The flecks of green in her eyes soaked up the colors of the dying sun falling over the Adair Estate. The smile on Arlette's lips pulled the fluttering from the depths of Brooke's stomach like a magnet.

"It's even better in the morning," Arlette continued. "The Lincoln Memorial is my favorite spot to catch the sunset, but this is my favorite spot to catch the sunrise." She gestured to the two chairs. Brooke smiled, knowing it was a privilege for Arlette to invite her into this sanctuary. "Maybe we can catch the sunrise sometime? I know it means waking up earlier, but I promise, it's worth it."

"I would love that."

Brooke closed her eyes, searching for the comfort and peace that Arlette seemed to find here. The humid air smelled like a mixture of water and summer. The only sounds were the waves, the night bugs, and doves harmonizing. Brooke's first visit to the Adair Estate was exactly what she'd expected: flashy, showy, and opulent as the sun. Her first visit, she'd felt small, standing on the periphery where she'd belonged.

However, when the people, suits, cocktail dresses, and champagne bottles that went for two hundred a pop fizzled away, she saw it: Arlette's home. The biggest house Brooke had ever stepped in, it looked like it was plucked from the French countryside and planted on Maryland's Eastern Shore. It was Grandpa Harry who made the difference. His love, acceptance, and understanding filled in all the spaces of the house. Arlette was one hundred percent herself around Grandpa Harry. A smile constantly brightened her face, and her laughter was filled with happiness, warmth, and confidence that made her presence louder in the room. When it was just Arlette and her people, the house was no different than her mom's two-bedroom end-unit condo.

Brooke didn't feel like an outsider when she was with Grandpa Harry and Arlette. She felt like one of them.

❖

"I swear, I was just feasted on," Arlette whispered as she led Brooke through the dark first floor and up the stairs.

She was only outside for a few hours, but the mosquitoes had thoroughly feasted on her legs and ankles as if they were ears of corn at her family's crab dinner.

The stairs creaked underneath them. Arlette came to a halt on the landing to ferociously scratch at her ankles. Brooke stumbled into her and grabbed her waist for balance. Arlette sprang straight up, not expecting Brooke to use her hips as a railing.

"Arlette, you can't just stop like that," Brooke said through a laugh. "I can't see, and you turned into a wall with no warning."

"I'm sorry, but I've been personally attacked by the mosquitos."

"Come on, let's get you upstairs so we can put anti-itch cream all over your legs."

Arlette fetched a tube of hydrocortisone from her bathroom and guided Brooke into her bedroom. She flipped on the lights and dramatically plopped on the bed. She pointed to her ankles, which were covered in white bumps and red scratch marks.

"You poor thing," Brooke said, snatching the cream and squeezing some on her fingertip. "I'll take care of you for now, but I do have to say, you should have known better."

"I know," Arlette whined playfully. "I just had FOMO while cleaning the dishes and wanted to join you two so much that I forgot my blood is basically sugar for them."

Brooke sat on the edge of the bed, pulled Arlette's damaged ankles into her lap, and applied the cream. Arlette sucked in a breath. She couldn't tell if it was because she wasn't prepared for the slightly cold temperature or the fact that she had her legs in Brooke's lap. Either way, she determined that getting feasted on by a swarm of mosquitoes was well worth it.

"You look like you have chicken pox," Brooke said. She dabbed some ointment on a bite that hadn't even begun itching yet.

Arlette looked down. She really did look like she was infected. She grunted and plopped her head back on the pillow in defeat. "I know. The mosquitoes like me a lot."

"They really do. I can't really blame them." Right as Arlette looked back down at Brooke after that comment, Brooke found one more bite next to her knee. She examined both legs one last time. "There. I think I got them all. Let it soak."

"Yes, Doctor."

Brooke walked over to her duffel bag, pulled out her pj's, and went into the bathroom while Arlette remained in her spot, waiting for the ointment to soak in. Brooke came back out in a heather gray T-shirt and black gym shorts, and Arlette had to remind herself to breathe. What was it about women in something as simple as pj's that was just as much of a turn-on as them in a sexy dress, teasing the smallest bit of cleavage?

After placing her folded clothes in the bag, Brooke glanced over, catching Arlette's lingering stare. Arlette got off the bed and hoped that would give her time for her cheeks to cool from the sudden eye contact.

"Um...you can take the bed," Arlette said and opened the closet door. "I have an air mattress right here that I can blow up." She pulled the air mattress bag, set it on the ground, and reached for the sheets.

"Arlette, this is a queen. Both of us can fit."

Honestly, Arlette was fine with the blow-up mattress. She didn't have to worry about accidentally touching Brooke, feeling her body heat, or her immense gravitational pull. The blow-up mattress was safe territory.

"It's really not a big deal," Arlette said.

"I don't bite, you know. We've slept together in the same bed before. Hell, the same tent when we all went camping in Shenandoah, sophomore year."

The camping trip was totally different. Brooke was just her friend and roommate. Arlette had stayed with her because Holly Davies had a giant crush on Arlette and was trying very hard to get her to sleep in the same tent. Arlette and Brooke didn't have palpable tension that followed them around like a shadow back then. Arlette hadn't known each spot on Brooke's body that made her squeak and moan. That camping trip was a much simpler time.

After Arlette changed and brushed her teeth, she found Brooke on one side of the bed, with the covers turned down for Arlette on the other side. Her throat was arid, and the glass of water on the nightstand offered ample time to stall.

"I'm going to regret that," Arlette said after she finished the glass and cautiously slipped into bed.

Arlette positioned herself on the farthest spot the mattress allowed without falling off, hyperaware of the space between them. Brooke's magnetic pull was stronger than it had ever been. The last time Arlette had slept in the bed, she had shared it with Sabrina, and it had felt like cramming together on a twin. But now, the bed felt too big. Brooke seemed too far away, and the space between them was too wide.

"I'm really glad you invited me today," Brooke said.

Her voice was husky from the laughter and joking earlier, and what remained seemed vulnerable. Arlette looked over, and the moonlight streaming through the window provided enough soft light to capture the rawness detailing Brooke's features.

"I'm glad too. I always wanted to bring you here. I always thought you would love it as much as I do. It's peaceful, isn't it?"

"It is. I mean, don't get me wrong. The first time I came here, it wasn't that peaceful."

Arlette laughed. "Same. I panicked. It was the one time I didn't want to be in the backyard. But I'm really glad it happened." She paused for a second, feeling her heart grow heavier. "Are you?"

Brooke's eyebrows pulled together. "Of course. I really missed this. I've really missed you."

Arlette turned over. Now, only a few inches separated them, and Arlette smelled the fresh mint toothpaste that laced every word.

"I've missed our pillow talks, our late-night walks, and *Jeopardy!*," Brooke said. "I miss all of it. Those were some of my favorite moments in college. Minus when you felt the need to tell me Willard ghost stories."

"Hey, those were fascinating, and you know it."

"Arlette, they were terrifying, and don't you dare mention the Carroll Hall ghost, or I'm walking back to DC."

"You wouldn't, though, because it's night, and St. Michaels has plenty of ghost stories too."

Brooke playfully shoved her arm. "Stop it."

"Hey, you brought it up. Not me."

"Did I ever partake in those scary movie marathons every October? No. I went to the art studio instead. It was much safer."

"Technically, it wasn't, since there was a ghost in that building too."
Brooke's mouth fell open. "What?"

Arlette bit her lip, trying to mask the grin. "Brooklyn, all of Willard is haunted. It's been around since the 1820s. It's, like, where all the ghosts on the East Coast spawn from."

"God, do I even want to know about this so close to midnight?"

"Of course you do." Arlette propped her head on her hand. "Before freshman year, I read up on Richmond's history. Obviously."

If it wasn't for the moonlight, Arlette would have missed Brooke's grin paired with the quick eye roll. "Of course you did. But continue."

"Well, you know the Raid on Richmond during the Revolutionary War? Benedict Arnold's forces marched into Richmond one night. He wrote Thomas Jefferson a letter saying he wanted the city's tobacco stores and military arms moved to his ships. Jefferson was pissed and said fuck no. So Benedict Arnold threw a hissy fit and told the British soldiers to torch all of Richmond. They followed his command and burned government buildings and even people's homes. Once the city was burned to a crisp, they moved on to this burning rampage to outside towns. Before Willard was a thing, there was a foundry on the grounds that produced supplies for the Continental Navy. I read up on the school's history before moving on campus too. But anyway, it was one of the first iron foundries in the US, and that prick burned it. Erased it completely."

"Leave it to you, Arlette Adair, to teach me the fascinating parts of history," Brooke said. "I never knew any of this."

Arlette's gaze slipped off Brooke's eyes and to that smile curving upward. It made her brain glitch. God, she was this close to Brooke, had a front-row view of her beautiful smile and those eyes that were so expressive, they pinned her to her spot. It wasn't until Brooke pushed her arm, making contact with Arlette's skin that she jolted awake like an AED had shocked her.

"I haven't even gotten to the best part yet," Arlette said and blinked into focus. "The legend has it that the owner of the foundry still wanders the spot where it used to be. You can tell it's him because he wears colonial attire. And where was the foundry located on the campus grounds? Dietsch Hall, your art studio. That's the story of the Dietsch Hall ghost."

"I heard that it was maybe haunted, but I always walked in the other direction when people were talking about it because I didn't want to hear about it. Ignorance is bliss."

"And that's why I never told you."

"But you had no problem telling me about the ghost that lives in the basement of Swanson."

"The ghost has a name, Brooklyn. Treat her with respect, please. Her name was Margaret Lanely."

"Stop," Brooke said through a slight laugh.

"One time, I was doing laundry, and the washer started going off, but I didn't start it, and I was the only person in the basement. Explain that."

"Ah!" Brooke covered her ears. "Why are you telling me this? It's dark, and there's a full moon. Things are scary right now."

Arlette laughed and tugged on Brooke's wrists. "If it makes you feel any better, this house isn't haunted, though I do know some great St. Michaels ghost stories. I'll tell you when the sun is out."

Arlette didn't notice that her hand had found its way into Brooke's until she stopped talking. She followed Brooke's gaze to where her thumb grazed the soft part between Brooke's thumb and forefinger. Arlette hadn't noticed she was doing it, and now she couldn't think of anything except how perfect their fingers looked when intertwined. Brooke didn't pull away. She didn't say to stop. She just lay there and seemingly let the moment encompass her.

Their connection provided an instant flashback to senior year, when Arlette had vented to Brooke about her breakup. Brooke had held her hand and had moved her thumb in the same comforting way as Arlette was doing. They had shared a heavy moment, and it had seemed like their entire friendship had exploded between them. Their exchange had been so raw, as if they had both flipped each other inside out. It was then that Arlette had allowed herself to acknowledge all the feelings inside her. When Brooke had kissed her and Arlette had kissed back, sinking into Brooke's soft lips, those anchors had come loose, and her feelings had floated freely to the surface.

Now, rubbing Brooke's hand, Arlette recognized that look from all those years ago. She saw Brooke inside out and could feel herself being turned too. If she was truly as transparent as she felt, she was going to capture the moment and put it into words.

"I've missed everything about you," she said.

They had careened over the friendship line so many times today that once-clear footpaths were becoming blurred. Those stolen glances, the stares that had lingered a little too long, the smiles crafted just for each other, the fact that it had been a full minute of brushing her thumb on Brooke's hand and the only thing that had happened was that Brooke allowed her hand to remain in Arlette's grip.

There was a hooded look in Brooke's eyes before they fell to Arlette's lips. Arlette felt as if her lips were glowing in the dark the longer Brooke scanned them. A million emotions battled for dominance. God, she wanted to close the gap and kiss her. A wave of intense want washed over her. She wanted more than anything to feel all of Brooke everywhere again.

"Brooklyn?" she said, her nerves clipping the rest of her words.

Brooke's grip around her hand seemed to tighten just a fraction more. "Yes?"

"Can I admit something to you?"

Brooke faltered as if nerves were causing her throat to close up too. "Yes."

Arlette brought their clasped hands to her chest, where her heart hammered away as if nailing her feelings on the inside of her rib cage.

Brooke glanced up with rounded eyes. "Your heart is racing."

"It is. You make me nervous, Brooklyn."

"You make me nervous too."

"I don't want us to be nervous around each other."

"Maybe being nervous isn't necessarily a bad thing," Brooke said. "Maybe it's just the friction of us readjusting."

Arlette gently squeezed the hand still flat against her chest. "I'm trying to be friends, but my mind keeps having other thoughts."

"What kind of thoughts?"

"Thoughts about how when I'm with you, I want to be close to you. When I'm not with you, I keep wondering about the next time I can be with you. Thoughts about how insanely attracted I am to you."

Brooke gently wiggled out of Arlette's grip. "Really?"

"If we didn't have a past, I'd be kissing you right now."

Brooke hesitated. "If we didn't have a past, I'd be telling you to kiss me." She scanned Arlette as if she was a painting hanging on a museum wall, trying to find the meaning. As if she found what she was searching for, she caressed Arlette's cheek.

Her touch completely unwound Arlette. She followed Brooke's pull and allowed her cheek to fall into Brooke's palm. Arlette desperately wanted to kiss her, to feel Brooke's hands caressing parts of her body that hadn't been touched in months. She wanted to be reacquainted with the sounds she knew she could pull from Brooke; she wanted their bare legs to be intertwined. She wanted to kiss and appreciate Brooke's every inch. And by the way Brooke held her face, Brooke wanted all of that too.

Arlette glided her fingertips up Brooke's arm. Goose bumps broke out beneath her touch like flowers emerging from soil after a drought. They spelled out one thing like it was a message in braille: keep going.

Arlette continued an invisible path up to Brooke's shoulders and danced her fingertips delicately across her collarbone. For the entire journey, Brooke's stare was fixed on hers. "Is this okay?" Arlette asked, her voice hoarse as she ventured up the column of Brooke's neck.

"Mm-hmm," Brooke said.

Arlette grazed her soft cheek and palmed her face. She couldn't believe it. She was holding her, and Brooke's stare never wavered. It bored into Arlette's so deeply, she could feel it squeezing her stomach muscles. "Can I kiss you?" Arlette said, barely above a whisper, afraid that Brooke would say no. She wouldn't have blamed her. Last time, each kiss they'd shared had tangled a tight knot in their friendship, and instead of finding a way to untangle them together, Arlette had run away.

Brooke nodded against her hand. "Please," she said as softly as Arlette's question.

That simple response shattered all the feelings compacting behind her chest. Arlette pulled her in until their lips finally met like a buckle clicking into place. She kissed her gently, feeling her own hesitancy brushing against Brooke's. At first, she thought Brooke would pull away. But as Arlette parted her lips, Brooke secured a hand on Arlette's cheek and kissed her back. An intense hum jolted through her stomach, like a firework that had been sizzling for so long, waiting for its turn to finally launch and color the night sky.

The gentle kiss felt like balancing on a tightrope, unsure and cautious with every movement. Then, once Brooke's lips unlocked memories from the last month of their senior year, Arlette refamiliarized herself with Brooke's kissing patterns. She followed them and sank into the kiss as if taking a deep, meditative breath. She opened her mouth and swiped her tongue along Brooke's. The longer they kissed, the more she found her footing on that tightrope. As the hesitancy dissipated, a flicker of arousal pulsated at her center, screaming for much-needed release. She crawled on top of Brooke, hovering over her and watching the hooded look in her eyes.

"Is this okay?" she asked breathlessly.

Brooke responded by grabbing a fistful of her shirt and pulling her back down, and fucking hell, it was hot. Their kissing resumed, scorching and sizzling. Arlette locked her hips onto Brooke's and rocked them, searching for any kind of release. Brooke responded with soft murmurs that hummed against Arlette's lips. God, those sounds. Hearing them again was like rediscovering a song she'd once loved.

Brooke rested her warm hands on Arlette's waist, securing her while they started moving together. Brooke slipped a hand under the hem of Arlette's shirt. Her fingertips teased and tickled, making Arlette's body break out entirely in goose bumps.

They kissed like they had never been apart. Hands wandered, hips rocked, little nibbles teased on necks, and like before, Arlette lost track of time. It didn't matter really because getting lost in Brooke's mouth and body could be an endless adventure. When she pulled away, her lips felt so different and refreshed that she wondered if they looked different, as if Brooke had kissed the color back into them.

She pulled away and collected a couple breaths, marveling at how Brooke's eyes remained closed a second longer, as if savoring the kiss.

Then Brooke opened them and gave Arlette the smallest trace of a smile. "God. I forgot how good you are at kissing," Brooke said between ragged breaths. She ran her thumb down Arlette's bottom lip.

"I forgot how well we kiss. Fuck, I mean, I thought I knew, but the memories don't compare to the real thing," Arlette said and fell back into her space on the bed. It took every fiber of her being to not peel Brooke's shirt off. That was the furthest they'd ever gone back then, making out in bras and underwear and dry humping. Lots of it. It was fucking hot, and Arlette knew, even back then, that if they had ever removed the rest of their clothes, that would be some of the best sex she would ever have.

One night, they had almost slept together before they had changed their minds. Arlette had felt the arousal from Brooke's soaked underwear on her thigh. The memory replayed as she felt her own arousal making itself known underneath her sweatpants.

As much as she wanted to continue to reacquaint herself with Brooke, endless exploring in her grandpa's house wasn't the right time, and Brooke agreed. So she apologized to her throbbing center in her head and planted one last soft kiss on Brooke's lips before she allowed the tiredness to take over her.

Arlette couldn't remember the last time someone had kissed her like that, so deeply and thoroughly. She couldn't remember the last time someone had made her feel so wanted, like she was the water they needed to cure their own drought. Kissing Brooke replenished her. She felt wanted again, which made her feel sexy again, which made her feel whole again.

CHAPTER ELEVEN

Hold the fucking phone." Stephen balked during morning coffee on the living room couch. "You made out with Arlette Adair for two hours straight?" He faced Abby, his mouth agape, both of them mirroring each other's facial expressions.

"I have no idea what is more surprising," Abby said. "The fact that you two made out when you said you weren't going to, the fact that both of you are back to your old habits of making out for hours and not fucking, or the fact that this happened six days ago, and we're just finding out."

"This is the first morning coffee we've had all week," Brooke said. "Busy schedules. Weekday bartending events. Dates for both of you."

Abby and Stephen exchanged a smirk.

"Amazing self-control. Very admirable," Stephen said to Brooke. He sipped his espresso, paused to look at it, then set the cup on the coffee table. "You know what, I don't need this right now. This news already has me wide awake. I'm invested."

"You can go back to your espresso," Brooke said. "That's it. We made out...for a long fucking time. That's the story."

"You two are really embracing the nostalgia," Abby said. "What happened to our chat two months ago? 'Nothing is gonna happen because I've been down that road before, and I don't need anything getting in the way of my art.'"

"A *lot* has happened since," Brooke said. "We've had so many moments that it just...I don't know. Felt right."

"It felt right?" Abby turned to Stephen. "Did you hear that, Stephen? It felt *right*. Okay, so that now means we must prepare. You'll go out and get the ice cream and wine. I'll start a list of comedies. Brooke's 'heartbroken party' will be ready whenever the time comes."

Brooke rolled her eyes and tossed a couch pillow at Abby. She wasn't sold on Arlette. That was very clear. But she'd never gotten to know Arlette like Brooke did. She'd never seen Arlette in her element, and she was on the other side of the planet from seeing Arlette peacefully sitting on the boat dock. Brooke just wished that Abby trusted her. She was older and wiser than the last time this had unfolded.

"Back then wasn't the right time for us," Brooke said, hoping her explanation would make Abby ease up. "We were about to go off on different journeys. Quite literally. I was moving back home to Charlottesville, and she was going to New York City, six hours away. Even if she'd come back and had talked to me at the party and we'd attempted to explore what was going on between us, we would have been doomed anyway."

"Fair," Stephen said. "I had a long-distance relationship with my boyfriend from college. I was here. He was in Philly. That's only three hours, and it was too hard for us."

"We're not those people anymore. We're more in sync, and it turns out, all that chemistry hasn't gone away."

"So what I'm hearing is that you're giving Arlette Adair a second chance?" Abby said.

Brooke laughed. "Abby, we just kissed. You're acting like I agreed to elope."

"I mean, you probably would if she asked," Abby muttered, and right as Brooke was about to go on the defensive, Abby finished, "Brooke, in all honesty, if this is what feels right and this is what you want, I'll shut up, I promise. But I can't help but worry that this is going to fuck with your art. Your show is in two months."

"I'm well aware."

"And I'm worried about her breaking your heart again. You were devastated."

Brooke patted Abby's knee. "And this time is different because I don't expect anything."

"I doubt that. I watched you two at the bar. You still look at her the same as you did in college."

Brooke rolled her eyes and hated how she felt the embarrassment streak across her cheeks. "Abby, it's going to be okay. Trust me."

Abby gave her a side-eye. "I'm still going to get that comedy movie list ready, just in case. Stephen can get that Taylor Swift playlist ready for when you need to sob into a pint of ice cream."

"You do that," Brooke said and got off the couch. "In the meantime, I have to go prep my studio for tomorrow's model."

"Yeah, I'm sure you already have plenty of inspiration to use," Abby said, waggling her eyebrows and sipping her coffee.

After Brooke showered and put her hair in a messy bun, she saw that she had two unread texts. One from Arlette and one from an unknown number.

Arlette had found a way to occupy her every thought the entire week: while she'd dropped off orders at the post office, had made drinks at two bartending events, or even when she'd painted in the studio. Arlette had slid into her mind and had kissed her senselessly and thoroughly in her head. When she'd returned home from work in the early hours of the morning, her mind had filled with visions of their kisses and Arlette's hands, mouth, and tongue mapping her body. It was like a black and white rerun Brooke wanted to play on an endless loop.

Yeah, she definitely went for Arlette's text first.

Please tell me that we can see each other this weekend.

Brooke bit her lip and texted back, *I have an event tonight and need to paint a model tomorrow but…I can be all yours when I'm done in the afternoon.*

Arlette: *I would like you to pencil me in right after you finish another masterpiece. I'll reward you with some dinner, maybe a movie, or maybe we can resume last weekend?*

Brooke: *I've been thinking about it all week, and while those thoughts alone are amazing, I would very much like to resume. The memory is starting to fade.*

Arlette: *I vote we refresh it.* Winky emoji.

Brooke changed into her yoga pants and a T-shirt and then checked the unknown number.

Hi Brooke, this is Julia. I'm so sorry to do this, but I'm no longer able to make it to your studio to model for your painting tomorrow. Just had a family emergency and will need to attend to that for the next week. Is there any way to reschedule?

Brooke deflated. Fuck, this changed everything. She needed to get the painting finished in the next week to stay on schedule while working on other freelance work and the bartending gigs. She sat on the edge of her bed as her mind started to panic while formulating a quick plan on how she could make everything work. It would be almost impossible to get a model for tomorrow or even next week. She couldn't necessarily switch to the fifth and final painting of the collection because she still had to think about what she wanted to do.

Her phone rang and pulled her from her tumbling mind. It was Arlette. Brooke had no idea why Arlette was calling, but her brain was too out-of-focus to question it. "Hey," Brooke answered a little flatly. She shook her head, disappointed that she couldn't mask the worry in her tone.

"Hey, I figured I would call because it's easier. I'm walking to work right now. Do you have a second?"

With a large part of her weekend now free, yes, she had all the seconds in the world. "I do, what's up?"

"I was going to ask about dinner for tomorrow, but you sound very stressed."

Brooke rubbed out the tension piling in her forehead. "I'm so sorry. I was supposed to paint a model tomorrow, and she just told me that she needs to cancel. So I'm in the panicking phase."

"Oh, shit. Can you find another one?"

"Not with this short notice. I was really hoping to have this piece finished by next week to stay on track. I have events the next couple of weekends that are going to get in the way of painting."

After a few moments of wind rustling, Arlette said, "Can I do it?"

Brooke frowned. "What? You want to model for me?"

"If it helps you stay on track, yes. Do I not qualify?" she said through a little laugh.

"No, I mean…you know it's nude, right?"

More wind filled the silence on Arlette's end, and despite Brooke's panicking, she couldn't help but smile when imagining Arlette realizing what she'd signed up for. "How nude?" Arlette asked cautiously.

"Not full-body but, like, I was going to have the model in a robe, exposing a breast…or two."

Just saying that while picturing Arlette in the robe made the words grate along her arid throat. Studying every inch of Arlette's body, searching for every unique detail, and capturing it on a twenty-four-by-thirty canvas was already sending a familiar zing from her chest to her toes.

Arlette cleared her throat. "I can do it if you need me. I trust you."

"Are you sure? You absolutely don't have to—"

"I know, but I don't want you to worry. We can fix this. I can help you stay on track."

Brooke blinked away the images filling her head. God, she didn't want to panic. She very much wanted to stay on schedule. Brooke's time-management skills were impeccable. She had everything planned meticulously, but the closer she came to the exhibit, the more stress flowed through her. Drawing Arlette would be so fucking difficult, but the more she thought about it, the more she thought how perfect it would be for Arlette to be the focus of her painting. The exhibit was about female sexuality, and Brooke wanted to showcase the nuances and beauty of the female gaze. Arlette had sparked Brooke's own discovery of her sexuality, and Brooke knew that only she could fully capture all of Arlette Adair in tiny, beautiful detail, the girl who she had memorized all those years ago.

Brooke had never been so nervous to draw someone. She hadn't seen Arlette since that Sunday after Grandpa Harry's. Saturday had involved so much kissing that her body still held on to some residual arousal, even a week later, that needed satisfying. Brooke had tried doing that herself, but only Arlette could successfully get the job done. Now Brooke had to fight against her libido while seeing Arlette topless for the first time. All those times she'd filled in the blanks and had enjoyed the image in her head, and now those thoughts would be brought to life in front of her.

And somehow, Brooke had to remain composed.

This was going to be the most difficult painting she had ever agreed to. Significantly harder than painting for Teresa Rosario.

When Arlette texted that she was there, Brooke's stomach sank like she was on a roller coaster, equally excited and anxious. When Brooke opened the door, Arlette gave a wary smile. Brooke wondered if her heart was beating a million miles an hour too.

"Hi. Your model is here," Arlette said and gestured to herself.

While her humor eased Brooke's nerves just a bit, Brooke knew all too well that she cracked silly jokes when she was nervous. Okay, so both of them were on the same level. Brooke could work with that.

Once Arlette stepped inside and Brooke closed the door, Arlette seemed to notice the fluffy down comforter and pillows over an air mattress against the windows. "So that's where I'm going to show you my boobs?"

Brooke smiled and grabbed her hand. "You're nervous. It's okay," Brooke said. "We can take our time. Just chat and hang out for a bit. I even brought mimosa supplies if that will help."

"I love mimosas."

"I figured you did. I hate to break it to you, though, it's not Dom Pérignon."

Arlette waved her off. "If you're holding a bottle of champagne in those clear-frame glasses and wearing that cute, paint-stained plaid shirt, then it's practically Dom."

Brooke pushed the glasses up the bridge of her nose. "I can put on that shirt if you want. I always try to make my model feel as comfortable as possible."

"I'm going to need the shirt, then. I won't be comfortable until it happens. That shirt with those sexy, clear-framed glasses? What a fantasy."

"I had no idea these glasses did something for you."

"Anything that touches you does something for me."

Brooke picked up her plaid shirt from the chair and buttoned it up, the exact opposite of what she really wanted to do with Arlette, but she was all about playing the long game.

Arlette smiled. "This is when I wish I was an artist. I'd capture you right here in this moment, exactly as you are right now, and hang it up on my wall so I can admire you whenever I want."

"You don't need to paint me to do that. However, now that I know you have a thing for glasses and plaid, I'll be sure to wear both more often. You want a mimosa?"

"Absolutely."

Brooke fished out the ingredients and poured them both a drink, one with a little more champagne for Arlette, and one that went easy on the bubbles for herself.

"My first time modeling, and my little baby bill gets debated next week." Arlette took her first sip. "So this mimosa will definitely help."

"I bet that has you in a ball of nerves."

"Oh, it does. A lobbyist warned me that it seems split, so that's spawned even more anxiety." She sighed and took another large drink. "I'll push it away for now. It's next week's problem. Now, tell me what I signed up for."

After Brooke explained how she wanted Arlette to pose, Arlette's facial features softened as if her nerves faded.

"What do you say to all of that? Are you comfortable?" Right as Arlette opened her mouth to reply, Brooke quickly added, "You don't have to do this at all, you know. Don't feel obligated. I'll be okay if you changed your mind."

Arlette reached for her hand and squeezed it. "I trust you. I feel more comfortable now that we talked it through, and this mimosa helped." She wiggled her empty cup. "I think I'm ready to do this. I have to say, though, I never expected this would be the first time you'd see me officially topless."

Brooke's mouth dried up from the sudden reminder, her brain filling in the blanks of Arlette's breasts. *Perfection*, she thought. *They're going to be absolute perfection.* "You and me both. I would have suggested we made out without bras if I knew this was going to happen...you know, a way to study for the test."

Arlette's eyebrows raised. "I mean...we can fix that right now, if you want."

Brooke snatched the rose-colored robe off the adjustable standing chair and handed it over. "If we do that, no painting will be involved. Work first."

Arlette nodded. "Work first. Play later. Got it."

"The bathroom is just around the corner. Oh, you can also leave your underwear on."

While Arlette changed, Brooke set up her canvas and pencils and fluffed the comforter and pillows. The sound of the door shutting pulled her away from setting up her station. Arlette had the silk robe wrapped around her, and Brooke lost a couple breaths. This was the softest and most beautiful Brooke had ever seen her. The lapels of the robe formed a vee right between her breasts, exposing her smooth skin and teasing her collarbone. Brooke imagined running her fingertips along the side of the lapels, feeling Arlette's warm skin, her collarbone, and slowly lowering the fabric to finally reveal her breasts.

A jolt hit her core and snapped her out of the daydream. No, she had to remain professional. She couldn't let herself get wet at the thought of touching Arlette. Arlette was a model, and Brooke needed to treat her as such. She had worked with plenty of models before. In college, nude models were part of her intermediate painting and drawing classes. Drawing partially—or fully—naked bodies wasn't anything new. It was part of her resume, and she handled it very professionally.

Except, with Arlette standing there in only a robe, Brooke could feel the temperature skyrocketing, and she tried so hard to mow over the lingering arousal that had been consistently throbbing between her legs all week.

"Wow, okay, we're doing this," Brooke said, not meaning for it to be a vocal thought, but with it out in the open, she shrugged and gestured for Arlette to lie on the air mattress.

"I have no idea what I'm doing," Arlette said as she sat on the edge of the bed.

"That's fine. I'll tell you how I want you."

An impish grin spilled on Arlette's face. "Oh really? I like the sound of that."

Brooke pointed. "Behave. Do you even have any idea how hard this is going to be for me? You get to lie there and look fucking gorgeous while I have to take in every single detail that makes you fucking sexy as hell and then translate that on the canvas."

Arlette blinked several times. "I think you should elaborate. A good ego boost will help me feel more comfortable."

Brooke rolled her eyes. "If it's going to help you, then okay. I'll lay it all out there. Seeing you in this robe and knowing there's nothing but underwear underneath is already making me feel things, and I haven't even positioned you…" Brooke facepalmed, realizing her error. "There are going to be so many accidental innuendos."

"This is making me less nervous. I'm enjoying how bright red your face is right now."

With her eyes closed, Brooke pointed to the pillows next to the large window. "Just lie on your back while I recover."

"Demanding, I like it," Arlette said in a salacious tone.

Brooke didn't open her eyes until she heard Arlette situate herself.

She opened one eye slowly, thinking that easing into the scene would tame her libido, but it didn't. As Arlette lay on her back, the lapels of the robe revealed the swell of her breasts. The hem of the fabric rode up her leg. Brooke imagined gliding her hands underneath the robe and feeling just how soft and toned Arlette's legs were.

Brooke cleared her throat and her mind. "So...um...how this is going to go is, I'm going to direct you. It's model ethics that I can't touch you, so I'll instruct you on how I want you." Arlette let out a prurient grin, and it was the biting of her lip as if to suck it in that sent another throb straight to Brooke's core. "Can you, um...lie fully on your back, head turned to look out the window?" Once Arlette positioned herself, Brooke continued, "And bend your knees and have them pointing toward me?" Arlette followed. "Okay...so...um...now can you untie the robe? I'm envisioning the left breast will be exposed and then the lapel will tease your right nipple."

A lump lodged in her throat as she watched Arlette untie the robe. Brooke fixed her stare on Arlette's hands pulling the robe back where her nipples budded through the silk. All Brooke needed was to see the tall peaks forming behind the fabric for another lustful thought to sweep through her mind: imagining pulling Arlette's nipple into her mouth...

She blinked out of the daydream once again. "Can you pull it back a little more?" Brooke said. Arlette followed, but it still wasn't enough. "One more centimeter." Brooke's breath hitched when she saw the start of Arlette's areola. She cleared her throat, attempting to dislodge the watermelon-size lump. "Perfect. Stay like that," Brooke said as she walked over to her digital camera. "Is it okay if I take a picture so I can use it as a reference for things like shading? It will stay on my camera, obviously."

"Yeah, sure," Arlette said, holding the pose and looking out the window.

It was when Brooke held up the camera and looked at the screen that she saw the raw beauty that made up Arlette. She lowered her camera and raked her gaze from the hem of the robe a few inches above Arlette's knees, past her belly button, the valley of her full breasts, to the robe pooling to the side and exposing her left breast. Brooke inhaled a cool, air-conditioned breath to calm her rattling nerves.

Arlette was beautiful. Brooke wasn't a master of words, but she was pretty decent at painting. God, Arlette was so fucking gorgeous that Brooke knew she had to take her time, making sure she got every single unique detail just right. If she was able to capture just a modicum of the beauty that made up Arlette, she'd consider the painting a very successful one.

She snapped a couple pictures and tried to steady her shaky hands. Then she adjusted her chair, pulling the lever so the seat popped up and gave her an elevated perspective of Arlette on the mattress. She picked up her charcoal pencil and gave herself a moment to breathe through the pressure mounting in her chest and her center. When she felt collected enough, she drank a big gulp of water and turned on her painting playlist on her phone.

"Draw me like one of your French girls," Arlette said, breaking the silence sparking with tension.

Brooke rolled her eyes but smiled. She was grateful for Arlette's silly joke to help her settle. "Shut it, or you're going to make me lose my concentration."

"I wish I could see you. Your concentration face was always so cute."

Brooke pushed her glasses up the bridge of her nose and started to sketch with the charcoal. "Oh, yeah? This is news to me."

"Only one eyebrow furrows, and you press your lips together. I knew you were in the zone when you were staring at your tablet like that. I remember one time going to shower, and when I came back, I swear you'd had no idea that I had left."

It wasn't until Arlette pointed it out that Brooke noticed her lips were already sealed together, and her right eyebrow was furrowed. She relaxed her face, tilted her head to both sides, and let out a sigh of relief when her neck cracked.

"Look at you being an observer," Brooke said.

"I know you pretty well, Brooklyn."

The mention of her full name at such a tantalizing time had so much more power than it ever did before.

For the next ten minutes, Brooke alternated glances between the canvas and Arlette, who lay completely still, looking absolutely gorgeous in the afternoon light. There was one point when Brooke paused just to stare at Arlette and how quickly she'd settled into being the main focus of the room. It was a sight Brooke had never seen before, one that Arlette had never allowed herself to be in when they'd been together, and yet there she was, taking control of a room and owning it so effortlessly. Brooke knew that was a reflection of her unwavering trust. Brooke knew how fragile it was, and it was imperative she made sure Arlette didn't feel a twinge of uneasiness.

"Are you doing okay?" Brooke asked as she drew the last part of Arlette's body and started sketching the mattress.

"I'm doing fine. That mimosa helped. It also helps that you're forcing me to stare out this window and not at you."

"You seem pretty relaxed, which is good."

"Why do you say that?"

"You're all out of dumb jokes," Brooke said.

"Hey, my jokes aren't dumb…most of the time."

"They're endearing. They also let me know when you're panicking on the inside."

Arlette hesitated. "You really do notice the smallest things, don't you?"

"I think my art degree trained me to take in all the details of everything and everyone."

"Like the flecks of gold in my eyes?"

"Exactly like the flecks of gold."

"Any other observances?"

Brooke studied Arlette as she looked out the window. The thing was, ever since she'd first drawn Arlette and the stunning complexities of her eyes, Brooke couldn't help but pay attention to all of her. Every day for four years. She couldn't help it.

"I have," Brooke said, keeping her eyes on the canvas as she penciled in the finer details of Arlette's nipple, though that didn't stop her mind from wondering how perfectly it would have fit into her mouth. "I've noticed how you make jokes when you're nervous. You clench your jaw when you're upset and holding something back. When you're anxious, you have a restless foot, and I could feel it shake whenever we shared a table at the library. That's also how I know, right now, you're not anxious anymore. Your foot stopped shaking like five minutes ago. When you're fighting back tears, your nostrils flare. They flared a lot when we watched the sunset. I think that's how I really knew how sorry you were for everything that happened between us."

Arlette flinched out of her position by turning her head. The movement pulled Brooke's gaze from the canvas. Arlette's stare was weighted, and the whole time, it made Brooke feel like she was standing under a spotlight, feeling hot pricks over her skin like in the summer heat.

"How do you know all that?" Arlette said quietly. "I didn't even know all that."

"You don't see yourself in every moment. I do, though. I see all of you." Arlette's eyebrows lifted in a silent question. "And your left eyebrow quirks when you're confused."

Arlette sat up. The robe fell open to reveal both breasts, and Brooke lost all the air in her lungs.

Brooke didn't just see Arlette. She felt all of Arlette, all over her body. Despite the couple of feet separating them, the tension tethered them together. She wanted to show Arlette, with her tongue, just how much she wanted and needed to appreciate her in all her entirety.

"You weren't supposed to move out of your position," Brooke said in a guttural voice. She cleared the hoarseness in her throat.

"Then come over here and put me back in place."

Arlette's demand snapped them out of the professional trance, as if they'd given up trying to fit a square peg into a round hole. One week after making out like teenagers, Arlette still had the power to make Brooke feel like a firework, ready to jet up into the sky and explode in colors she'd never seen.

"You know I'm not supposed to touch you," Brooke said and attempted to tame the throbbing between her legs. "It's, um…it's not ethical."

"What if I want to be touched?" Arlette said. Brooke swallowed and shook her head, trying to stay on track. Arlette pursed her lips. "What if I desperately *need* to be touched?"

Brooke closed her eyes for the quickest moment and willed the aching to go away. When she opened her eyes, the chartreuse in Arlette's eyes had darkened and practically begged Brooke to touch her.

Why had she asked Arlette to be a model? It had seemed like a great idea in a hopeless attempt to stay on schedule, in a desperate attempt to also share another day with her, in a despairing attempt to see how stunning she looked in a robe.

"Arlette…" Brooke said, then trailed off into silence, not sure what she wanted. To direct Arlette back on the bed to finish the sketch before turning the canvas into an *alla prima* painting? Or to coax her over so Brooke's hands could finally feel how fucking gorgeous she was?

Before Brooke had the chance to decide, Arlette stood. The fact that she sauntered over to Brooke, full of confidence, made every part of Brooke feel like it was dipped in fire. She dropped her stare along Arlette's collarbone, down to those beautiful breasts. She scanned those legs that were toned enough to straddle her face.

Brooke snapped herself out of her tumbling thoughts and looked into the eyes of the beautiful woman standing in front of her. Arlette had stepped into the studio cracking nervous jokes and worrying about her work but now had no trace of any anxiety. She stood in front of Brooke, the smell of sandalwood wafting off her skin and luring Brooke into a daze. Brooke was balancing on the tightrope of treating Arlette like a model and treating her like the woman she'd adored since she was eighteen.

Brooke parted her legs and allowed Arlette to step in between.

Arlette lifted her chin with two fingers and grazed her cheek with her thumb. "Am I allowed to do this?"

Brooke nodded. Looking like that, Arlette could do whatever she wanted. Brooke was a marionette controlled by Arlette's beauty and the bottled-up tension over the last nine years.

"What if the model wants to touch the artist?" Arlette said. "What do the rules say about that?"

"I…um…"

Arlette ran her thumb down to Brooke's lips, and they opened at her touch. A soft moan escaped Brooke's mouth, and the noise planted a smug smirk on Arlette's face. Just that one murmur of pleasure revealed Brooke's cards, and she was at the mercy of Arlette and anything she wanted to do.

Arlette leaned in and hovered a breath away from Brooke's lips. "Is all of this okay?" Brooke nodded. "Good."

That seemed to be all Arlette needed. The kiss scorched Brooke's lips. Arlette's tongue glided along her lips, beckoning for them to part. When their tongues danced together, the heat took over. Brooke whimpered while Arlette combed her hands through her hair, gently tugging and wrestling yet another murmur from her. Arlette kissed down the column of Brooke's neck. She swirled her tongue and punctuated the most sensitive spots with nibbles that caused Brooke to whimper. God, Arlette knew how to undo her so effortlessly and easily.

"I want you," Arlette whispered and gently bit Brooke's earlobe. Brooke moaned just imagining Arlette kissing her most sensitive parts the same way she methodically kissed her earlobe. "I want to feel all of you, I want to finally taste you—"

Brooke pulled back to see if Arlette meant what she said, and by her darkened eyes that glistened with determination, Arlette was just as desperate as Brooke was. "Arlette," Brooke said through ragged breaths.

God, she desperately wanted her. She needed her. It had been such a long time since she'd had sex. She had spent so long admiring every detail of sexiness that comprised Arlette Adair that she wasn't sure how much longer she could live with the pent-up frustration.

Arlette looped her fingers around the band of Brooke's yoga pants. She waited. The throbbing became so much, Brooke caved. She needed Arlette. She lifted her hips and allowed Arlette to slide her pants and underwear down her legs. Brooke blinked slowly as Arlette tossed the offending items aside.

"Brooklyn," she whispered as she fixed her stare on Brooke's naked center.

The way Arlette's fragmented breaths wrapped around her full name like that, so raw and yet so careful, Brooke was desperate for her body to wrap around her in the same way.

"Can I see more?" Arlette said.

Brooke nodded. Arlette methodically unbuttoned the paint-stained plaid. When she tossed that on the ground, she gripped the hem of Brooke's shirt and slowly lifted it over her head. The shirt knocked her glasses. She started to remove them, but once Arlette discarded the shirt, Arlette said, "No, keep the glasses on."

A simple demand like that made Brooke feel the sexiest she had ever felt.

Brooke could feel Arlette's stare all over her body, and it left a trail of goose bumps in its path. As if their roles had been reversed and Arlette was the artist, she took in all of Brooke as if searching for beauty in her smallest details. Being the subject of her unwavering admiration tugged countless breaths from Brooke, and the airier the exhales that escaped, the more they turned into moans.

When Arlette pressed her cheek against Brooke's ear, Brooke almost came undone. Arlette took her earlobe between her teeth, and her free hand wrapped around Brooke's back to unhook her bra. Brooke's breasts collided with the cold air and hardened as she melted into Arlette's grip.

"You're so fucking beautiful, you know that?" Arlette said.

Brooke had never felt so desired in her entire life. She skimmed her fingers down the soft silk lapels, working her way toward Arlette's hips, but before she could reach them, Arlette grabbed her wrists and lowered them.

"You're not allowed to touch me, remember?" Arlette said as her breaths staggered over Brooke's lips. "So let me touch you. Okay?"

The desperation and hoarse tone undid the last reservations Brooke had. She let out a heavy exhale while Arlette lowered herself to her knees. Arlette reached for the lever on the side of the chair and pulled it, then locked the wheels in place. Brooke and the seat dropped so Arlette had perfect access to her. Whatever version of Arlette was in between her legs, Brooke loved her. Her confidence suffused the entire studio. Arlette took control of the entire room, the chair, and she was about to take control of Brooke. Brooke was so ready. She didn't care that she was in her studio or that she should have been slathering the first layer of paint over the charcoal sketch. She wanted and needed Arlette. After nine years of foreplay, her clit couldn't take it anymore.

Arlette scooped Brooke by the hamstrings and tugged her to the edge of the chair. Brooke's dangling legs draped over both her shoulders, and she took Brooke into her mouth. Brooke gripped the armrests, and Arlette sucked a cry from her that filled the studio. She covered her mouth, not wanting her sounds to filter into the hallway.

Arlette pulled away. "I want to hear you," she said and put her tongue back on Brooke's clit.

Brooke lowered her hands and secured them once more around the armrests. She closed her eyes and rested her back against the chair, and Arlette's fingers filled her with absolute ease. She arched her back at the contact and rocked. Brooke pressed her lips tighter to muffle a moan. She opened her eyes and absorbed the sight of Arlette staring up at her.

This was happening. Arlette was touching her, tasting her, and moving inside her. She'd never longed for anyone so much. She'd never thought they would get to put their chemistry to the test, and here they were, with electricity lighting up all her nerve endings.

Brooke undulated her hips, desperate to cure the mounting pressure between her thighs. Soft moans fell from her lips, punctuated with whispers of expletives. As Arlette curled her fingers upward, Brooke cried out, and warmth flooded her. The orgasm lit up her whole body, from the top of her head all the way to the soles of her feet.

"You know, I always thought the noises you made when we kissed were hot," Arlette said, standing to kiss her lips before tracing a trail of kisses along her jaw to the other side of her neck. "But that…that was sexy as hell. You're sexy as hell."

Brooke felt the compliment color her entire face. "You're…that was…hard. It was so hard not to touch you."

"I didn't make the rules. I just followed them," Arlette said and hovered over Brooke's mouth. "It's a shame about those rules, though, because I'm so incredibly turned on right now."

That alone had Brooke wet all over again.

Arlette closed in and kissed her, slipping her tongue into Brooke's mouth and repeating the same patterns she'd traced on her clit. Brooke pulled away before she melted in the same spot for the second time.

"I can take care of that, you know." Brooke tugged on the robe to pull Arlette in, but Arlette stopped her.

"You have a painting to create," Arlette whispered against her lips.

"The sketch is practically done," Brooke said and gestured to the canvas. Arlette looked over. "I can either start painting now or table that so I can make you come. You decide."

Arlette pulled away. "Fuck, Brooklyn."

Brooke took off her glasses, rested them on her easel, and pointed to the air mattress. "Resume your position."

With rounded, intrigued eyes, Arlette moved to obey. Brooke was shocked by how up-front she was, but at the same time, she wanted this to continue. She wanted to feel every inch of Arlette the same way her eyes had already done. She wanted to hear and feel Arlette come undone in her grip.

Arlette lay in the same spot. Brooke crawled on top and watched as her pupils dilated. Her smile faded as the weight of the moment covered them like a blanket. Brooke slowly peeled the robe to the side and finally took Arlette in like a piece of art she'd never seen before.

God, she was so fucking beautiful. She didn't have the words, but luckily, words weren't needed.

She caressed Arlette's cheek with her thumb. She'd spent all of college wishing that Arlette would look at her the exact way she was looking at her right now: soft, desperate, and at Brooke's mercy. Now she had Arlette's full attention, and she planned on enjoying every last second of it.

Brooke lowered herself, pulled a nipple into her mouth, and flicked it with her tongue before moving to the other. Arlette tossed her head back, lips parted, and soft moans escaped her as breaths. Every kiss Brooke planted on her body sounded like untying a knot inside Arlette until Brooke found something beautiful underneath, like undoing Arlette's robe to find her gorgeous body. When she finally reached the top of Arlette's black underwear, Brooke skimmed her tongue along Arlette's waist before slipping them off. When she tossed the underwear aside, she found Arlette's stare locked on her, so beautifully delicate. Brooke lowered herself to kiss her and deepened the kiss so she could trace patterns on Arlette's tongue, a quick preview of what she could expect on the spot where she needed it the most. Brooke felt Arlette's arousal on her leg, letting her know exactly how much Arlette wanted her.

God, it was sexy as hell to know that she could make Arlette feel that good. This was Arlette Adair, the woman she'd pined over all through college. The same woman she'd watched sneaking into their dorm freshman and sophomore year, late at night, after spending time with several unknown girls. The same woman who other girls in the dorm had crushed on much more openly and obviously than she had. Despite all of that, and a five-year hole punched out of their timeline, Brooke loved that she still had the ability to affect Arlette that much.

Brooke kissed her way down. When she reached Arlette's clit, she glanced up and noticed Arlette watching her. Brooke held her stare as she covered her center. Arlette tossed her head back and cried out the sexiest sound. Brooke wanted to hear more, until the studio was filled with her moans. Brooke slid into her warmth and moved slowly. She wanted to take her time. She wanted to memorize the feel of Arlette's body the way her eyes had long memorized the sight of her. She wanted to push Arlette to the edge, then pull her back in like a wave against the shore. When Arlette's sounds quickened, her back arched, and she twisted the sheets, Brooke pulled away and slowed. She teased her a few more times until Arlette glanced down with desperation in her eyes.

"Brooklyn...please," Arlette begged through ragged breaths. She slipped a hand into Brooke's hair. "Please, I...I need you."

"You have me," Brooke said. She loved how desperate Arlette sounded. She wanted to hear what Arlette sounded like when she exploded into bliss. When she put her mouth on her again, Arlette tightened the grip in her hair as her free hand searched for support. Brooke grabbed her hand while the other tugged her closer. Arlette's lips parted, eyebrows folded, back arched, and she held on to Brooke's hand and hair tightly as she cried out her orgasm.

Brooke hadn't ever created anything more beautiful than when Arlette lay there, collecting her breath, her body limp while her sounds still clung to the room just like the smell of old wood and paint.

"Fuck," Arlette muttered and tossed an arm over her eyes.

Brooke plopped in the space next to her and rested her head against Arlette's chest. She smiled when she heard how fast Arlette's heart hammered.

"Arlette?" Brooke said softly, grazing her opposite cheek and guiding her to look down. Arlette lowered her arm. "You're fucking beautiful, do you know that?"

There was so much vulnerability in Arlette's eyes. She stared for a second before leaning in and giving Brooke a long, soft kiss, almost as if thanking her. "Come home with me," Arlette said a whisper away from Brooke's mouth. "Let's order food and then stay in bed for the rest of the weekend."

She kissed Arlette's forehead. "I'm sold."

They finished up at the studio, went to Arlette's, and crawled back into bed for another round, only leaving the bedroom for bathroom breaks, food, and hydration.

At night, while Brooke's body pleasantly hummed from all the tension and frustration that had been released, Arlette held her in her arms. Her face was buried in the nape of Brooke's neck while she'd wrapped her arms around Brooke's middle. Brooke let out the longest sigh, pushing out the remaining hurt from years before.

Everything felt so right for the first time in a long time.

CHAPTER TWELVE

Arlette wanted to scream. The bill she, her team, and Teresa had worked so hard on was killed in the House by four votes. It was a bill that could have easily gone to the Senate, and the most aggravating thing was that three of those votes came from ancient Democrats, including Uncle Henry.

Arlette wasted no time sprint-walking across Independence Avenue and into the Cannon Building. She needed time to process everything. Her mind spun around so quickly she was dizzy. She needed to sit and breathe. She plopped on the couch in the main room of Teresa's office. She only had a couple minutes until the rest of the staff came back. So she inhaled deeply, held it, and then exhaled, repeating the cycle.

She wanted to cry. This was a tipping point in her career that had her wedged between a rock and a hard place. The unfortunate part was that these games in Congress were part of her job. She should have been fully equipped to weather the lows. Every job had them. The fact that she could no longer emotionally handle the lows was the most obvious sign that she had to leap far from Capitol Hill. It wasn't for her, and she wasn't meant for it. She couldn't be in a field where she spent months thoroughly researching science and facts and solving a very serious issue only for politicians to ignore all those facts.

What was the point?

Once she let out a heavy exhale, she noticed Brooke's painting on the opposite wall. The painting added beauty and color while Arlette felt like hers had been drained from the debate. It was the one thing that made the racing thoughts halt for a moment.

"There you are. I've been looking for you."

Arlette looked up and found Teresa and the rest of the team walking in. Arlette sat up straight, trying to undo any wallowing they might have witnessed.

Teresa quirked a dark eyebrow. "You doing okay, Arlette?"

The question held immense weight. It wasn't a cordial "how are you" as they passed by each other in the hallway. She could tell by the way Teresa's eyes held hers with sympathy that she wanted the absolute truth.

"I'm fine," Arlette said. It was easier to say than the truth. Everyone was reeling from the disappointing loss. She didn't need to air her own internal issues on top of it.

"Let's go talk in my office," Teresa said and headed to her door. When Arlette raised her eyebrows, Teresa gestured for her to get up. So she followed her inside, and Teresa shut the door.

"Talk to me," Teresa said, sitting at her desk. Right as Arlette opened her mouth, Teresa raised a hand. "This is real talk. I'm not your boss right now. I'm your friend. We've known each other for…what, two years? I hope that you know you can talk to me about anything. Like right now, I know for a fact that you're not fine. It's all over your face. Talk to me."

The last thing Arlette wanted to do was cry in front of Teresa Rosario. Teresa had bigger things to worry about than what was wrong with her. However, so much filled her chest that she was desperate to get it out and relieve some of the pressure. "If we're being honest and this is off the record—"

"It's all off the record," Teresa said.

"I'm at a loss. I feel like I've been lost for quite some time."

Teresa leaned into her desk. "Why do I feel like there's more to this than just the bill?"

When Teresa said that, the tears threatened, and Arlette felt her nostrils flare. She looked at her lap, willing her eyes to dry up and for the ball in her throat to unravel. But after one tear slipped past the seal, Arlette knew she wouldn't be able to keep up the stoic act anymore.

"Arlette?" Teresa asked in a soothing, sympathetic voice.

She shook her head as more tears fell.

Teresa wheeled her chair to the other side of her desk. "Talk to me."

Arlette swatted away the pesky tears that were quick to multiply down her cheeks. "I really don't think I can do this anymore."

"Do what?"

"This," Arlette said and gestured to the room. She cleaned her face with the back of her hand. "I'm really sorry that I'm bringing it up at the worst possible time, but it's been weighing on me for a while. I've tried fitting into this political mold. I really tried, but it's not for me, and now, I just feel so lost."

"Why?"

"I should have a clearer idea of what I want to do with my life. I'm twenty-seven. I shouldn't be hitting a fork in the road at twenty-seven."

"You can hit a fork in the road whenever in your life."

"It feels too early in my professional career to hit a fork in the road."

"I think it's more common than you think. You think I woke up when I was, like, ten and decided that I wanted to be a congresswoman? No, I had no idea that it was an option until I was twenty-eight. I was some nobody living in Washington Heights who decided just two years before that I wanted to become an immigration lawyer. So three years after college, I hit my first fork, and I thought the same thing you are right now. 'Shouldn't I have thought about this when I was in college?' I decided to forget it and study for the bar. Several months after I passed, my best friend's father was deported, and I was pissed. I wanted to do more, and that's when I decided to run." Teresa rested her hand on Arlette's wrist. "Forks in the road are scary when you find them in the dark, but when you find that switch and turn on the light, they're exciting. They show you a new perspective. You found yours in the dark, and what I see is a chance for you to finally grasp something that you love. You can't think that there are age limits on opportunities. They happen at all ages, and that's okay. We're constantly evolving as humans. We pick up passions and discard others multiple times in our lives. I know that wherever you end up, you're going to shine. You're destined for great things, Arlette. All you have to do is turn on that light and see all the things within your reach."

Arlette swiped her eyes as the tears fell. Teresa had so much hope and confidence. Somehow, despite the major setback that had occurred an hour before, a smile found a way to land. It felt like Arlette was looking at a mirror. The way Teresa saw her—the way Brooke had always seen her—reflected back the confidence that she should always have. Maybe if she looked at the mirror long enough, she would absorb it.

"What about you?" Arlette said. "What about the bill? The reelection campaign next year?"

Teresa waved her off. "I'll be okay. I promise. It doesn't sound like you're okay, and you need to focus on you right now. I want to see the Arlette Adair I met two years ago. What happened to her? Where's that tenacity?"

Arlette let out a hollow laugh. "I've been asking myself that since I was twenty-two."

"Arlette," Teresa said with a lower voice. "You want to know what made you stand out? The second that I wanted you on my team?"

Arlette used her blazer sleeve to wipe her eyes. "What?"

"When I found out that—despite the famous Adair military legacy—you decided to forge your own path and studied environmental science at a college I'd never heard of. You broke the mold, and it takes a lot of determination and confidence to do that. I wanted my team to be made of people who weren't afraid to rock the boat in that stale Congress. You've got the passion to make bold decisions. And honestly, in my opinion, that's bolder than getting off the Hill. You might think you're miles away from being happy, but I don't think you are. I think you're within a push's reach, and guess what? This is me pushing you. Hurling you, in fact."

Arlette let out a small laugh. "Hurling me?"

"I'm chucking you across the National Mall like a football. I'll miss you terribly, don't get me wrong. You're leaving behind big shoes to fill, but I care about you and want you to be happy. If getting out of politics has been your dream, then you need to do it. Get online and find that job that's going to fulfill you in all the ways this job hasn't. Just promise me one thing."

"What's that?"

"Please stop by and visit once in a while. That's my only requirement."

Teresa told everyone they could take the rest of the day to recoup from the devastating blow. Arlette went home, lay on her couch, and tried to process where to even begin looking for other opportunities. Teresa's advice and the fact that she truly believed in Arlette felt like a fresh breath of spring air during winter, a reminder that all bad things ended eventually. But Arlette knew that before she cleared her mind enough to start working on her résumé, she needed to sort through the mess of feelings inside her.

On her walk back home, she checked her phone and noticed texts pending from Jackie and Brooke. She looked at Brooke's first.

I just heard about the bill. Can I come over to cheer you up? Cheetos, Jeopardy, and cuddles?

The sudden text was the one thing that tweaked out a smile and made her push away the disappointment at the lack of texts from her parents. A part of her hoped that they would have messaged despite getting ready for the second debate in San Antonio, but considering her last interaction with her dad a month before, the lack of communication spoke volumes about how her dad was still bitter about her decision not to attend any debates. That, or he was truly swamped with prep and events. It could have been a mixture of both.

Arlette decided to table those thoughts for the time being, right next to the anxiety of looking for another job. Brooke was on her way over, and she would be able to pick up those worries weighing on Arlette's mind and—hopefully—kiss them away.

Brooke walked into Arlette's fresh from the studio. Specks of paint dotted her hands as she handed over a bag of Flamin' Hot Cheetos, black cherry seltzer water, and even a brownie.

Arlette held it up. "Is this from Eastern Market?"

Brooke settled next to her on the couch. "Maybe. I'm an observer. I know you like these brownies."

"I do," Arlette said, wasting no time unwrapping the baked chocolate and taking a bite.

Brooke kissed her softly on the cheek. Arlette exhaled. Brooke was next to her; that was all that mattered at the moment. "Hi, how are you?"

Arlette lowered the brownie and slid a hand along Brooke's soft cheek. She planted a delicate kiss on her lips, one that lingered just a bit. "I'm not doing well, but you're here, so that's something. I missed you."

Brooke grinned. "I missed you. Do you want to talk about it?"

"Not in the slightest bit. It's a lot. It's a lot to think about."

"Well, I'm here whenever you want to talk."

"All I want to do is hear about the paint on your fingers," Arlette said and threaded hers with Brooke's. She pulled them up and kissed each splatter of paint.

"I put on the second layer of your painting," Brooke said; each kiss seemed to make her smile wider. "It takes about a day for oil paint to dry, so it's not finished yet, but it's getting there."

"I can't wait to see it." Arlette tucked a piece of hair behind Brooke's ear. "Am I allowed to come to your exhibit?"

Brooke laughed. "I think the fact that I painted you almost naked automatically gives you a ticket to my show."

"I would hope so, or that was all for nothing."

"Oh please, I think you got an amazing deal out of it," Brooke said and playfully pushed her arm. "At least, it sounded very much like you enjoyed it."

Heat slammed into Arlette. "I mean…" She almost wanted to hide from being called out, but when she thought back about how amazing that entire day had been, there was no point in even denying it when her face was that warm. "Yeah, I enjoyed it. Very much. Haven't stopped thinking about it, actually."

"Oh really?"

"Really." She guided Brooke's face closer and kissed her, slow and measured. Brooke's tongue brushing against hers reignited a tingly feeling that kept humming anytime Arlette's mind wandered back to the weekend.

"I have an idea," Brooke said and then kissed and gently sucked on the most delicious spot on Arlette's neck. Arlette closed her eyes and reveled in how Brooke's neck kisses were powerful enough to dilute all the stresses, anger, and worry from the day. Yup, she needed to bottle this feeling and save it as a magical elixir she could store in her medicine drawer. "If you want to forget about your day, that is."

Arlette moaned softly as Brooke kissed her neck. "I would love to forget about this day."

Brooke slid a hand under Arlette's sweatpants until she reached Arlette's folds, discovering her lack of underwear. "Seems like you're all ready."

Arlette looked down and smirked. "Underwear is restricting."

Brooke pressed a thumb on her clit. Her breath hitched, and her head rested on the back of the couch. "Well, just lie here and let me help you forget." Brooke withdrew her hand and twisted her hair up into a messy bun on top of her head.

Arlette gulped at the universal sign. She was conditioned to get even more aroused whenever a woman looked at her with hungry eyes while putting her hair in a bun. Brooke dropped to the floor and tugged Arlette's sweatpants down. She discarded them and stared at Arlette's center like it was a destination she was desperate to get to. She grazed her fingertips up and down Arlette's legs and then teased her clit with one thumb. Arlette sank into the couch, feeling herself become wetter at Brooke's touch. God, Brooke was so sexy between her legs, eyeing her like she had the strongest urge to taste her again. Brooke put her mouth there, and Arlette gasped.

Brooke had been quick to learn all the ways to move, suck, and lick Arlette to get her to completely lose herself. With those insistent strokes driving her, all Arlette could focus on were the wonderful sensations firing from her center and traveling up her body and down her legs. Arlette circled her hips, searching for that perfect release that would finally push her over the edge. The orgasm rippled through her. She moaned as she clutched a couch pillow, and out came all the frustrations that had gathered inside her since the last time Brooke had gone down on her.

Fuck, that was exactly what she'd needed. The next thing she needed was Brooke.

They migrated to the bedroom, and Arlette pushed Brooke onto the bed and was quick to return the favor. Brooke threaded her hands in Arlette's hair and steered her to the spots she wanted Arlette to pay attention to. She tasted like something Arlette had always craved and sounded like her favorite song. Her sexy cries filled the bedroom, sending another rush of warmth between Arlette's legs just from hearing how fucking sexy she sounded when she came.

"This was a genius idea," Arlette said as she cuddled Brooke and kissed her neck.

"Dean's list every year, remember?" Brooke said through fragmented exhales.

When they recouped their energy, they watched an episode of *Jeopardy!*, ordered Thai and, while waiting for the delivery, jumped back in bed for another round. Arlette donated clothes for Brooke to sleep in. Then they cuddled into each other, taking turns rubbing each other's arms and hair while talking about everything, anything, and nothing.

She spooned Brooke to sleep and smiled as Brooke twitched in her arms. Tiredness weighed heavy on her eyelids, and Arlette was thankful that Brooke had helped detangle all her worries, so she didn't have to worry about frayed bouts of sleep. Instead, she drifted off, feeling half as light as she had when her day had started.

She woke up to the sound of her phone going off and demanding knocks from her front door. She shot straight up, her heart pounding in her chest, and her pulse racing.

Brooke sat up. "What the hell is that?" she asked in a groggy voice.

Arlette looked at her phone and noticed it was almost six a.m., and Jacquelyn's name took over her phone. "Hello?" Arlette asked in her half-asleep voice.

"Arlette, answer your door."

She got out of bed and sluggishly walked through the living room to the front door. "It's fucking six a.m. What's going on?"

When she opened her door, she found Jacquelyn dressed in maternity yoga pants, a Navy T-shirt, and with her dark hair thrown up in a messy bun. Her purse was slung over her shoulder, and her keys dangled in her hands.

"Arlette, get dressed," Jacquelyn said in a low, worried tone that smacked the residual tiredness out of Arlette's eyes. "Grandpa's in the hospital."

And just like that, Arlette's whole world went fuzzy.

CHAPTER THIRTEEN

Fluorescent lighting and the stench of disinfectant filled the long hospital hallways. As Arlette and Jacquelyn wandered toward the waiting room, a haze warped Arlette's vision. She wondered if it was from her body equalizing to the possibility of a new future: life without her grandpa. She knew that her time with him was borrowed. She'd seen it in the way he'd slowed down over the last several months. She could feel memories becoming warnings, and it soured her stomach. But it still hadn't prepared her to accept that she would eventually lose her biggest fan, her longest supporter, and her best friend. All she could hope for was more time.

While they waited for her parents to fly in from the debate, they took turns being with Grandpa Harry in his room. Arlette got to avoid Uncle Henry when he first arrived and spent an hour in the room with Jacquelyn. Grandpa Harry was asleep in bed, wires connected to his body and a nasal cannula in his nose. Even though she had seen him a few weeks ago, he already looked so different.

Arlette hoped that their connection was strong enough to will him awake. She had no idea how many more moments she would have with him. The last time she had seen him was with Brooke, and she'd thought they'd have so many more moments. She hadn't even had the chance to ask what he thought of Brooke. That would warrant a deep talk, either on the boat dock or in his study with a glass of scotch, Arlette in the leather chair next to the bar holding the crystal decanters of liquor and Grandpa Harry at his desk.

But instead of having that talk and seeing the grin he always wore when they gossiped, he stayed asleep, and the heart rate monitor replaced the ticking of the clock on his desk.

After their hour, Jacquelyn and Arlette headed back to the waiting room where Christian and Charlotte sat next to their parents, and Ron, Angela, and Sabrina McKay filled the once-empty seats.

Arlette's stomach bottomed out.

Her cousins headed down the long hallway to Grandpa Harry's room, leaving Jacquelyn and Arlette stuck waiting with Uncle Henry for the first time since the House vote, and the McKays.

The hospital waiting room chair wasn't comfortable when it was less crowded, but now as Arlette sat in the only empty seat next to Sabrina and Jacquelyn, it felt like sitting on asphalt on a hot August afternoon. She could feel every layer of problems pushing down on her. The conversation she'd just had with Grandpa Harry. The bill that Uncle Henry had helped kill. Her ex-girlfriend sitting an inch away from her. Knowing she'd see her father in a few hours after not speaking to him for a month.

The only relief she had was Jacquelyn. She wished Brooke was there. Brooke had offered to come, and God, did Arlette want her there, but then she would have had to explain her to the entire family. The hospital wasn't the place or time.

"I'm really sorry about Gramps," Sabrina whispered to Arlette after a few minutes of silence.

Arlette kept her eyes on the stack of magazines on the coffee table. "Thank you."

Another minute of silence.

"Do you want to go on a walk? It's a bit stuffy in here."

Arlette was so desperate for any kind of relief that she nodded and led them out of the waiting room. Taking a walk with her ex-girlfriend was a much better deal than being crammed in a small room with everyone who had their own opinions about her.

They headed outside and started doing a lap around the hospital. Arlette inhaled deep breaths of mid-September air. Even though it was humid and felt more like an early August afternoon, she hoped the fresh air would unclench the knots of nerves. She needed to free herself from the many emotions piling inside her. The anxiety of Grandpa Harry asleep in the hospital and the uncertainty if she would get one more moment with him. Their last conversation still clung to her like the sterile chemical scent now clinging to her shirt. Her worries spiraled back to yesterday and clasped on to the anger from the failed bill and the uncertainty of her future career. The anxieties of what Sabrina had to say followed them around like a shadow.

She was dangling over the edge and balancing on the last grip she had. She needed to take as many laps as she could around the hospital to walk away from that edge.

"How are you doing?" Sabrina said.

The question hit Arlette hard. She knew just how serious the situation was if Sabrina was asking that question, something she hadn't done since before they'd dated. Sabrina wasn't an emotional person, and Arlette had often sensed that she couldn't be bothered. Her life was too wrapped around her career to let anything else in.

But she was genuine now. Arlette heard it loud and clear. So she decided to embrace the comfort. She didn't want to push Sabrina away completely. She hated burning bridges, and while they were no longer together and Sabrina wasn't the right match, she still cared about her and wanted to be friendly.

"Not well," Arlette said.

Sabrina rubbed her back three times, more than she'd probably ever done in their relationship, and then took back her hand. "I'm so sorry, Arlette. I'm really hoping he pulls through."

"Me too. I just saw him a few weeks ago. He seemed fine. I just...I don't know how he suddenly took a turn." She swatted at her tears. "How have you been?"

Sabrina let out a hollow laugh. "Not well." Arlette saw the troubles in her faraway glance. "I've missed you. A lot. I've thought about us these last couple of months, and I get it. I get why you left. I got swept up in it too. Family, work, expectations."

It was the very thing they had bonded over. Sabrina was the only person who understood the pressure the family name put on her. The only difference between Sabrina and Arlette was that Sabrina went with the wind and wanted to be a part of it, and Arlette's attempt to escape it had caused a riptide in her family. But despite those differences, Arlette understood completely.

"I never meant to hurt you, and I definitely never meant for you to feel like you weren't enough," Sabrina said, finally meeting Arlette's eyes.

"I know you didn't."

Sabrina raised an eyebrow. "You do?"

"I do."

Sabrina faltered as she continued walking. "I'd love to talk…when the timing is more appropriate. Maybe over drinks or dinner or—"

Sabrina was trying, Arlette would give her that. The only problem with Sabrina's plan was that the time to try had passed long before.

"I'm open to talking," Arlette said. "But I should let you know that I'm seeing someone. Well, kind of. It's still a bit new, but it's exciting. It could very much be something."

Sabrina nodded slowly as if accepting defeat. "I just hope she makes you happy."

"She does."

Sabrina looked over and seemed to force a smile. "I'm glad."

They didn't say much on the rest of the walk. They did two more silent laps around the hospital before heading back into the waiting room where Arlette found her parents greeting everyone.

She hadn't seen their dad in a month, and it wasn't until that moment Arlette recognized the terrified look in his eyes; it matched exactly how she felt. It was another reminder of how similar they were, despite all their differences. Her dad's eyes resonated with pain and sadness, breaking the residual hurt he'd caused her. Apparently, it didn't matter how distant they had been, not only the past few months but for most of Arlette's life. Her heart burst open as she wrapped her arms around him tightly and buried her face in his blue dress shirt. When he placed a gentle hand on the back of her head, she broke. She cried into his chest and felt his tight, protective embrace catch her mid-fall. He swaddled her and held her close. Something in that hug reassured her that the supportive dad she'd once known was still alive somewhere in him.

When she really needed him, he was there. It was translated fluently in that embrace.

She pulled away and swiped at her eyes. He placed both hands on her shoulders. "Hi, hon," he said and forced a weak smile.

"Hi, Dad."

"Have you seen him yet?"

She nodded. "I did, but he was asleep."

"He's up, you know," Charlotte said from behind.

Arlette's heart sped up. "Really?"

"Really."

Arlette faced her dad. "You go ahead."

He gave her a thankful smile, patted her shoulder, and walked down the hallway, holding her mom's hand.

Arlette settled back into her seat in between Jacquelyn and Sabrina. She closed her eyes, pinched her temples, and tried to tame a budding sharp headache. The emotions were rising in her and tasted like bile in her throat. She thought that if she closed her eyes hard enough, she would find herself in bed, wrapped up in Brooke, the last scene she'd been immersed in before Jacquelyn's pounding on the front door. Arlette squeezed and then squeezed some more, and when she opened her eyes, she was still surrounded by blue-gray hospital walls, fluorescent lighting, disinfectant that smelled stronger with each passing hour, and Uncle Henry.

After twenty minutes, her parents walked back out. Everyone looked up, eager to hear an update.

"He's awake and talking," her dad said. "So hopefully, that means something." He eyed Arlette. "He specifically asked for you. How about you go back and see him?"

She wasted no time speed walking to his room. The chemical smell and stale air were even more potent in there. His eyes were open, and she followed his stare to the empty seat beside the bed. She wondered if it was the god-awful fluorescent lighting that made him seem ten years older. His skin was more translucent and wrinkled, the age spots darker on his arms and face. Some spots she had memorized over the years, and some she was discovering for the first time.

"Don't look so scared," Grandpa Harry said and inhaled a gulp of air. It sounded like he struggled to get the words out, as if each one grated along his throat.

"How can I not be scared?"

"Is this not a good look on me?"

She wanted to tell him his jokes were inappropriate, but she clung to the fact that, despite his shortness of breath, he hadn't lost his sense of humor. She desperately hoped that meant he would be coming home.

His hospital alert bracelet dangled as he extended his arm. Arlette clasped his hand in both of hers. His once-firm grip had weakened to a little squeeze. Tears brimmed in her eyes at how weak he was. She'd seen him slow down over the last two years, but it had never felt more apparent than it did now.

"Arlette?" he said and followed it with a cough. "That heart of yours...everything you have to offer the world...use it," he said, taking his time with each word. "Stop hiding behind expectations."

"I'll use it, Gramps. I promise. I'm ready to change course."

"I'm glad. Go do something that soothes you...find a woman who soothes you." His grip hardened just a little more.

Arlette considered her next words. She didn't want to gamble with time and decided to open her heart completely to her grandpa. "You remember when we first smoked those cigars on the boat dock and how I told you I was upset because I ruined things with a girl?"

"I do."

"Brooklyn's the girl."

He offered her a weak smile. "Do you feel it? In your chest? With Brooklyn?"

She ignored the tears falling freely down her face. Remorse for ever having swatted her feelings for Brooke away hung heavy and large in her chest, but at the same time, thinking about their last couple of weeks together inflated her with happiness.

Brooke filled in all the cracks Arlette had collected over time. Brooke made her whole. Her unconditional love threaded Arlette's broken pieces back together. Her feelings ran deep, the deepest they'd ever traveled. Brooke made her feel everything she'd ever wanted to feel and then some.

"I do," Arlette said and wiped away the pesky tears. "I feel it in my chest. All over, even when she's not around."

He smiled. "She feels the same way about you. I saw it in her eyes."

"You did?"

He nodded and patted her hand weakly. "It was clear as day. I like her a lot. Make sure you don't lose her this second time around."

"I don't plan on it."

"Good. I hope you hold on to that feeling and keep it. You'll find that it's one of the greatest feelings in the world." He took a second to breathe. "I love you, Arlette."

A cry escaped her. She brought their intertwined hands to her face and kissed his. He cleared her damp cheek with his fingers. "I love you too, Gramps. You've been my best friend my whole life."

"You've been mine for twenty-seven wonderful years."

She sat with him until it was time to let him have a word with Christian and Charlotte. She didn't want to let go of his hand, worried that her absence would make him decline, but she knew she had to for the rest of her family to get their moments in with him.

The Adairs took turns visiting with him for the next two days, but his strength waned each day. His ability to talk weakened. The amount of time he was awake thinned. He was fading away, and Arlette couldn't help but wonder where he was fading to. She hoped he was searching for Grandma Dot, the missing piece to his puzzle. At least, she kept telling herself that as his breathing slowed. She hoped that as he slipped away from this life, he was about to start another life with her grandma. She hadn't ever been religious or spiritual, but she desperately hoped that whatever happened after death, it involved people reuniting with their soulmates, that maybe he wasn't necessarily leaving his family. Maybe he was just trying to find the love of his life, and together, they would start a new life somewhere in the universe.

After three days in the hospital, Grandpa Harry died in his sleep, surrounded by his entire family.

❖

When Brooke got the text from Arlette about Grandpa Harry's passing, her heart sank. She couldn't believe that it had been just weeks since she'd spent the evening with him, and now he was gone.

She offered to send food, borrow a car to drive out to St. Michaels, volunteered to talk whenever Arlette needed, even if it was three a.m. Brooke hadn't seen her in a week, hadn't heard her voice, and God, she missed her. She missed all of her.

Arlette wrote back: *Thank you, but I don't think I can see anyone right now.*

Brooke felt like the pieces of their summer had been scattered everywhere, and she had no idea how to stitch them back to where they were. It felt like an anchor hanging from her chest. Arlette was pulling away, and part of Brooke couldn't help but worry that falling back into their loving patterns would also mean falling back into the complicated and messy ones. Arlette had every right to her space, Brooke kept telling herself that, but she missed her, as simple as that, and she decided to manifest all the racing thoughts into her art.

Brooke stepped out of her room one morning and found Abby and Stephen sitting on the couch with bottles of champagne and orange juice on the table.

"Voilà," Stephen sang and gestured to the coffee table like a model on a TV show.

"What's all of this?" Brooke asked.

"It's to cheer you up," Stephen said. "Mimosas and I've curated a playlist of Taylor Swift songs."

Brooke lifted a skeptical brow. "Why?"

"Because you've been sad for a week," Abby said. "Champagne for breakfast should cheer you up, right? It certainly cheered me up." Abby and Stephen clinked their plastic flutes together.

"Is this the start of my heartbreak party or something?" she asked. Abby and Stephen exchanged a glance. She suppressed an annoyed eye roll. "I'm not heartbroken. I'm sad for Arlette. Her grandpa just died, and he was her everything. Two very different things. Thanks, but I've got work to do. I'm going to the studio. I'll be back late."

She appreciated her friends looking out for her, but she was still annoyed that they took Arlette's grieving as something horrible she was doing to Brooke. She snatched her keys from the kitchen table and left, leaving more mimosas for Abby and Stephen.

Once Brooke made it to the studio, she locked herself in, put her headphones on, and let her mind wander all over the canvas. She went through every single emotion she'd collected over the last few months as if they were old documents she had to sort through, deciding which to keep and which to discard.

Sometimes, she knew exactly what she wanted to paint because she had so much inspiration that it splashed out on the walls of her mind. Other times, she dove in blindly. Those times, her thoughts spun like an endless whirlpool that dripped onto the canvas. Once upon a time, she had allowed herself to get caught up in the tide and get sucked under. Up until recently, she worried that she would fall back in if things became too much. The black and blue art from her depressed years after college were hidden in her studio behind other paintings she

THE HUES OF ME AND YOU

had yet to sell, tucked away like a stack of boxes underneath a sheet. Just because she couldn't see them didn't mean she hadn't noticed the strong presence in the corner. Back then, when she'd found a way to translate the heartbreak into art, she had let her mind wander, leaving strokes of oil paint in its path. She didn't necessarily know where she'd been going with it until each inch of the fabric had been coated. It was a more extravagant form of doodling, just with more room to travel aimlessly. What she'd created was abstract art of blacks, dark blues, and the occasional lighter hues breaking up the darkness.

Just like back then, Brooke allowed her mind and heart to spill onto the canvas. She sketched the outline and immediately colored it. She mindlessly mixed different shades of pale blues and whites before streaking the brush across them. She repeated this until she felt the clenching in her chest loosen. Once lightness filled her rib cage, she added a splash of chartreuse and lowered her headphones.

She stepped back from the easel and stood in her usual observational spot. Two women wrapped around one another, naked under bedsheets made in coral paint. One had her head in the crook of the other's arm, only the side of her face showing, a pop of chartreuse detailing her eye.

Brooke didn't need any models for this one. The image in her head was vivid enough for her to grasp every detail. The feelings that had been accumulating in her chest were tangible enough to transform into a vivid memory.

She walked over to the paintings propped against the brick wall, searching for the black and blue ones from five years prior. When she found them, she lined them up and alternated glances between them and the one she had just created. While the ones from five years ago were dark, visually and emotionally, when she looked at the one she had just created, it eased the heaviness the old ones possessed. She focused on the contrasting green and how mesmerizing it was against the pale hues. This one had sadness in it, but there was also hope and comfort. The woman's eyes matched Arlette's, and Brooke longed so much to be the one holding her like that.

It hit her all at once. While comparing the new piece with the old, emotions washed over her again, so many that she needed to take a seat, which reminded her of the salacious memory Arlette had forever pinned to that chair.

Arlette was everywhere.

Fuck, Brooke had done it again. She knew exactly what the continuous dropping feeling in her chest was. She had just painted it. She was falling for Arlette.

Again.

Brooke woke up the next morning to her phone ringing. When she saw Arlette's name, she shot straight up, rubbed the grogginess out of her eyes, and answered.

"Hey, Brooklyn," she said with sadness in her tone that Brooke could tell she was trying to fight against.

"Arlette? Hi, how are you?" She sat back against the pillow.

"Struggling. It's kind of silly how debilitating it is. Like, he was eighty-six. I knew he wasn't going to live forever. So why does it hurt so much?"

"Because he was your grandpa. He was your best friend."

"I thought I was going to have more time with him. I mean, we'd just seen him."

"I know. I keep thinking about that too."

Arlette exhaled what sounded like a million thoughts. "His funeral is Friday. It's going to be at the National Cathedral, and he's going to be buried in Arlington. I...um...would it be too much to ask you to come with me?"

For the first time since she'd last seen Arlette, the clenching in her chest relieved. Arlette wanted Brooke there as much as Brooke wanted to be there for her.

"What? No, not at all."

"It's going to be a whole thing. Like, presidents, vice presidents, and cameras, so I completely understand if you don't want to go. It's giving me anxiety too, but I'm allowed to bring someone, and I thought—"

"Arlette, do you want me to be there?"

She hesitated. "I do. I...um...I really need you."

"Then I'll be there. I promise."

Grandpa Harry's funeral was a bigger who's who of DC than Marc Adair's campaign launch party at the Adair Estate. Since Brooke wasn't part of the family, she camouflaged herself toward the back of the cathedral, lost in the sea of formal black attire. She watched as former presidents, vice presidents, and the current president walked down the aisle to their spots up front. She'd even seen all the Democratic nominees sitting several rows back, which seemed a little odd, given they had just picked Marc Adair apart a week and a half ago at the second Democratic debate. She even spotted Teresa Rosario, along with other recognizable representatives and senators, as well as the McKays.

The organ started playing, the melancholy sounds filling the cathedral. The grandkids were the first family members to walk down the aisle. All the cousins wore their formal Navy dress whites with Arlette as the only one in a black dress. It was the first time she'd seen Arlette in ten days, and the look of raw grief on her face sent a pang of hurt through Brooke. She willed the service to speed up so she could hold Arlette and ease as much pain as she could.

After the service, Brooke met Arlette outside where Jacquelyn, her husband, and another young man and woman—who Brooke assumed were cousins—huddled around a black Escalade. When Arlette looked up, she offered Brooke a half-smile. She ditched her family and met Brooke halfway. Brooke wasted zero time opening her arms and bringing Arlette in. Arlette held her tightly, and she reacquainted herself with the soft scent of sandalwood that she had desperately missed. She sank into the hug, closed her eyes, and relished Arlette in her arms.

"God, I've wanted to do this for the last ten days," Brooke whispered in her ear. When she opened her eyes, she noticed Arlette's sister and cousins eyeing them with faint curves around the edges of their mouths, as if they were intrigued by what was unfolding in front of them. She turned to her right and found Sabrina McKay eyeing her as well from next to Uncle Henry and his wife.

Brooke quickly took her eyes off their spectators and back to safety from the crowd of judgment. She broke the hug and looked at those beautiful eyes she'd missed so much. They glistened in the sun, residual tears from a service that had been a wonderful tribute to a wonderful man, father, grandfather, and leader. "How are you doing?" Brooke asked. "It was a beautiful service."

Arlette looked around, and Brooke followed, taking in each camera catching the funeral for national TV and the rest of the Adairs and the McKays closely watching. Arlette placed her hands on Brooke's shoulders and spun them around so their backs faced everyone. "I'm better now that you're here. I'm sorry about everyone staring."

Brooke could feel the eyes piercing her back. "They knew I was coming, right?"

"My parents and sister did. Don't worry, the rest will get over it. I promise to treat you to some very needed mimosas when we have lunch at Jackie's. Grandpa Harry would have insisted you have one. It's the only way to tolerate Uncle Henry." The little tweak of a smile from her was comforting. "You want to head to the car?" Arlette turned and stared at where her family was watching them as if they were the only source of entertainment they'd seen in days. She leaned in close. "Ignore them. They're all nosy."

She placed a hand on Brooke's back, shifting them back to where they'd been before they'd lost Grandpa Harry. Her hand always felt so perfect there.

She guided Brooke over to the Escalade. "This is Brooklyn. Brooklyn, this is everyone. My cousins, Christian and Charlotte." Right as Charlotte opened her mouth, Arlette said, "We will not be taking questions at this time."

A man in a suit opened the door and gestured for them to get in. Brooke had never had a man in a suit help her inside a car before, but there was a first time for everything. She was the first to crawl into the back, and even though they had the entire seat, Arlette sat close to her in the middle, while Jacquelyn and her husband took up the middle row.

Once their Escalade pulled out to follow the others in the procession, Arlette pulled Brooke's hand into her lap and held it right where their legs touched. "Thank you for being here. It means a lot to me," she said against Brooke's ear.

Brooke squeezed her hand. Arlette's lips were coated in dark purple lipstick that Brooke wished she could kiss to let her know how much she had missed her. Instead, she leaned in to whisper, "I'd do anything for you, you know that, right?" When she pulled away, the longing in Arlette's eyes cut her deeply, as if what she'd said was brand-new information.

But it seemed to settle quickly as Arlette's eyes softened. "I'd do anything for you too," she whispered. "I really want you to know that."

The words landed in Brooke and blossomed. They exchanged a

weighty stare, and something passed between them. She wondered if Arlette felt it too because she smiled, squeezed Brooke's hand, and rested her head against the back of the seat, her fingers not once leaving Brooke's.

The rest of the ride to Arlington was silent, and it continued that way while the Navy soldiers brought over the casket. Two of them folded the American flag and presented it to Marc while the military band played taps. Brooke looked at Arlette again, checking on her, and saw tears in her eyes. Once the twenty-one-gun salute shot into the air, Arlette grabbed her hand and didn't let go.

The funeral ended after the salute, and the family took the Escalades back to Capitol Hill, where Jacquelyn and Ben were hosting lunch. Brooke was extremely nervous. She had no idea what the rest of the family thought about her presence at such an important and emotional event. Given by their constant stares outside the National Cathedral, some were definitely curious. No one who was just a friend showed up to a nationally televised funeral.

Once inside her sister's townhouse, Arlette headed straight for the kitchen table and the mimosa supplies. She nudged Brooke's arm and handed her a flute. "You're going to need this," she said softly. Her eyes were red and puffy, but at least there was a hint of a smile on her face. "Don't worry. I plan on heading downstairs in, like, an hour. That's a reasonable amount of family time, right?"

Right as Brooke opened her mouth to answer, Arlette's mom made her way over, a friendly smile in place. "You must be Brooklyn," she said, a knowing tone ringing through her voice. Kathryn Adair could very well be the next First Lady, and here she was, acting like any normal mom would when meeting her daughter's…whatever the hell they were. Friend? Friends with benefits? Person she was dating? What the hell were they? "Arlette talks about you so much that I feel like we should just hug. Would that be all right?"

Brooke couldn't turn her down even if she wanted to. She nodded and allowed Kathryn to give her a warm embrace.

When Kathryn broke the hug, she held Brooke at arm's length. Her smile grew. "It's so nice to finally meet you."

"It's nice to finally meet you too."

"Thank you for being such a good sport today. I know it was probably a lot, but I also know that you being here means the world to Arlette. She was all nerves, asking if she could bring someone, and I told her, if that special someone"—Kathryn flashed a stern look at Arlette before placing the warm smile back on—"makes your day a little easier, then by all means, invite her. Just please, can you do me one favor, Brooklyn?"

"Absolutely."

"Please get her to eat something. She won't listen to me, but she might listen to you. I haven't seen her eat a full meal in the last week and a half."

"I'll try my best. I promise."

"I'm right here, Mom," Arlette said, waving as if her mom must have forgotten.

Marc Adair walked up to his wife, slipped a hand around her back, and gave a much more reserved smile to Brooke. He commanded the room, and Brooke wasn't sure if it was because he was running for president or if it was because of all the stories Arlette had told her over the years.

Either way, she was thankful for the mimosa. She took her first sip and suppressed a wince at how strong it was. It was more like champagne with a splash of orange juice, just like how they'd made drinks in college.

"This must be the famous Brooklyn," Marc Adair said in a tone slightly less excited than his wife's but still cordial. He had just buried his father, so Brooke didn't take it personally.

She straightened her back, lowered her flute to her waist, and extended her other hand. "Mr. Adair, it's very nice to meet you."

His handshake was strong, confident, and professional. When he broke contact, he let out a chuckle. "You don't need to hide that mimosa from me, Brooklyn. In fact, I'm going to ask you where you got it."

Brooke hooked a thumb at Arlette. "It was this one, right here."

"I'll get you one, Dad. Extra strong?"

"Please," he said.

"Okay." Arlette downed the rest of hers, then leaned into Brooke, "I'll be right back. I'll make it fast." The words tickled her earlobe, causing warmth to flitter across her face right in front of Arlette's parents, a very possible future President and First Lady.

She sipped her mimosa to help hide her face, also buying time to figure out something to say. She knew Marc Adair was a tough man to please. She could already tell that all the Adairs were questioning what was going on between them, maybe as much as Brooke had been questioning it herself. "I'm so sorry for your loss," she said, pushing through her discomfort. She figured trying was better than not. "I met Harry a couple of weeks ago, and he was the sweetest."

"Oh, you met him?" Kathryn said, sounding confused yet grateful, maybe that Brooke had the opportunity. Marc raised a curious brow. *Damn, Arlette really doesn't share much with her parents.*

"I did. We had dinner with him." Brooke figured being one hundred percent honest would give them a good impression of her if things ever escalated with Arlette. They exchanged a glance. "I see why Arlette speaks highly of him. I've been hearing so much about him since the beginning of college, and he certainly lived up to all the stories."

Marc Adair gave her a thin, yet friendly smile. "That's very kind of you. My father was a great man. I'll certainly miss him. The whole family will. I know Arlette will. Those two had a really special bond. It was pretty remarkable."

Arlette came back and handed them mimosas.

"Arlette, we had no idea you'd brought Brooklyn over to meet Grandpa Harry," Kathryn said.

Arlette shot a quick glance at Brooke and then turned back to her parents. It was getting incredibly warm in there. Brooke wondered if she'd said too much. "Yeah...um...he invited us over for dinner, and I wanted Brooklyn to meet him and see the place. We've been friends for so long, she practically knew Grandpa, and we thought it would be a nice getaway for a night." She tossed back a large gulp.

"I'm glad you got the chance to spend time with him," Marc Adair said. "I'm sure you'll hang on to that memory extra tight."

"I will, for sure," she said.

Just then, Uncle Henry approached, and Brooke could feel Arlette tense. He tacked on what looked like a forced smile and extended his hand. "You must be Arlette's new...friend."

How he said it was less than welcoming, but she shook his hand a little looser than Marc's to save face. "Hi, I'm Brooklyn."

"And how do you know Arlette?"

Her parents and Henry eyed them, and Brooke couldn't help but glance over to see how Arlette reacted. Her eyes widened, and her cheeks flushed. "She's...um...a good friend. We go back."

Brooke hated how she deflated at Arlette's response, even though she knew she had to say whatever she needed to prevent Uncle Henry from saying something unhinged.

"Oh yeah? Back when?"

"Before Sabrina, that's when."

Uncle Henry's eyebrows rose. "So that's really done, huh? No McKay? No politics? No Navy? Hmm." He sipped his mimosa, and his judgmental stare that flicked between Brooke and Arlette made Brooke burn in her spot.

Marc looked at him. "Henry, knock it off."

"Just pointing out the obvious, Marc."

Marc leaned in, and Brooke noticed the tight jaw as he mumbled something. She tried making out what he said. She thought she heard, "This is not the time. Stop it."

Arlette downed the rest of her mimosa. "And on that note, I'm going to head downstairs."

"Arlette—" Kathryn said.

"No, it's okay. I'm not hungry and don't really need this right now. Let's head out, Brooklyn."

Brooke gave an apologetic look to Kathryn and ignored Henry. She was happy to not be anywhere near him or the reminder of how different she was from the Adairs.

Arlette grabbed her hand and led her out the back door, circled around to the front, and snuck into her basement apartment.

Once she'd shut and locked the door, she fell on the couch and let out a long grunt of what Brooke could only assume were pent-up emotions that she had been bottling since the morning. "It's okay to strongly dislike a family member, right? Because I very much dislike my uncle."

Brooke sat next to her. "You're asking that question of someone whose dad walked out on her, so I'm going to have to say, yes, it's completely all right."

"Good. God, I'm so sorry you had to hear that."

Brooke rested her hand on Arlette's wrist and rubbed her thumb along her skin. "I'm sorry you did too. Do you want me to order some food? Your mom gave me a task, and I'm obligated to complete it."

"I'm not hungry. I'm too tired and drained and angry."

Brooke got off the couch and knelt. Arlette lifted an eyebrow.

Brooke removed Arlette's heels, tossed them aside, and massaged one foot.

Arlette exhaled and relaxed back into the couch. "Ah, that feels amazing."

Brooke had never given a foot massage. She wasn't sure what she was doing, but she was willing to figure it out for Arlette's sake. Anything to get her mind off her uncle and the grief. When she was done with the right foot, she moved to the left. "How about I draw you a bath so you can relax a bit," Brooke said. "Would you like that? I feel like you need time to relax."

Arlette nodded.

All Brooke wanted to do was take care of her. It was an urge that had strengthened more each day they spent together, and once Grandpa Harry had been admitted to the hospital, the urge had become a desire. So she filled the tub with water warm, enough to make Arlette sink into the bath and melt away some of her pain. She shopped through Arlette's selection of bath bombs and chose a lavender one to help draw out each layer of weight she'd been carrying for too long. She collected the candles scattered around the basement and positioned them along the tub. Then she called Arlette in and handed her a clean towel.

"The tub is all yours," Brooke said, gesturing to the steaming bath.

Arlette reached behind her back for the zipper to her black dress, but Brooke stopped her. Arlette lowered her hands. Brooke slowly unzipped the dress and backed away when the zipper reached the end. What she really wanted to do was plant a path of kisses from the top of Arlette's neck and down her spine to where the zipper ended on the small of her back. But she refrained. She was still so unsure of what they were, and based on how Arlette had reacted and responded to her uncle, she seemed as confused as Brooke. But now wasn't the time to figure it out. She would follow Arlette's lead and just be there to help her get back on her feet.

Arlette turned and flashed a thin smile. "Thank you, Brooklyn. For everything. For being here, dealing with my family, and my uncle. Just…thank you."

"Go relax in your bath," Brooke said and nodded toward the tub. "I'll be in the living room…if you want me to stay."

"I want you to stay."

Brooke left her to soak for as long as she needed. She decided to follow through on the favor Kathryn Adair had asked for. She ordered pizza, and by the time Arlette got out of the bath an hour later, it had arrived, smelling so delicious that Brooke's stomach grumbled its happiness.

But Arlette curled into one side of the couch underneath a blanket and muttered, "I'm not hungry."

"Come on, it smells amazing," Brooke said and took a bite. It tasted even better than it smelled. She let out a moan to hopefully get Arlette's attention. She snuck a glimpse at her, noticing that Arlette was carefully watching. "It tastes amazing too. Have one slice, please."

She put a slice on a plate and handed it to Arlette, who nibbled on half until she set it on the coffee table and laid her head on the pillow. It was better than nothing. Brooke accepted defeat for now and put the slice in the box and saved the rest in the fridge for later.

She joined Arlette underneath the blanket, and Arlette flipped around so she could rest her head in Brooke's lap. They didn't say much for the rest of the day. They only communicated through small bouts of laughter while watching *Friends*, and Brooke raked her fingers through Arlette's hair and up and down her arms. At one point, Brooke needed to go to the bathroom, but she felt Arlette's body loosening. She breathed deeply too, as if Brooke's fingertips had swept away the pain. So she couldn't just get up. As shitty as the last several weeks had been, an unexpected peace had settled over them, and it felt like a warm blanket after walking through a blistering cold night.

Arlette's dark hair pooled over the pillow and onto Brooke's lap. Slight waves coiled in her hair from the messy bun she had worn while enjoying her bath. The tips of her hair were damp, and while Brooke combed through them, she smelled the remnants of lavender wafting with each stroke.

Fuck, I'm in love with this woman.

It was the last thought she had until her eyes flew open at the sound of a soft knock on the front door. Arlette was so out of it, she didn't wake, not even when there was a second knock. She wasn't surprised that it hadn't woken her. Arlette was a sound sleeper. Brooke didn't want to get up. She knew it was a family member. She almost didn't answer because she didn't want to risk the chance of being face-to-face with Uncle Henry without Arlette awake. But something in her gut told her to answer. *It could be Kathryn or Jacquelyn.*

She slowly slipped out of her spot and guided Arlette and the pillow to the seat. When she quietly opened the front door, she was greeted by Marc Adair. He gave that thin smile, just like a few hours before, one that held grief and a bit of insecurity, as if he knew that he wasn't exactly welcome.

Shit. A presidential candidate stood in front of Brooke, and she felt severely underdressed in his daughter's jogging sweatpants and old Willard T-shirt. She wondered for a split second if he could tell those were Arlette's clothes.

She needed to make up for her lack of fashion by straightening her posture. "Mr. Adair, hi, how are you?"

He glanced over her shoulder toward where Arlette was passed out on the couch. "I'm okay. I was hoping to check in with Arlette before her mom and I headed back. She's asleep, I take it?"

"Yeah, she's out. She's exhausted."

He paused, as if searching for his next words. "Okay, I'll let her rest. I know there's been a lot on her plate recently. I just...um..." He exhaled. Was Marc Adair nervous? Whatever he was feeling, it made him less intimidating. It made him seem normal, a dad worrying about his youngest daughter. By his furrowed brows, Brooke could tell he wrestled with a few thoughts. "I'm worried about her. I...um...yeah, I'm really worried about her."

Arlette had never shied away from telling Brooke stories about how she and her dad had butted heads throughout her life. His job took up a lot of time; his upbringing and his father and grandfather's lives had shaped who he was and what he and his brother wanted and expected from their own kids and nieces and nephews. But now, Brooke saw something that she wondered if Arlette had missed all this time. Despite their differences and approaches to life, one thing was certain: Marc Adair loved his daughter. She could see it all over his face. She could feel it as he looked into the apartment to catch a glimpse of her. Brooke's heart swelled, envious of the love she could see in his eyes, a look she had never seen from her own father.

"She's having a hard time," Brooke said. "And I think the last thing she needed was that comment."

Marc rubbed his forehead. "I know, and I agree. I'm very sorry about that, Brooklyn. My brother...well...he's a bit hard too hard sometimes. I know I haven't helped, either." He shook his head. "Today was a tough day. I know she's been struggling the last two weeks." He paused again. He was always so fluent and composed on TV. He acted like how anyone would want their governor or president to act: calm, collected, intelligent, and articulate. Brooke had never expected she would witness him unravel. "Hell, things have been really hard on her the last few months."

Brooke nodded. "They have."

He pulled back as if surprised. "I hear that, recently, she's been happier, like she's starting to find herself again. At least, that was one of the last things my father told me. I haven't had the chance to see it until today, though, when she was with you, and he was right. I can't imagine what it would have been like if she didn't have someone important next to her. I'm glad you're looking out for her. She's a good one."

"Yeah, I know. She really is."

"Can you take care of her, Brooklyn?"

"Of course. That's what I'm here for."

He gave another thin smile. "Just let her know I stopped by, and I would like to talk. I'll check in a bit later. It was nice meeting you. Thank you, again, for looking after my baby girl. Take care."

Once he walked up the steps, Brooke closed the door and rested her head against it, stealing another peek at the woman she was in love with sleeping peacefully on the couch.

CHAPTER FOURTEEN

Arlette studied the backyard of the Adair Estate. It had only been two weeks since Grandpa Harry had died, but she felt him everywhere on the property.

She wandered to the boat dock and sat in an Adirondack chair, wondering if she could feel him sitting next to her. The once enjoyable peace and quiet was too silent. She didn't want to hear every wave lapping at the dock or the different number of birds chirping in the maple tree. She couldn't help but wonder if Grandpa Harry had taken a piece out of the scenic backyard, and that would be all she could focus on moving forward. That missing piece, smack-dab in the middle of something that was once beautiful and complete. It still was beautiful, but without her grandpa, the beauty had faded like paint in the sun.

She wished she felt him next to her. She remembered telling Brooke a month ago that there wasn't a single ghost on the property, and that she was safe from any haunting. But Arlette wanted to feel his presence so much. Maybe over time, she would feel him everywhere, but that moment wasn't it.

She headed inside the house where the rest of the family had started sorting through Grandpa Harry's things, figuring out which they wanted to keep as family treasures and which to sell in the estate sale. Her dad had texted her the day after the funeral, telling her that if she had anything special she wanted to keep, she should stop by.

Inside, the home was disheveled, with boxes and the organized chaos of different piles of items dispersed throughout the first floor. She stopped inside Grandpa Harry's study where she knew her keepsakes would be: Grandpa Harry's burl wood humidor and his crystal decanters.

That was where she found her dad, sitting in the leather desk chair and going through papers scattered all over the desk.

He looked up, gave her a weak smile that couldn't reach his eyes. Not with the bags underneath, at least. Seeing him going through this was just as painful as losing her grandpa. She and her dad might not have seen eye to eye on a lot of things over the course of her life, but she'd never stopped loving him and wanting the world for him.

"Hey, hon," he said and lowered a stack of papers. "How are you doing?"

She stepped inside. It felt like a distorted version of a room that was familiar and also one she'd never seen before. It still smelled like cigars, books, and whiskey, three things that would forever remind her of him. A bunch of cardboard boxes littered the hardwood floor around his desk.

She shrugged. "As good as one can be. This whole place just seems…empty and weird."

"I know. It's going to take a lot of getting used to. I remember it feeling like this when Great-Grandpa Charles died. But Grandpa Harry eventually made his own memories here, and your mom and I will too. Soon, Jackie and Ben's little one will be scampering all over the place, and she'll help restock everything we lost."

Arlette took a seat in the leather chair next to the bar with the crystal decanters. Even Grandpa Harry's whiskey, scotch, and bourbon were still inside. She was half tempted to pour a glass to help her through the conversation, and if it wasn't for the fact that she planned on driving back to DC that night, she would have helped herself.

"So…I hear you wanted to talk to me? At least, that's what Brooklyn said the other day when you stopped by."

"Yeah, I did," he said and rubbed his temples. "I just wanted to check in, see how you were doing with everything."

"I'll find my way."

He gave her a thin smile. "You always do, Arlette."

Something oddly heavy suffused the room. It was more than just Grandpa Harry's absence and the unresolved tension she and her father needed to address eventually. Something was going on inside her father's head. He seemed utterly defeated, in more ways than one, but she couldn't quite figure out the reasoning, besides mourning his father.

"I want to tell you something," he said. "I think it's important that you hear it first."

She frowned. "What is it?"

"This isn't an easy decision. I've thought about it very long and hard, and I'm still struggling with accepting it, but my gut tells me that it's the right thing to do."

Okay, now he was officially scaring her. "What's going on?"

He met her eyes. "I'm going to drop out of the race."

Her chest plummeted. "What? Why?"

"For many reasons, hon," he said, the defeat the loudest she had ever heard.

She had no idea what to expect. Maybe something like, he had heard she was quitting her job or something about Grandpa Harry. She'd never expected him to drop out of the presidential race. It was his lifelong dream. He'd worked so hard to be able to eventually get to the point where he could run for president, and while Arlette had her own concerns about privacy, she still wanted that for her dad.

"Dad, you can't drop out," she said, her heart picking up speed. "You just announced it. You're on top in the polls right now. Your campaign is on fire—"

"I know that, hon. I know. I said it wasn't an easy decision. It's probably the hardest decision I've ever had to make, but I think it's the right one."

"How is it the right one? This is what you've always wanted to do."

He gave a thin smile. "There are many things I wanted to do, and I feel like I'm failing at those."

She leaned back in her seat. "Like what?"

He faltered for a couple of moments, each tick from Grandpa Harry's analog desk clock adding more panic behind Arlette's sternum. "I had a long talk with my father a few days before he was in the hospital. We were out on the back porch, talking about regrets and how he couldn't think of a single one."

He looked at the picture on the opposite side to the clock. Though Arlette couldn't see it, she knew it was the family photo they'd taken six years back at the family crab feast when he had just turned eighty. It felt like a million lifetimes ago.

"My father said he loved his wife, had a successful sixty-four-year-long marriage with her. He had a family and tried to form a relationship with every one of his kids, grandkids, and their significant others. He specifically said that he was grateful to have found an unlikely companionship with two of his granddaughters, you and Jackie. He said he felt like he struck gold with you two."

Arlette thought she had cried enough the last several weeks. Between the bill failing and Grandpa Harry, she'd thought there was nothing left. But there she was, feeling the all too-familiar-stinging in her eyes and finally noticing how her nostrils flared when she tried to swallow the cries back, just like Brooke had pointed out.

"He asked if I was proud of my relationships with my family, and I reflected a lot on it and what had transpired between us recently, and I said no, I couldn't say the same thing. He asked if I knew that you were unhappy with your job, asked if I knew that you worried about my not accepting you for who you were, and then he asked if I knew that you had someone in your life that you looked at like she hung the moon, and I was speechless because I didn't know any of that."

She swiped at her eyes. "You knew some of that, Dad. I told you I didn't want to go into politics when I was a teen."

"Hon, I thought you'd grown out of it."

"I didn't. I didn't join the Navy because I had no interest in being in the military. I went to Willard because it was a place I thought I could finally be myself at, and yes, my internships with the EPA and UN were two internships I wanted to do, and working for Teresa Rosario was amazing, but I realized that I'd tried fitting into this mold of what I thought you wanted me to be. We'd gotten close over the last few years—"

"We have," he said, nodding.

She looked at her lap, picking her cuticles with her thumb. She felt silly for considering her next question, but it was one she needed the answer to so she could hear if she needed to hold on to it or let it go. "Was that because I had a job on the Hill and was dating Sabrina? Because I can't help but feel like it was."

"That absolutely was not the case, Arlette," he said sternly.

"I have a job interview next week. It's an animal welfare nonprofit, Paw Aid. I'd be doing policy work and campaigning but at the community and grassroots level. It's a big change, but I know I can do it. I'm actually really excited for it."

He thinned his lips and slowly nodded. "I just want you to have a good job that you love and that makes you excited to wake up every day. I've realized now that I didn't do a good job with that, and that's why I'm pulling out of the race."

"You don't have to pull out because of that—"

He raised his hand. "I do because I want to be present. I want to be with my family and be that reliable support system that I apparently haven't been. I love that we've gotten closer, Arlette. But I'm very envious that my father had a special relationship with you. I've given you the impression that my love is conditional for all these years, and that's my own damn fault, and I'm very sorry."

She wiped a tear away, but one immediately fell in its place. All the weight she'd been carrying on her shoulders throughout her childhood began to lift the more her father apologized. She could hear the remorse in his tone and see regret sparkling in his eyes. She knew that it would take time and actions for her dad to completely erase the hurt he'd caused her over the years, but this was a first step, one Arlette was willing to take alongside him.

"My first grandchild is coming in two weeks," he said with a twinge of a smile. "I want to be an amazing grandpa to her, like how my father was to you. I can't take back the feelings I've caused you, Arlette, but I can start. I can start being that support system for you, Jackie, and my granddaughter. I don't see how I can be the father or grandfather I want to be if I stay in the race. Now isn't the right time. Maybe in another four or eight years, but not right now. I'm proud of you, Arlette. I know I haven't shown it, but I'm so incredibly proud of you for always being your own person, going to the college you wanted to go to, all the passion you have in your heart. I'm so proud of you, and so is your mother, so was your grandfather, and you should be proud of yourself too."

It was one of the only times he'd said that he was proud of her. She blinked, breaking the tears that fell down her face. "Really?"

He gave her a thin smile. "Really. I once had dreams for you kids that matched too closely to my own, and that's not fair to the two of you. I want you to take the job that makes you feel happy. I want you to be with a woman who makes you feel loved. As much as I wished you and Sabrina had worked out, I'm sorry that you didn't find that in her."

She shrugged. "It happens. I hope she finds someone who makes everything worth it."

"Have you?"

"Have I what?"

"Have you found someone who makes everything worth it? Grandpa Harry said you found someone who looks at you like you hung the moon, and I have a strong feeling that person is Brooklyn."

The mention of her name elicited a rush in her chest, as if she was free-falling. It must have been transparent on her face because he grinned and opened the top drawer of the desk. He pulled out a small black velvet box. Arlette fixated on it, knowing there was only one thing that lived inside a box that size.

"Um, what's that?" she asked. He opened the box to reveal a ring. A white gold band, a square diamond in the middle and two round diamonds on the side. She recognized the ring, and knowing who it belonged to made her heart drop. "Is that Grandma's ring?"

He nodded. "It is. After your grandpa asked if I knew about the new woman in your life, he said he wanted you to have this ring and told me you would appreciate it the most."

He slid the box over. She plucked the ring out and studied it. While the ring needed to be polished and touched up from the sixty-four years' worth of memories and love that came with it, it was still breathtakingly gorgeous. Tears pooled in her eyes because of how honored she was to be given her grandma's wedding ring. It might have been just a ring, but it was the very thing that symbolized the kind of love Arlette desperately wanted for herself.

"You know what you're supposed to do with that ring, right?" her dad asked.

She wiped away a tear. "I know exactly what I'm supposed to do with it."

"Hearing how my father described you and Brooklyn, watching the way you looked at each other, I see how wrong Sabrina was and how right Brooklyn is for you. It explains why Grandpa Harry was very adamant about giving you this, and this was before he went to the hospital."

She twirled the ring between her fingers. "I care about her more than anything. She's…she's everything to me. She's the closest friend I've ever had outside of Grandpa and Jackie."

"I think that means something, don't you?"

She looked up and noticed his genuine smile. He'd given it to her whenever he'd used to speak about her and Sabrina, and it pleasantly tugged inside her that Brooke was the reason for it now. "Absolutely," she said.

He stood and walked around the desk. He placed his strong hand on her shoulder. "Hold on to this ring, and when the time is right, give it to the woman who makes you the happiest, the woman you want to spend the rest of your life with."

"I will, Dad. Thank you."

She stood, and his grip tightened. His eyes glazed with a mixture of pain, regret, and a little bit of hope. "I love you, Arlette."

"I love you too, Dad."

She closed her fist around the ring, wrapped her arms around her dad, and for the first time in a long time, there was more of an understanding tying them together.

She walked into the kitchen to grab some packing supplies for the humidor and the decanters. On her walk over, she got lost in observing the ring. When she glanced up, she spotted Uncle Henry packing china in Bubble Wrap right next to the empty boxes and all the packing supplies. She suppressed an eye roll at his sudden appearance.

"Oh, hi, I didn't know you were going to be here," he said.

"I'm sorry for the terrible surprise."

He looked at her and then the box in her hands. "What's that?"

She closed the box and tucked it in her back jeans pocket. "An heirloom."

"Is that Grandma Dot's ring?"

She didn't say anything. Instead, she collected a box and some Bubble Wrap and headed out of the kitchen.

"You broke up with Sabrina two and a half months ago and now you're going to propose to someone else? To who? The artist?"

Arlette turned back around. "Excuse me?" She had no idea how Uncle Henry knew anything about Brooklyn, but it didn't matter at that exact moment. "You know what? I'm so tired of this."

"I think we're all tired, Arlette. Tired of making public appearances where you're the only one not in a Navy uniform. Tired of hearing about how you left the Hill because the bill didn't go your way."

"You really need to let the Navy thing go, Uncle Henry. It's been almost ten years. You know, I'm a good person. I haven't done anything wrong except try to be myself. I've gone against what I was taught from a young age about what I should do with my life, and I've created a life for myself that I'm proud of. I'm authentic and passionate, and I'm a good person who works hard, and that's something that should be more admirable than a Navy uniform or a job title. I might not live up to your expectations, but I really don't need your approval, do I? I don't care about it anymore, quite honestly. Grandpa Harry was proud of me, and I'm proud of me for sticking true to my morals and beliefs. So I'm going to take this," Arlette said and wiggled the ring box, "and leave."

She turned her back on his shocked expression, packed up the humidor and decanter, and got the hell out of the house.

She drove back to DC, proud that she'd finally stood up to Uncle Henry. For so long, she'd let her father and uncle's expectations warp her idea of what it meant to be successful. She'd taken stock of her life over the last few weeks, and even though her life was still settling into place like the autumn leaves outside, she was looking forward to jumping in the pile. She had an exciting job prospect, and God, did she want that job. She still ruminated over her father's words of approval that she'd longed to hear so much. She was about to be an aunt, and she would make sure that her niece was loved and accepted, no matter what she wanted to pursue in life.

Though she still had to sift through bouts of grief and immense loss without Grandpa Harry, she could carry on during the hard days ahead, knowing how proud she'd made him and how much their friendship had meant to both of them.

To top it off, she had an amazing woman by her side.

Anytime she thought about the ring over the next few days, Brooke's beautiful face appeared in her mind. She was the only one Arlette could see wearing it. Part of her thought it was wild to imagine that when they were only a few months into whatever it was they were doing, but she didn't want it to end.

She smiled when the excitement zapped through her chest like a pinball. Yeah, she felt it in her chest all right. She might have never told

Brooke exactly how she felt about her, but she was ready to grab on to every aspect of her life and turn it on its head.

She wanted to be with Brooke. That ring didn't belong to anyone but her: the roommate, the artist, and the best friend, and Arlette was so in love with all three.

❖

"Oh my God, Brooke...honey," Brooke's mom said, standing in front of her five pieces hanging on the wall at the exhibit.

She was only mildly embarrassed that her mom had driven two and a half hours from Charlottesville to stare at her oil paintings of nipples and naked women. But the look of pure amazement and pride on her mom's face was something for the record books. She knew her mom would never say her art was bad, but as an artist herself—and the one person who knew probably more about art and art history than Brooke—Brooke also knew that it would be incredibly hard for her mom to mask her opinions. Her opinion mattered so much, and while seeing the joy widen her eyes and smile, Brooke felt completely filled with pride herself.

"Thanks, Mom," she said. "I'm really glad you're not appalled by my naked women paintings."

Her mom laughed and gave her a tight hug, and when she pulled back, she placed her hands on Brooke's shoulders. "Remember when we took the trip out here?"

"Did you have any idea that you would be back twenty years later to see my stuff on an art gallery wall?"

"I might not have known exactly, but it doesn't surprise me. You have talent. I've said that all these years." Her mom looked over her shoulder and smiled again at the paintings. "And you know what? I'm sure we'll be talking about this moment in another few years, when you have a whole gallery to yourself or have a piece in the Met."

"I still think that's wishful thinking, Mom, but thanks for believing in me."

"I'm pretty sure you said the same thing at your senior art show in college when I told you to just wait until the day comes when you have an exhibition. And look where we are. Really, Brooke. Look around and really take in where you are right now."

Right as she did so, her favorite pair of eyes snagged her attention. In the midst of crowds snaking through the exhibit and admiring the other nine local artists, she found Arlette with a program in hand, looking breathtaking. She wore dark skinny jeans and a black blazer over a white blouse. Simple yet classy and sexy. Arlette quickly found Brooke through the slow-moving crowd, as if Brooke's stare was the opposite magnetic pole of her own. The connection made Brooke's stomach tighten. Arlette smiled on her walk over, and she had the amazing ability to make Brooke's face heat for her mom to witness.

"Hi, Brooklyn," Arlette said and then turned to Brooke's mom.

"Mom, you remember Arlette?"

Arlette smiled. "Mrs. Dawson! It's so nice to see you again."

Brooke's mom offered her a hug. "It's nice to see you again. It's been a while."

"I know. I was hoping to see you tonight. Aren't you proud of this one?" Arlette pointed the rolled-up program at Brooke.

It hit Brooke all at once when she saw amazement sparkling in her mom's dark eyes. There were a lot of things Brooke didn't have growing up. She'd never had a father, and that had taken away so much of her childhood. She and her mom didn't have a lot of money. They'd had enough to get by, but not enough for Brooke to have a "childhood home," with her growing height marked on a door or photo albums of countless vacations all over the country. But she felt extremely wealthy when it came to a support system. It always came back to her mom… and then Arlette. The two people who made breaking into the subjective art world seem like a breeze because their support was that strong and unwavering.

"I'm incredibly proud of her," her mom said.

"Me too. She's absolutely amazing, isn't she? I always thought so." Arlette turned to the wall and stepped forward, taking in each piece in what seemed to be great detail. It was the same look Brooke saw when they admired the modern art at the museum.

She glanced over at her mom, who raised her brows in return. A mother's intuition, which meant Brooke had embarrassed herself more in that moment by probably giving massive heart eyes to Arlette. Brooke hadn't told her mom she was sleeping with anyone. There was a line she drew in the sand. Her mom didn't need to know about her sex life, and the last time her mom had asked about her dating life, she and Arlette hadn't yet slept together.

Except there was nothing about Arlette that was casual. Brooke's body lit up like a night sky on the Fourth of July anytime she was around. Those weren't casual feelings.

After the exhibit, when they'd go out to dinner, her mom would ask about her love life. She always did when they had time to catch up, and now that her mom had caught her staring at Arlette, she knew she would have to fill her in. There was no hiding it now, and frankly, Brooke was done hiding. God, she just wanted to figure out what the hell they were.

She leaned into her mom. "I'll explain later."

"You better," her mom whispered and gestured between Brooke and Arlette.

When Arlette turned, a bigger smile on her face than before, Brooke and her mom backed away from each other.

"Wow, these are…wow."

Brooke's mom smiled. "I'll let you have a moment with the artist. I'm going to do a lap. Plus, I think I see Abby over there." She pointed to Abby and Stephen walking in. Abby must have noticed them because she waved over the crowd. "I'll make them take a lap with me. That way, I can get all caught up with your life. I know that she'll be honest with me. I'll see both of you later."

When Brooke's mom left them alone, Arlette filled in the space. A light blush blossomed on her cheeks as if she was also embarrassed by Brooke's mom calling them out, "So your mom knows something," Arlette said with a smug smirk.

"Apparently. All you have to do is show up like this, all sexy and liberal with the compliments, and I'm affected instantly."

Arlette scanned her dark navy dress. "You think I'm unaffected? Brooklyn, you're stunning. So is your art, but you're…wow."

Brooke laughed at how speechless Arlette seemed to be. It was definitely an ego boost.

Arlette looked back at the paintings. "I really like this one," she said and pointed to the last one Brooke had created, the one with the chartreuse eyes.

Brooke nervously scratched the back of her head. "Um, thank

you. That one came to me out of nowhere. I just sort of painted it and thought it fit."

Arlette glanced at her. Her beautiful eyes held Brooke captive. "You just mindlessly painted this masterpiece?"

"I did."

"It looks a bit familiar," Arlette said knowingly.

Brooke shrugged. "I've had someone on my mind recently. She's occupied so many thoughts that she needed to be captured on more than one canvas."

When Brooke studied her collection, she saw Arlette in each piece, even the ones she hadn't intended on. People connected with art because it made them see and feel things that hadn't been apparent to them before. Maybe that was why Brooke was especially proud of every single painting hanging in front of her. Arlette was hidden in every stroke. She had been such an important part of Brooke for the last several months, it had spilled onto five canvases that formed a whole collection.

"You know how impressed I am by you, right?"

Arlette's compliment was so tender that Brooke forced her eyes to the ground for a moment to capture a breath. "I think I have an idea," she said softly.

Arlette slid her hand into Brooke's, and her thumb caressed Brooke's hand a couple of times before she let go. The feeling of having her so close, holding her hand on one of the most important nights of Brooke's art career, inflated so much happiness that Brooke felt like she could float away at any moment. As someone who'd grown up constantly questioning her worth, Arlette made her feel invaluable, worthy, and extremely desired. That was why their senior year of college, the hurt had cut Brooke deeper. But over the last few months, she'd not only gotten her best friend back, she'd gotten her best friend's heart, and it was more beautiful than she had ever thought. She needed to capture those feelings and secure them before it was too late.

Brooke tightened her fingers around Arlette's and pulled her closer. "Do you think we can talk after this?"

Arlette gave her a half-smile. It seemed half-worried yet half-excited about the plan. "I would like that very much. I've been meaning to ask you the same thing."

Brooke nodded at that major piece of info, her mind starting to race with all the possibilities. "I'll meet you outside then. Eight thirty?"

"I'll be there. I promise."

While Arlette continued with the rest of the exhibit, Brooke's mom brought over Abby and Stephen, who gave her big hugs, championed her art, and demanded they celebrate with Brooke's mom after they went to dinner. "We've got a bottle of wine," Abby said. "We need to properly celebrate this achievement. Are you in, Mrs. Dawson?"

"Of course," her mom said.

While Abby and Stephen took good care of her mom and continued to the rest of the exhibit, Brooke entertained all the other exhibit-goers who stopped to admire her work. Some asked about her painting process; others inquired about purchasing. For anyone interested in buying, she handed them her card and told them to contact her with any questions or inquiries. She had more interested buyers than at her June exhibit, and it made her heart race knowing she was still climbing in the art scene instead of stalling or tumbling backward. Selling the entire collection would put a large influx of money into her bank account. The pieces required more time, more supplies, and they were on larger canvases. The collection was worth almost double what the June collection was, and the fact that she had a handful of names seriously interested in purchasing put her on a higher cloud than before.

At exactly eight thirty, the crowd thinned. Brooke told her mom that she needed fifteen more minutes. She found Arlette waiting in the lobby, playing on her phone. When she looked up, Brooke's heart pounded so hard that it almost ached with worry at the possibility of revealing all her cards to Arlette only for her to take the jackpot and run.

Brooke told herself this was a different time. This wasn't five years ago. The last few months had been a journey they had been on together. There was a force pulling them together rather than apart. Brooke had no intention of going against the force. She wanted to cave into it and into Arlette. She wanted this more than she had their senior year, and she sure as hell was going to make sure Arlette understood that.

Arlette stood and met her at the front door.

"I told my mom we were just going to be a second," Brooke said. "She's in good company with Abby and Stephen. Want to walk?"

They walked through the front doors and into the early October night. A cooler wind swept through the city, reminding them that fall weather was just around the corner. Arlette snatched Brooke's hand and guided her across the street to the National Mall. They walked the dark paths in silence until they reached the back side of the National Gallery of Art. Brooke smiled at the memory and how far they had come since that night, when they'd first lowered their guard with each other.

They took a seat on a bench, hidden underneath two trees and a curtain of darkness. It shielded them from the rest of the world, allowing them the pocket of privacy Brooke needed to lay her emotions bare.

"Listen, I don't want to keep my mom waiting by slowly leading into this because honestly, I can't hold it in anymore," Brooke said.

Her heart sprinted so fast that she worried it would fly into Arlette's lap. She sucked in a deep breath. She felt the admission dancing on the tip of her tongue. The same three words she'd felt for years. Reuniting with Arlette had made those words absorb a delicious taste, much different than the taste they'd had back in college.

"I'm in love with you, Arlette. I have been since I was eighteen, and there hasn't been a moment since then where there wasn't at least an ounce of you in my mind."

Arlette bit her lip, looked at Brooke's hand, and took it in hers. Arlette rubbed her thumb over each finger. Brooke had never said those words out loud before, then again, no other woman had made her feel as much as Arlette did. Her admission knocked down her walls, leaving her the most vulnerable she'd ever felt, and that meant all her senses were heightened. She heard every second of silence, she felt Arlette's thumb caressing every nerve ending, and she saw every emotion that Arlette had bottled over the years sparkling in her eyes, shining in the streetlights.

"Right when I was losing my grip on my life, you showed up," Arlette said, still rubbing, her touch easing the rapid beating of Brooke's heart. "Our love went up when I felt my world was crumbling down. It kind of reminds me of this building," she said and nodded to the National Gallery of Art. "You were the one who saved me from falling completely, especially after my grandpa died. I've been trying so hard to find the kind of happiness I had back at Willard, before I lost you the first time, and I told myself I wouldn't lose you a second time. And while times have been really hard these last few months, I feel like

I'm the strongest I've ever been. I stood up to the things that made me uncomfortable, I quit my job, and I've been offered a new one."

Brooke's jaw dropped, and her grip tightened around Arlette's hand. "Arlette, are you serious?"

She smiled and nodded. "They offered it to me this morning. It was the other thing I wanted to tell you after your exhibit."

Brooke placed both hands on Arlette's cheeks. "Tell me everything!"

Arlette laughed, lowered Brooke's hands, and kissed them. "I mean, I was in the middle of declaring my love for you. Talking about my new job can wait. I'll tell you all about it later. I just want to say this first: I'm all in, Brooklyn. I want to do this with you. I want to be with you. I want you to be my girlfriend, and I don't ever want us to lose that part of ourselves again. I'm in love with you too. Actually, I think I've been in love with you for a while."

"Really?"

She caressed Brooke's cheek. "Really. Grandpa Harry was right. It's not as scary as I thought it would be. It's actually really amazing."

Brooke's smile rooted in place. "I feel the same way. So you want to do this? For real?"

"Absolutely," Arlette said so confidently, it turned Brooke inside out. "You're the only person who's ever made me feel like this. I tried to find it in others, and no one even came close. Without even trying, you give me everything I've been looking for and wanting."

Brooke kissed the back of Arlette's hand. "I feel the same way about you. I would absolutely love to be your girlfriend."

Brooke slid her hand against Arlette's cheek and brought her in for a kiss. Kissing Arlette for the first time as her girlfriend elicited the same rush as the first time they'd kissed back in college.

Brooke pulled away and rested her forehead against Arlette's, inhaling a deep breath of that sandalwood perfume she now got to look forward to wrapping herself up in every day. "Let's go have dinner with my mom and celebrate your new job. Do I even get a little hint before we pop the champagne?"

"It's at an animal nonprofit," Arlette said as she stood and offered her hand.

Brooke allowed Arlette to help her up. "An animal nonprofit?" She tossed her free hand over her chest. "Be still my heart."

"Oh, yeah? Does that do something for you?"

Brooke held up an invisible inch with her thumb and pointer finger. "Maybe a little bit."

They started walking back to the exhibit, hands interlocked. With Arlette as her girlfriend, Brooke planned on holding her hand for as long as possible.

The silence between them settled like a flannel blanket during the winter. They exchanged glances, smiling with shy smiles until they found Brooke's mom waiting in the lobby.

"There you are," Brooke's mom said. She glanced at their intertwined hands before looking up with a wide smile.

"Mom, this is Arlette, my girlfriend."

EPILOGUE

One and a half years later

Arlette was very impressed with her girlfriend, her girlfriend's two best friends, and her girlfriend's mother.

It was Brooke's second crab feast, and she navigated the crabs, the bowls of butter, and the crackers like a seasoned pro. She even instructed her mom, Lori, Abby, and Stephen on the proper techniques Arlette had taught her the year before. Abby caught on very quickly, but Stephen struggling and squirming every time he cracked a crab provided Arlette with a much-needed distraction from her nerves.

She bounced her knee, half to entertain her niece, Harriet, to prevent her from snatching a crab off the table and playing with it like she'd done countless times already, and half because she needed to release some nervous energy. She had a lot of it. Excited nervous energy, like she was finally ready to conquer the Capital Wheel at National Harbor.

Her dad nudged her side and leaned in. "How are you doing?" he said, soft enough that when Arlette looked at Brooke, Lori, Abby, and Stephen, they were still in their own world of crab-feast basics.

"Harriett is doing a fantastic job distracting me. My favorite niece by far."

Harriett reached for a crab again. Arlette pulled her away.

"You got this," her dad said softly. "I know you do. You've put a lot of thought into this."

"I don't know what words are anymore," Arlette whispered to him as another wave of sweat washed down her spine.

He laughed and rested a comforting hand on her shoulder. "I'm sure you have the words in you. Just speak from the heart, and they'll come to you."

She looked back at Brooke as she helped Stephen collect all the meat from a crab leg. Arlette smiled, remembering how the summer before at Brooke's first crab feast, Arlette had given her the same tutorial. Watching her struggle with the cracker had been adorable, a sight she missed as much as she loved the sight of her womanhandling the cracker like a champion now. After a few errors, Lori, Abby, and Stephen took off and caught up with the rest of the Adair family. And by the end of the feast, they were in the same slouched position, with a buttered napkin tossed over their plates in defeat.

"You know, Mr. Adair, if you ever decide to run for president again, which, by the way, you have my vote, I would love to have the honor of serving you a drink," Stephen said.

"Stephen," Abby said with a tight jaw and nudged his elbow.

"Don't mind him. He just has this bartending bucket list," Brooke explained. "One item includes making a drink for the president."

Arlette's dad laughed. "I'll make sure you'll be the first to know, Stephen. In the meantime, you can serve me a drink now if that helps with your list. I won't complain."

His eyes widened. "Really? I can serve up a mean old-fashioned. Ask Brooke."

Arlette's dad raised his hand. "I'm joking. You're my guest. You sit, relax, and enjoy. I'll make the drinks. I'm impressed by all three of you, by the way. You all made a nice dent. My father always expected each person to eat their fair share of crab. He didn't want too many leftovers."

"You're officially part of the family now," Arlette's mom said.

Abby and Stephen exchanged an excited glance as another wave of nerves swirled in Arlette's stomach. She looked over at Brooke and Lori, Brooke seeming completely unaware, which Arlette was thankful for. Inviting Brooke's mom and her two best friends to witness the special night had other benefits, like distracting Brooke from paying close attention to the details around her. She seemed oblivious to Arlette's silence and seemed so grateful about Arlette and her family inviting Abby and Stephen to their crab feast that she didn't put the pieces together as to the real reason why.

Arlette wanted all of Brooke's favorite people around when she proposed.

As the evening sun started to weaken, Arlette's nerves started to awaken even more. She caught her family members sneaking glances, probably checking in with how she was doing. Any time she met their stares, she got an encouraging smile, a thumbs-up, or a supportive nod. Even Uncle Henry had offered good luck when he had arrived and was even nice enough to chat with Abby and Stephen. She appreciated his acceptance on one of the most important nights of her life.

Though they would never be close, he and Arlette had eventually found an in-between, and she really believed that it was because she'd finally defended herself to him. They'd gotten to a point of cordial hugs and shared moments...but with a distance. Arlette removing herself from Capitol Hill had helped tremendously with that. Her policy and campaign work with Paw Aid was far removed from her uncle's work in Congress. It put incredible space between them, so she didn't have a full window into his life, and he didn't have a full window into hers. They could wave at a distance and keep the peace, which she liked. Uncle Henry going from once calling Arlette "the black sheep of the family" when she was in college to pulling her aside to wish her luck and give her and her guests the respect they deserved showed just how far they had come.

Once the first streak of color started bleeding into the evening sky, it was time, like the lights darkening signaled the end of an intermission. Though there were so many nerves swarming inside her that she struggled to get out of her seat, she somehow found a way.

"Good luck, sweetie," Lori said from her seat on the elevated patio.

Arlette turned to where her parents were sitting next to Lori. They flashed her heartwarming smiles, and she noticed a thin layer of gloss in her mother's eyes.

Arlette faced the rest of the backyard: Brooke and Abby versus Stephen and Ben in cornhole. Charlotte and Jacquelyn chasing Harriet. Uncle Henry, Aunt Denise, and Christian in the kitchen, tasking themselves with cracking the remaining crabs to save as leftovers.

Arlette sucked in a humid breath of early July air and held it; the freshness could calm her excitement so it didn't turn into shaky or stumbling words during the speech she'd rehearsed countless times since her dad had given her the ring.

Now was the time.

She walked over to the game. Brooke tossed a bag perfectly into the hole. She threw her hands in the air and celebrated with Abby, who caught Arlette waiting and nodded at Brooke to look over.

"Did you know your girlfriend is a pro at cornhole?" Brooke said to Arlette.

Abby, Stephen, and Ben eyed them with knowing looks, as if Arlette should brace herself to replace the title "girlfriend" with "fiancée" in a matter of minutes.

"We'll add cornhole to your list of amazing talents," Arlette said. "You want to go to the boat dock with me?"

"Is it cigar time?" Brooke said.

Arlette smiled. She wished Grandpa Harry had been there to watch Brooke last year at her first Adair crab feast. She'd eaten a lot of crab, they'd enjoyed plenty of beer, and Brooke had been eager to smoke her first cigar. Arlette wasn't necessarily sold that Brooke was a cigar lover, but it always made her smile when Brooke made an effort.

"Something like that," Arlette said.

"Can I finish this game first? I need to make it one more time, and Abby and I win."

"How about we take a break? I really need to run to the bathroom," Abby said, though Arlette knew it was a lie.

"Oh, and I'm extremely parched," Stephen said. "All that crab and beer and not enough water. Break and then I'll be able to accept defeat."

Brooke shrugged and then turned to Arlette. "Cigar time it is."

Arlette led them to the boat dock. The maple tree supplied them with a half-private view of an Eastern Shore sunset. With Arlette's entire family, plus special appearances by Brooke's mom and best friends, she knew everyone would try to catch a glimpse of the scene unfolding through the pockets of space between the leaves.

They both took a seat in the Adirondack chairs and looked out at the water. Since it was the Fourth of July, there were more boats than usual ready to enjoy a front-row view of the St. Michaels fireworks display that launched across the river.

Arlette tried combing through her rehearsed speech and wondered if she should wait or just get right to the most important question she would ever ask. Her grandma's ring was in her pocket, freed from the black velvet box because not only would it not fit in her shorts, but Brooke noticed every single detail of a scene—that was, when she wasn't instructing three people in how to eat crab. She surely would have noticed a ring-shaped box bulging in Arlette's pocket.

No, she couldn't wait anymore. This was the thing she wanted most in life. Ever since her dad had given her the ring, she'd fallen asleep every night picturing the ring on Brooke's left hand. She wanted to see it in front of her. She wanted to feel Brooke's hand in hers. She wanted to seal the promise that she was all in…again…for the rest of their lives.

So she slid out of her seat and stood. Brooke looked at her with a smile that hadn't dimmed the whole day. Arlette loved that smile and how she got to start and end her days with it. She slowly eased to one knee and watched as Brooke's smile faded just a bit, but intrigue still glistened in her eyes.

"Um…what are you doing?" Brooke asked suspiciously.

"Brooklyn…" Arlette said through her arid mouth, feeling the weight of the moment in her throat closing around her words.

Brooke scooted to the edge of the chair. "Arlette…what are you doing down there?"

The suspicion in her voice hinted that she knew exactly what Arlette was doing on one knee while in her favorite spot in the whole world.

"I'm trying to tell you something." Brooke glanced over her shoulder, but when Arlette grabbed her hand and intertwined their fingers, Brooke looked back. "We met each other almost eleven years ago next month. It didn't take me long to realize that I trust you more than anyone, that all I want to do is be around you. Ever since we reunited in this backyard two summers ago, I haven't been able to get you out of my head. I know we went through a lot in the beginning, but the fact that we both got through it together made me even more certain that this was always supposed to happen—you and me. You make things easier. Everything seems less scary with you, and I know those years without each other were the scariest parts of our lives, and we don't ever have to go through them alone again." She pulled the ring out of her back pocket and held it up. Brooke covered her mouth. "My grandparents were married for sixty-four years. They had a love that I've always admired. My grandpa said that he knew he loved my grandma because she constantly made him feel something in his chest. You know what one of the last things he asked before he died was?"

"What?"

"He asked what I felt with you. His question made my chest swell, and I realized right then and there that it has always been like that since the day I met you. You've always made me feel safe, you always saw every part of me, even the parts I didn't know I had. Every day feels like the first day, and that's something I've only experienced with you. All the things that you make me feel are so apparent, my grandpa saw it when we were together. My dad said my grandpa knew you were the one because shortly after meeting you, he'd told my dad to give me my grandma's ring. I've been peeking in my drawer and looking at this ring ever since, and every time I looked at it, my chest swelled even more with this feeling of absolute happiness that I want to experience for the rest of my life, the rest of our lives. You've been on my mind since I was eighteen, Brooklyn, and I would very much like to keep it that way. Will you marry me?"

The question broke the seal. Tears streamed down Arlette's face. Brooke's mouth hung open as she alternated glances between Arlette and the ring. She slid off the chair and joined Arlette on her knees on the dock. "Arlette, this ring...it's gorgeous."

"It can be yours if you say yes."

She met Arlette's gaze, a thick layer of tears brimming in her eyes as her firm smile remained intact. She palmed Arlette's face and wiped the moisture from her cheeks. "I'll absolutely marry you, Arlette," she said and pulled her in for a kiss.

Arlette slid her free hand along her fiancée's cheek, holding her in place long enough to seal a lifelong promise.

When Arlette broke away, she took Brooke's hand and slipped the ring on her finger. Finally, she was able to absorb the sight of their love bringing Grandma Dot's ring back to life.

"Arlette," Brooke said, staring at the ring, then back at Arlette. "Is this really happening?"

Arlette kissed the backs of her fingers. "It's really happening. That means your mom, Abby, and Stephen are going to eventually become a crab feast pro just like you."

Brooke pulled back. "Is that why you were so insistent on all of them coming here?"

Arlette shrugged. "They're your mom and best friends...plus, Abby mildly threatened that if I didn't invite her, the next cockroach she finds in her apartment is becoming our first pet. So I kind of had no choice on that."

Brooke laughed and shook her head. "Thank you for staying with me even though my best friend is a lot."

"I can handle her. I think we should share the news because I can see Abby and Stephen peeking through the leaves, and it almost made me stumble over my words. I'm not sure if they can wait anymore." Arlette stood and offered Brooke a hand. She then cupped her face and sealed the promise with another searing kiss. Almost two years into their relationship, kissing Brooke never got old. Brooke still found a way to awaken the butterflies in Arlette's stomach, and she was so ready to feel them for the rest of their lives. "Let's go tell everyone that you didn't say no."

When they walked off the boat dock with hands intertwined, everyone cheered and clapped. Arlette raised their clasped hands right before everyone swarmed around them, wanting to see the ring and to offer congratulations.

"My baby," Lori said as she held her daughter's face and gave her a tight hug. "I'm so happy for you, sweetie. I'm so happy for both of you."

"I've curated the happiest Taylor Swift playlist for all of us to listen to on the way back," Stephen said.

Abby barreled into them and squeezed them tightly. "I'm so glad I don't have to keep this a secret anymore."

"There's only one proper way to celebrate," Arlette's dad said and extended a bottle of Dom Pérignon and two flutes.

Arlette passed the bottle to Brooke. "You do the honors."

Brooke smiled and got the bottle into position. Arlette stood back, watching her soon-to-be-wife handle that expensive bottle of champagne. Being with her for a year and a half had made Brooke more comfortable around the champagne that Arlette's family loved so much. She remembered how reluctant Brooke had been at first when Arlette had treated her to a bottle two summers before. She had to do so much convincing just for Brooke to accept a glass of Dom Pérignon bubbles. Now, Brooke clasped the bottle and popped the top off like it was no big deal.

Arlette was incredibly proud.

Brooke poured the champagne into the glasses and then encouraged her mom to take a sip. Abby and Stephen were quick to try it and exchanged a glance.

"I've never felt as fancy as I do in this exact moment," Stephen said.

"Good, because I think we just peaked," Abby said. "We'll never be able to drink twenty-dollar champagne again."

"And I promise to make sure you stay away from the cheap champagne," Arlette said. "You're better than twenty-dollar champagne. Always tell yourself that."

Lori sipped and smacked her lips. "It's like each bubble is worth fifty dollars."

"That's exactly what I said," Brooke said with a laugh.

"You two go share your bottle by the dock if you like," Arlette's mom told them. "The dock is all yours tonight."

The boat dock was prime real estate for the Fourth of July fireworks. The closer to the edge of the property, the more beautiful they were. Usually, everyone pulled up chairs or blankets and sat on the dock or on the grass behind. The best spot on the property was carved out just for the two of them.

"Thanks, Mom," Arlette said.

"You all going to be okay over here?" Brooke asked her mom, Abby, and Stephen.

"Oh, of course," Lori said. "I'm in very good hands. Abby and Stephen have challenged me to cornhole, and even little Harriet is starting to befriend me. Go on. This is a night to remember. Enjoy your moment."

With her mother's approval, and another hug from both Abby and Stephen, Brooke looked at Arlette and smiled. Brooke led Arlette back to the Adirondack chairs. They sipped champagne while watching as the yellows, oranges, and purples streak across the sky, and vivid pinks puffed up the clouds. Arlette smiled at how beautiful the sunset turned out to be during one of the most important nights of her life, of their lives. It made her wonder if Grandpa Harry and Grandma Dot had anything to do with it. She hoped it was a sign from her grandparents that their presence was everywhere on the property, cloaking them in colorful warmth, just like their hugs had always done.

They had come such a long way in the last two years. They'd found each other again, had formed an even stronger bond than in college. Arlette had escaped Capitol Hill while Brooke had escaped her bartending job four months ago and was fully a freelance artist, just like she had always strived to be. They'd moved into their first apartment on U Street, which meant Arlette got to wake up and fall asleep next to Brooke every day. She came home to watch Brooke's freelance business take off, and Brooke's art started to fill coffee shops, boutiques, and galleries in the city.

Arlette was so proud of her fiancée. She was so proud of both of them.

Now the love of her life sat next to her, her face bathed in the bright sunset colors. Her family sat behind her, surrounding them with love and support. Her grandparents seemed to be painting them a beautiful scene for their special night. The excitement of going back to DC and working at a job that filled her with happiness and pride every day was perfection.

Arlette exhaled and held Brooke's hand. Brooke looked back, winked, and gave her the most beautiful smile, as if she was just as content as Arlette was.

This was exactly the life Arlette had always wanted.

ABOUT THE AUTHOR

Morgan Lee Miller started writing at the age of five in the suburbs of Cleveland, Ohio, where she entertained herself by composing her first few novels all by hand. She majored in journalism and creative writing at Grand Valley State University.

When she's not introverting and writing, Morgan works for an animal welfare nonprofit and tries to make the world a slightly better place. She previously worked for an LGBT rights organization.

She currently resides in Washington, DC, with her two feline children, whom she's unapologetically obsessed with.

Books Available From Bold Strokes Books

Catch by Kris Bryant. Convincing the wife of the star quarterback to walk away from her family was never in offensive coordinator Sutton McCoy's game plan. But standing on the sidelines when a second chance at true love comes her way proves all but impossible. (978-1-63679-276-7)

Hearts in the Wind by MJ Williamz. Beth and Evelyn seem destined to remain mortal enemies but are about to discover that in matters of the heart, sometimes you must cast your fortunes to the wind. (978-1-63679-288-0)

Hero Complex by Jesse J. Thoma. Bronte, Athena, and their unlikely friends must work together to defeat Bronte's archnemesis. The fate of love, humanity, and the world might depend on it. No pressure. (978-1-63679-280-4)

Hotel Fantasy by Piper Jordan. Molly Taylor has a fantasy in mind that only Lexi can fulfill. However, convincing her to participate could prove challenging. (978-1-63679-207-1)

Last New Beginning by Krystina Rivers. Can commercial broker Skye Kohl and contractor Bailey Kaczmarek overcome their pride and work together while the tension between them boils over into a love that could soothe both of their hearts? (978-1-63679-261-3)

Love and Lattes by Karis Walsh. Cat café owner Bonnie and wedding planner Taryn join forces to get rescue cats into forever homes—discovering their own forever along the way. (978-1-63679-290-3)

Repatriate by Jaime Maddox. Ally Hamilton's new job as a home health aide takes an unexpected twist when she discovers a fortune in stolen artwork and must repatriate the masterpieces and avoid the wrath of the violent man who stole them. (978-1-63679-303-0)

The Hues of Me and You by Morgan Lee Miller. Arlette Adair and Brooke Dawson almost fell in love in college. Years later, they unexpectedly run into each other and come face-to-face with their unresolved past. (978-1-63679-229-3)

A Haven for the Wanderer by Jenny Frame. When Griffin Harris comes to Rosebrook village, the love she finds with Bronte de Lacey creates a safe haven and she finally finds her place in the world. But will she run again when their love is tested? (978-1-63679-291-0)

A Spark in the Air by Dena Blake. Internet executive Crystal Tucker is sure Wi-Fi could really help small-town residents, even if it means putting an internet café out of business, but her instant attraction to the owner's daughter, Janie Elliott, makes moving ahead with her plans complicated. (978-1-63679-293-4)

Between Takes by CJ Birch. Simone Lavoie is convinced her new job as an intimacy coordinator will give her a fresh perspective. Instead, problems on set and her growing attraction to actress Evelyn Harper only add to her worries. (978-1-63679-309-2)

Camp Lost and Found by Georgia Beers. Nobody knows better than Cassidy and Frankie that life doesn't always give you what you want. But sometimes, if you're lucky, life gives you exactly what you need. (978-1-63679-263-7)

Fire, Water, and Rock by Alaina Erdell. As Jess and Clare reveal more about themselves, and their hot summer fling tips over into true love, they must confront their pasts before they can contemplate a future together. (978-1-63679-274-3)

Lines of Love by Brey Willows. When even the Muse of Love doesn't believe in forever, we're all in trouble. (978-1-63555-458-8)

Only This Summer by Radclyffe. A fling with Lily promises to be exactly what Chase is looking for—short-term, hot as a forest fire, and one Chase can extinguish whenever she wants. After all, it's only one summer. (978-1-63679-390-0)

Picture-Perfect Christmas by Charlotte Greene. Two former rivals compete to capture the essence of their small mountain town at Christmas, all the while fighting old and new feelings. (978-1-63679-311-5)

Playing Love's Refrain by Lesley Davis. Drew Dawes had shied away from the world of music until Wren Banderas gave her a reason to play their love's refrain. (978-1-63679-286-6)